PRAISE FOR JODY SCOTT'S BENAROYA CHRONICLES

"[*Passing for Human* is] one of the ten weirdest science fiction novels you've never read."

— Charlie Jane Anders, *iO9*

"Anyone who appreciates the offbeat (and the off the wall) will enjoy Scott's [Benaroya]. Benaroya is a visiting alien, whose mission (to save the human race from an evil alien invasion, and to have a good time while she's at it) is complicated by her inability to understand why human beings make a fuss over such inessentials as death, pain and the physical universe. Wearing an attractive assortment of bodies, including those of Emma Peel and Virginia Woolf, Benaroya shows herself and the reader a riproaringly magnificent time. ...Quite unlike anything anyone else has ever done."

— Neil Gaiman

"Protagonist comes to alien world whose natives and absurdities are of course not at all 'alien' but refractive of the human condition. The tilt of alien perspective however enables the insanity of that condition, perceived by a faux-naif, to be the more clearly perceived... This is the greatest employment of science fiction in the service of satire; we've had notable satirists — but Scott alone refuses to sentimentalize."

— *The Magazine of Fantasy & Science Fiction*

"This satire was first published in 1977, but its biting commentary still registers strongly today. Scott carries on the tradition of Mark Twain, using outside observers to remark on society. A light touch keeps the moralizing from getting too ham-fisted, and this cautionary tale calling for a better world is a message needed now more than ever."

— *Publishers.Weekly*

"A joyously and at times scatologically tangled Satire of the post-industrial Western world from a Feminist point of view that wittily verges on misandry."

— *The Encyclopedia of Science Fiction*

"The rapid non-sequiturs Scott puts into Benaroya's mouth and her aside justifications combine sha   and great humour. Those who seek to deric   it is too serious, po-faced, but Jody S   ngly scattershot but tightly controlle   rdly comic romp of unexpected juxtapositions and witty asides."

"Jody Scott does it again [in *Devil-May-Care*]. Her latest book, presents us with a startling vision of life on planet earth as seen through the eyes of alien beings, disguised as famous humans. Fasten your seatbelts and brace yourself for a tumble through the universe with Virginia Woolf, Abraham Lincoln, Nancy Reagan, Douglas MacArthur, General Patton, Heidi's grandfather and, of course, our favorite vampire. [*Devil-May-Care*] is the third book in The Benaroya Chronicles and I promise it will keep you on the edge of your seat."

"Jody Scott is like a mad cabby who knows most of the streets in town and knows where the laughs are — get into her rig and she'll take you on a fast and furious spin through America's ideological terrain."

"I liked *I, Vampire* enough to check it off on the Nebula ballot. I'm still of the humble opinion that it is the equal (in a couple of cases, the superior) of the books that are apparently on the final ballot."

"Scott is a superb social satirist."

"The best unknown SF writer."

"Jody Scott [has the] amazing ability to look askance and detached at humanity and human affairs, all the while passionately involved. Huge enjoyment of Scott's vitriol, her hilarity, her delineations of action and excitement (and indeed, one can read for these facets alone and gain many times the price of admission). A further, truly remarkable achievement of hers is her ability to describe a steamy, passionate love sequence without being explicit. My. How unfashionable. How very refreshing!"

THE BENAROYA CHRONICLES

JODY SCOTT

I, VAMPIRE

THE BENAROYA CHRONICLES II

Strange Particle Press

INTRODUCTION

by Theodore Sturgeon

Benaroya on "Insurance":
A prime test for madness and paranoia is called "insurance." If a species has "insurance," it is patently doomed. Only a toylike, salivating, pent-up bunch of gruntlings could conceive of such a sociopathic type of gambling.

Sterling O'Blivion is the manager of a big-city dance studio (not *Dance* dance, but ballroom dance) who was born in the thirteenth century and is a vampire. She has invented a kind of time machine, which she is too timid to use; she is timid about nothing else in any universe. She falls quite madly in love with Virginia Woolf for motivations not entirely literary, and it may be that it isn't really Virginia Woolf, but an extraterrestrial that is not at all human, but rather a great gray porpoise-like thing which, or who, chooses to be like, or even to be, Virginia Woolf.

Sterling O'Blivion is a vampire, and makes no effort to conceal it from the reader, though she is pragmatically discreet elsewhere. Let it be understood that this is, however, not a vampire novel in any usual or expected sense. As O'Blivion herself says:

Without being aware of it I was inventing, and I mean personally creating, that baroque dramatization known as "the classical style." I wore yards of black lace. I spoke Spanish, kept bats in the tower, sucked in my cheeks to look hollow, and carried blazing candelabra up and down winding staircases. I slept in a canopied bed…

At the time of narration, some 700-plus years after her birth in old Transylvania, she is the manager of that dance studio. Though she has not—cannot, actually—abandoned the necessity for ingesting six ounces of arterial blood at regular intervals, the parallel between this and her current occupation is obvious, painful, and hilarious. The studio, she says, "does business in the time-honored way. We go for the jugular." If this astonishing book is about anything, it is about this kind of parallel: about Jody Scott's amazing ability to look askance and detached at humanity and human affairs, all the while passionately involved. And if that be paradox, make the best of it. Of greed, of murder, of betrayal, she makes something joyful; of love, something pyrotechnic. More about this last, later.

The longer I write, the more I teach, the more aware I become that the very essence of meaningful, if not great and lasting, literature is metaphor, simile, parable, proverb. If fantasy, no matter how far-out, has no relationship (however subliminal) to the human condition, then it is trivial, cannot be great, and will not last.

Examples are many: Alice's shout "You're all a pack of cards!" is a very great deal more than the description of an irritated little girl dreaming; it marks one of the most profound comments on the nature of reality ever uttered. Aesop's improbably vegetarian fox, leaping for grapes, deals neither with foxes nor with grapes. Evidence of the other, evanescent uses of fantasy can be found in the current glut of trilogies, tetralogies, monotonologies (if I may coin a word) blurbed on their be-dragoned, be-unicorned, be-princes-with-daggered dust jackets with the words "In the tradition of Tolkien" or Dunsany or Robert E. Howard (without having paid Tolkien or Dunsany or Howard a rusted nickel for the use of their illustrious names). These overwritten, overpriced literary sausages run heavily to convoluted court intrigues, heroes who always win, slime-and-scale beasts that do not, after all, horrify; and in the end, if you ever get to the end, It All Comes Out Happily, which you should have known before you started. Little of this is usable or useful as metaphor.

(In fairness, I must add that not all contemporary fantasy deserves this scourging: the works of Anne McCaffrey, for example, or of Elizabeth Lynn, Marion Zimmer Bradley, John Ireland, and some others don't...Further thought re: useful metaphor: Couldn't these remarks extend to the bulk of contemporary fiction? All of it?)

Which reminds me — and the following may have evoked the above — here is one of the few passages in which Sterling O'Blivion refers to her vampirism:

By the Beast! I've been shattered so many times I feel like an experi-

mental windshield. And for what? For six ounces of blood. These turkeys protect their carcasses as if they were the Holy Grail wrapped in pluto- nium foil. Which makes me laugh, because in just a few years they die anyway, despite all that frantic "health care," and they die without ever having lived; and all that ruby blood pours into the undertaker's sink. This is called "going through channels." People seem to love it. It means they never have to think. Just follow the herd.

And so Sterling O'Blivion meets Virginia Woolf, who is not really Virginia Woolf but a sea pig of indeterminate sex from some distant planet or continuum, and, after a wild fistfight in a ladies room, Woolf tells Sterling, "You're as commercially debased as the rest of them, and crazy as a bean besides, but get past all that and you're very old, very wise, and not only a damned good theoretical physicist but a square shooter." And she asks Sterling's help. And Sterling falls in love. Which brings us to good old Topic A.

But worst of all, she was a natural murderer. Or at least a careless, gross animal — a fish, for Godsake! I was having an affair with a fish. How could I be "in love" with this demon from hell? Was I out of my mind? (Answers: I could. I was. I didn't care. I wished I'd never met her. On the other hand, I was so in love I couldn't stand it.. But was it "love," or a demonic mesmerism?)

Love is so simple, so easy to grasp. As a Supreme Court justice once said (about obscenity, not about love), "I can't define it, but I know it when I see it." Does he? Do you? You love your one- and-only, of course you do. And you love chocolate mousse. Your mother. The Dodgers. The one with the pearly curves. The one with the ropy muscles. What the hell *is* it that you love?

I think it was Pascal who wrote: "The heart hath reasons, rea- son knows not of." Try to use reason on love, the ways of love, the levels of love, the activations and — yes — the cessation of love, and you'll find it slippery indeed. At least as slippery as an extra- terrestrial sea pig.

This bears out my thesis on literature and metaphor. The re- mark "How on earth could she/he fall in love with a nerd like that," is one we've all heard from our contemporaries, in one form or another, at one time or another, and there seems always to be no answer, because there is indeed no *reasonable* answer, which is, of course, the very point M. Pascal and Ms. Scott are making. There is, however, an answer embodied in the question "What is love?" even if it can't be stated in reasonable terms. One has to sidle up to it, which is what metaphor is for. Permit me then to sidle.

A passage in one of the more remarkable books of our time, *The Female Man* by Joanna Russ, deals with a girl of the far future and her house, her miraculous but purely technological house. In this house there is a young man, perfect in face and form, who (when she wants him to) lolls at her feet, allows her to rumple his hair while his head is in her lap, and generally decorates her surroundings. One evening, the fondling reaches an ignition point, and when a writer of the Russ caliber sets out to do an explicit scene, she doesn't fool around. At last, spent and content, she looks up and becomes aware of her three guests, who have been watching in various stages of astonishment. "Ah," she says. "I see you're shocked. Well then, perhaps you ought to know that this young man isn't what *he* appears to be. He is merely another artifact of this house, which also supplies me with food, comfort, music, and a good many amenities...Ah; I see that you are still shocked. Well then, forget that explanation, and let's say that he is not an artifact, but flesh and blood, springing, through genetic manipulation, from a species of anthropoid apes, and bred to be what you see here...Ah again! I see you are still shocked! Well then: tell me which of these two explanations shocks you the more. And then—tell me why."

The question is not answered; Russ leaves it to the reader to answer; and this episode defines, for me, the *writer at work.*

(I am aware that I have quoted Russ clumsily, but I do not at the moment have her book in hand; I recommend the brilliant original.)

Writing—real writing—is not about setting up situations to be deftly resolved or destroyed. The writer—what I am calling the *real* writer—at work, is, like Russ, giving clear, not obscure, questions to ask of oneself and the world, to find one's own answers, whether that is done by agreeing or disagreeing with what the writer has posited.

In dealing with so flickery and mutable a thing as love, Jody Scott flashes at us the existence of same-sex love, something that an increasing number of people are becoming able to confront, but immediately flips past that and presents the concept of a flaming passion for an extraterrestrial sea pig. One becomes aware immediately that her layered description of love objects is confronting the one thing in this process that is the denominator of all these expressions of love in action, and that is love itself. And this, the confrontation with love itself, without being confused with ways of loving or with what is love, is, I think, what Jody Scott is about, and why I call her processing "the writer at work." (A further, truly remarkable achievement of hers is her ability to describe a steamy, passionate love sequence *without* being explicit. My. How unfashionable. How very refreshing!)

After the huge enjoyment of Scott's vitriol, her hilarity, her unexpectedness, her delineations of action and excitement (and indeed, one can read for these facets alone and gain many times the price of admission), one has the freedom to search for and to find the bottom line. And to me, it emerges from this:

Frank Herbert, in a recent novel, makes the point that "normal" means only "like me" and/or "like us"; and that stretching, as does his mind (and yours, or you wouldn't be reading this kind of book) across an infinite spectrum of monstrosities here, in the future, and across the universe anywhere, any time, and realizing that each and any of them defines "normal" in exactly the same way—like me, like us—one may at last get past prejudice and rejection and discover that at base, for all, and for each, there is love. And perhaps the use of that word in English, applying it to babies and God and flavors of ice cream and that darling hat is not after all an impoverishment, but the profound expression of the fact that love is everywhere.

ONE

"Get out!" Papa thundered.

"And go where? And do what?" I howled.

"You are not our daughter. You are a limb of Satan," screamed my fat pretty little mama.

The uproar went on all night. I had made the childish mistake of confessing to the crime, then retracting the confession, and on and on until they shrieked: "You swore you sucked that priest's blood!"

"I lied! I tell lies; everyone knows that."

Snow had begun to fly, and torches blazed, but my parents were adamant about not letting me back into the house. I'm sure they had been dreading this scene since the day of my birth. Maybe earlier. We all knew in our bones that I, Sterling O'Blivion, had "it," that unspeakable "it" — the defective gene that runs through our family. Something was tragically wrong with me; something that terrified others, but was minor, natural, and even quite pleasant as far as I was concerned.

My old nanny Blescu screamed the Lord's Prayer for hours, crossing herself and rolling her eyes. That nanny used to make dolls for me ("They come to life when you sleep, my little pet," she often told me) and I was her loved one, her adored favorite. But now the crass old hypocrite had gone completely barmy. She held up a crucifix and pleaded with Jesus to kill me on the spot. (Which, I am happy to say, he did not do.)

The most shocking thing was what had happened to my parents' faces. Fear had burnt away every trace of love; indeed, of everything familiar. They looked at me with such cold distaste that I could hardly believe it. They had become like the peasants, certain I was going to perform a ghoulish miracle that would destroy them.

"Papa!" I wheedled. "Please, there's nothing to worry about. You're jumping to conclusions—"

I used every bit of the charm and persuasiveness God had given me (which even then was quite something) and spoke carefully, not wanting to betray myself with the wrong words. "The superstitions are a bit misleading. It's not as bad as it sounds."

Papa's mustache trembled. He wanted to believe me, but the crime was far too disgusting; he couldn't stomach it. He made an irritated gesture with his index and little finger outstretched. It meant I was disowned, of the devil, and should go far away and die and let them forget the Gorgon monster they had spawned. Of course dying was the last thing your correspondent was planning to do.

All this took place 700 years ago. Nothing is left of our estate in the town of Sibiu, in Transylvania, except a ghetto that stands on the site today. Actually, 130 years later but still bowed with grief, I was in Munich wrestling with plans for a time portal. I longed, absolutely *yearned* to go back and see my dear parents and make things come out right this time.

Yet that eruption of evil, which seems like a week ago, actually happened when I was thirteen. It was well below freezing but Papa told the servants to nail every door shut and drop rocks and boiling water if I tried to climb the bastion, which I had done all through childhood for sport.

Dozens of peasants were up there clicking rosaries and whispering, or throwing aprons over their heads when I stared a little too boldly. To keep myself from crying (because I had lost love, because I saw the handwriting on the wall, because my heart was broken) I stuck out my tongue and chanted, hair tossed back and fists on hips:

Tattletale tit,
Your tongue is going to split,
And every little dog in town
Will have a little bit.

Then, absolutely determined that Papa and Mama must believe my side of the story, I hid in the barn. I was terribly unhappy about no longer being loved, but not a bit guilty. Why should I be? My "crime" was a normal act. God had made me this way. My parents and nanny were the cruel ones, not myself. I figured out a little speech that might convince them, then cried myself to sleep between two warm, friendly cows.

The morning seemed most peaceful after that hideously tortured night. I gazed at the house, its walls rosy-tinted by the dawn, and its spires and turrets capped with fresh snow. I bowed my head and commended my soul to Saint Jude the patron saint of bloodsuckers (wherever did that idea come from? I can't imagine) and with hands clasped, while stared at by several curious ravens, I prayed: "*Omnes gurgites tui et fluctus tui super me transierunt.*"

Then I washed in the pig trough, combed my tawny hair, and figured out what words to use.

As I approached the house, a rock or two whizzed past my ear.

"Summon your master, you preposterous, miserable, quivering nincompoops!" I shouted.

I had all the arrogance, all the wild humor, the enormous vitality and scornful cruelty of my race; and the servants adored me for it. Or so they had done, up to now. *Now,* they thought me eerie. *Now* I was despised and rejected. But my eye flashed fire, and in a minute came a rattle of locks and squeak of hinges and out rushed Papa and Mama who both looked all puffed and haggard, as if they had slept in separate beds, unwilling to face each other.

I made a courtly bow and said: "Let me stay, and I thank you from my heart. Send me away and the pain of separation will kill me. Either way I bear no malice; indeed, I will love you forever."

It was the absolute truth.

Then...I still don't know how I pulled it off. Papa had been a knight in the last Crusade and was tough and ruthless, but with that sales pitch I had worked out so sincerely in the barn, and which would be called "hard sell" in today's jargon, I convinced him that:

1. The man who said I put him to sleep and sucked his neck was lying. Or partly lying.

2. He was a parish priest, so what? Priests have been known to lie. This one exaggerated my crime. Why? I could only guess it was because of my fine complexion, well-built body, and the

certain something I possessed that charmed everyone (including Papa).

3. It was the priest's word against mine. Would they take the word of a baseborn ruffian against an O'Blivion of noble blood?

4. See for yourself, that confessor was alive and kicking. He was fit enough to bring false witness against the innocent. So what was all the screaming about?

The upshot was they let me back in; they were under the wonderful impression that a vampire drains every drop of blood and therefore I couldn't be one. Illogical, but I did not argue.

After that I learned to be sneaky enough not to get caught in the act for a whole year; although I did "it" every chance I got, being hungry — O! so ravenous — in those wild, wonderful, windy young years. And I scanned the night skies constantly from my small window under the eaves.

It was then I became absolutely certain and positive that one fine day a woman from the stars was going to land in our pasture. She'd be piloting a beautifully crafted starship. And wearing fantastic star-clothing. And we would fall deeply, passionately in love; because she, unlike everyone here in Sibiu, didn't care a rap about my "evil nature."

Then we'd zoom off in her galactic cruiser and have thrilling adventures on strange worlds, with plenty of swordplay and romance, and we would couple ourselves for love, and live happily ever after.

It's now the tail end of the twentieth century and I'm still waiting. Where are you, my light-of-wonder? this is Sterling O'Blivion sitting at her desk at the Max Arkoff Studio of Dance in Chicago. For you, soul mate and lustrous star-woman, I've kept myself alive and gorgeous (by tooth and claw! I might add, and don't you ever forget it; for after that night came a wild, savage hand-to-mouth existence that it sickens me to remember) for the better part of the millennium.

Haunted by shadows, but unbowed.

The logic of my nature tells me "something terrible is going to happen." Swift as the storm-blast, destiny comes full circle; warning signals are flashing. I'm having premonitions and the weirdest dreams. A part of me longs to break free, not only of the wheel of life and death but of my "compulsion." Not that it hasn't been a joy and a delight, after the first shock.

I'd never knock vampirism. Without it I'd be nothing, less than nothing, a bag of bones in some European crypt. My compulsion is all that sets me above the ruck of women: that scent of conquest, the noble chase, a game of wits, figuring out how I can penetrate and feast without getting my neck broken. And then the thrill of victory forever new, the ritualized ecstasy as I master the unconscious victim and at long last that slow, marvelous caress on the tongue as the Ruby slips down my throat…

Ough! Just thinking of it makes my heart pound like a triphammer.

I adore being a vampire. I love the lore, history, rich tradition and sense of fabulous majesty it confers upon an otherwise simple, sentimental, and perhaps boring older woman. The only part that wearies me is the convulsive outrage and vain lamentations, the barbed words of cruel slander, as a selfish world fights to hang onto that few lousy, crummy, measly drops of blood.

And I'm sick, too, of getting the crap beat out of me, which happens oftener than one would like to believe.

I suppose the bottom line is, I'd love to be "cured" (how I despise that vulgar, vulgar word!) without losing any of the miraculous powers and thrills that come along with the perils of my compulsion.

But…are things ever that easy?

TWO

The students stood talking in groups; the teachers, in separate knots of two or three. The P.A. had announced a break (in Johnny File's familiar, folksy drawl).

I had an appointment at seven to interview a certain Patsy Cox, job applicant who'd insisted on the phone that she was "mad and desperate" to become a Max Arkoff dance instructor.

The time: two minutes to seven.

I walked from the main studio past the elevators to my office. An elevator stopped, and a woman got off. It was Patsy Cox. I knew her at once. I had seen that face every night for weeks in those dreams I mentioned; or to be more accurate, those nightmares.

According to ancient lore, it would take some kind of colossal pressure to drive a vampire mad. I'm not the least bit crazy. I am sane beyond ordinary sanity, despite an obvious and terrible split: I, a product of the Middle Ages, immersed in the trivia of being a Today Person and earning shekels to pay the rent.

True, I am like a Giotto fresco painted on the side of a pizza hut. But I carry it off—and why not?—for I am prodigiously adaptable. A survivor in every sense. So now, cool as a snowdrift, I smiled and moved toward her.

"Patsy Cox?"

"Sterling O'Blivion?"

In my office I went over every detail of that dream, smiling and nodding as Patsy extolled her own virtues. In the dream, I surprise this woman as she rifles the desk in my apartment. She's searching through a box of scientific papers and research notes. She whirls, pulling out a gun. We wrestle. The gun goes off. To my horror it blows away half her face.

I drag the body to the freezer, brains and blood dripping on my new carpet. I hoist the body up and with great difficulty hide it under the packaged vegetables. Then I do a Lady Macbeth number trying to get the stains out of the rug.

It's a nightmare, but not the worst I've had recently. The very worst takes place in an emergency room. It's always the same. Johnny File, my husband in the dream (but not in real life, God forbid), is rushing me to a hospital. There is a cascade of blood; it spurts, can't be stopped, and suddenly I die in the most heart-wrenching and tragic circumstances.

Another awful one is Johnny as a Thought Police agent who tracks me relentlessly for centuries until I finally kill him. In another one, I'm thrown into a cart full of naked corpses resembling the plague victims I often saw in the past. Whoever originates these hallucinations knows exactly what will upset me the most. They strike at any time. They are vivid, solid, intense daydreams. They come from outside and are propelled into my time track. They hit like shockwaves, complete with unspeakable visions that make my head spin.

Now, who could pull off a trick like this? Only an inter-dimensional sniper. This diabolical fiend can rip bits from my memory bank, mix them with ordinary scenes from the lives of ordinary people I don't know, and slam them into my brain like missiles. No other explanation makes sense.

It's my own fault, admittedly. By my very nature I'm prone to attract "alternate worlds" but, worse, I've set strange forces in motion by perfecting what Herbert George Wells used so quaintly to call a "time-travel machine" which I'm too scared to use.

This ultra-new new physics is dangerous territory. Even on the level of mass psychology, there are forces beyond our reckoning. But I've gone my own sweet way, ignoring public opinion and the work of other (more cautious?) theoretical physicists until... Patsy Cox phones up and tells me she's "desperate" to get this job.

Nothing strange about that part of it. Hundreds of good-looking dames would give their eyeteeth for a job here; Max Arkoff is a passport to instant money, parties, glamor, and (perhaps) even a listing in the Chicago *Social Register*. But... I know that I am now skirting a psychic wormhole.

Patsy said she was attending U.C. in poli sci and needed this job right away, and would do "anything" to get it. I tested her. A truly great dancer. Tall and bony, she whipped her shiny locks in orbits of abandon when the Sledgehammer, our latest blackmarket tape from England, was played.

"You'll give up your studies, your chance to become a real intellectual, for this?" I shouted.

"Socioeconomic dialectics," she shouted back, at once detecting the irony and putting me in my place. The class was doing turnabouts to loosen up, so I ushered Patsy back to my office and closed the door. It was blissfully quiet except for the ceaseless boomBOOM, boomBOOM, boomBOOM which has driven us all deaf as doorknobs (fortunately it does not matter, as nobody at the Studio listens to anyone else).

Patsy was out of breath and all pink with job-lust. She sat primly erect and called me "Ma'am" about 500 times too many, and waggled her foot to the music while pleading in twentieth-century jargon;

"Meaningful paradigm basic viable alternatives?"

"Sharing, caring, and other buzzwords," I soothed. (I'm considered one of the best managers in the business.)

But the sweetness was all on the surface. I was not only chilled with apprehension but my jealousy was awakened, for what did this me-generation child know of hunger, of fear, of persecution? She was a plastic doll, well-fed, and had a pack of artificial mannerisms like most of the Today People.

Try as I may I can never copy them faithfully, can never really fit in, and it's sad. But on the other hand it is not Patsy's fault. The present is far, far better than the past. I recall watching women claw each other's eyes out just for a chance to sit next to some skinny, drunken duchess or other; and so what if my hearing is being destroyed by anti-music? Never shall I forget the winter I spent in Heidelberg begging for pennies, faking epilepsy, chewing pieces of soap, falling down in foaming fits, then grabbing the coins and scuttling off to buy one roasted potato and a mug of ale, my only food in a week.

Yes, today is much nicer, even though we are universally forced to conform to a malignant mass psychosis underpinned by latent violence and hysteria.

I told her, "It's a difficult line of work, my dear. We play phony roles. You'll get blisters and attacks of the blues but it beats clerking for a chain store, *if* you can get them to sign that little old all-important contract."

"Alternatives! Paradigm." Patsy hardly listened to me; she'd fit in nicely. I continued,

"You'll meet important men, a relentless flow of rich, lonely bachelors. Can you handle it? By which I mean, can you get them to sign that contract for twenty or forty or sixty lessons and write us a nice big check?"

"Viability," nodding firmly.

I explained the virtues of hard work and shallow relationships. She paid no attention, but seemed tenser than the situation called for. Her foot tapped furiously. I gazed into the nicely decorated shop windows that were her eyes, and got a feeling that she *knew*. Luckily that was impossible. And even so, it shouldn't frighten her. My hunger is always there ready to spring out, but never with someone from work; that would be like incest. Unthinkable. Then I had a feeling she was recording our conversation on a little gadget stuffed in her heel or somewhere, but that was also absurd.

I forced an airy laugh and rasped in my tough whisky voice, "Our clients aren't learning to dance for fun, kiddo. They come here out of desperation. Why are they desperate? That's for you to find out and take care of with a course of lessons."

That seemed to put her at ease, so I blundered on, "This joint may look like a social club, but it's not. Oh, there's plenty of mummery and farce and after hours we make merry at Leon's downstairs, but during office hours this is hard computer circuitry, baby; this is recombinant DNA, a tough and competitive business. I'm looking for a strong closer who can sell courses day in and day out and never get emotionally involved. By that I mean neither for nor against, understand?"

No doubt she could teach steps, knuckle under, work hard, attract clients, train like a boxer and do what I commanded, but could she sell? That was the bottom line: could she insert those silver nails into the place where her student hid his checkbook and his American Express card? Could she deal in the frailties that keep the wheels of commerce humming?

Caught up in such problems, I'd half forgotten the premonitions.

Patsy was every inch the Competition Female; wonderfully made-up, perfectly groomed, a copy of *Cosmopolitan* under one arm; no doubt utterly unscrupulous, unless I was just projecting my own sins onto her...but...something was throwing me off.

Angst, angst.

I haven't been in this business long. I'm forever on the move, an expert in forged birth certificates, scared to death "they" are going to find me out again; nerves always stretched beyond the breaking point. And for this reason, my study has been the study of human character as it really is, not as we wish it could be.

Miss Cox stood with her face to the window. I tried to analyze her simple mind — and drew a blank. But she had no intention of losing the advantage. She looked at me out of the corner of her eye and said, "I need this job, Sterling. Give it to me."

I was stunned. First names already? Somehow we'd made a sharp turn in the conversation and it all had happened below my level of comprehension. It seemed like a tremendous effort to pull myself together and get her to fill out the insurance forms. I'm enough of a telepath to know that something was troubling the surface of Patsy's mind, aside from our shared, superficial snobbery, formed by layers of intense fear. No; I suspected her of —

What?

I must be crazy.

I went over and patted her cheek, saying, "You'll have your answer tomorrow morning, darling."

Of course the answer would be "yes." With a little effort on my part, the woman would be semi-ravishing. A real moneymaker. A real break for the Studio. These spectacular dancers who can toss their hair in a perfect circle, who can wring out their entire body like a shirt in a windstorm, who are empty as if waiting to be filled up; they always do well under my tutelage.

Another promising sign. I had forgotten to tell Patsy that Johnny File, my assistant, was supposed to be my, as it is called, "boyfriend." So the little thief immediately got her claws into him. Then I heard her discussing Johnny with another teacher as they changed costumes in our somewhat unhygienic dressing room. She said, "You should dance the *tango* with him. You'd go out of your *mind.*"

So I, Sterling O'Blivion, who by now should know every trick in the book, smiled my inscrutable smile and was taken in.

Blam, what a gull.

But that's the awful thing about "fate." When it chooses to set a trap for you, there is nothing in the world you can do to avoid it.

THREE

The Max Arkoff Studio does business in the time-honored way. We go for the jugular.

Smiling, flattering, soft of speech, we operate on your wallet. Or as my assistant puts it: "I don't teach disco for my health." Not that Johnny's any greedier than the next man but as he says, when you work for The Public you've got a rich tyrant for a boss.

Johnny's the only person at the Studio who has the least inkling that I'm a vampire. Even Max Arkoff himself—dear wonderful old balding Max, who lit up the dark cave which is America's heart with his twinkletoes routines during the Depression—even Max does not know. I made it a rule never, ever, to tell anyone—since the first time I was tarred, feathered, and pierced with pitchforks by a howling mob.

But Johnny (every inch a Today Person: an ex-cop, a skilled cross-examiner, and a thoroughly bad poet with dozens of awards to prove it)—yes, Johnny did something nobody else has been able to do. He wormed the truth out of me one night in the Pump Room after too many gin slings.

It's tough to keep a secret for 700 years. We all need to trust someone. Besides, who is he going to tell? They'd laugh in his face.

Normal humans, in my view, have an elitist attitude about themselves. They can do any horror they like to other species, but when it comes to their own persons that's a different matter.

I was born in Transylvania in Romania in the Year of Our Lord 1282. I'm a Gemini with a badly afflicted chart. I've faced despicable enemies. Even my own parents detested me. Both of them so-called normals (ha ha, what does the word really mean?), they accused me of inheriting "the unspeakable quirk" (again it's their phrase and not mine) from my maternal grandmother Mimi de la Huguelet, a beautiful woman who died in what they always called "a mysterious accident" (be honest, Papa, it was matricide) shortly before I was born. And if my actual history sounds like outtakes from a tacky B movie, or worse, well, that's not my problem. I am what I am, as God and Popeye both say when you wake them out of a sound sleep.

There was a time when I was furiously jealous of every non-vampire in the world, including hunchbacks, dwarves, ugly prostitutes and condemned murderers, but that time is long past. I was born to a French-Irish family of rank and fortune, the O'Blivions, who didn't exactly turn me over to the mob; they just sat back and buffed their nails when the time was ripe.

What would you do if your 14-year-old daughter suddenly began thirsting for the blood of the family confessor? What would you do if she *scored*?

Truth is truth. It can't be manipulated by popular opinion. To remain young and adorable, I must drink six ounces of human arterial blood once a month. This is not an ethical choice. I was born this way. If society wants to kill or cure me, that's not up to me. I'm an alchemist, a Hermetic Master, and a Unified Field scholar, and I will never betray my principles.

I went to find Johnny and he was nowhere in sight. That was peculiar; he's always around at this hour. I watched Patsy Cox leave, slithering between rows of hopeful disco freaks, craning her head on its slender stalk, as the voices of this incredible century engulfed me.

"She went through hell with Ralph's drinking problem. She wore hidden microphones."

"Bondage, Craig, but is Bruce lying to Susan about the gen-vats?"

"She sniffs snow in the sunset with her man from Merrill Lynch."

"Bondage Bondage Bondage, Deborah!" (Bright laughter.) "Sabrina drank a dish of recombinant DNA and left mangled remains on the sidewalk."

"She was off the wall. Had all these magnetic discrepancies.

Anyone holding snow?"

I hate to eavesdrop, but the distortion patterns intrigue me. After all, this is not my native language (or milieu, thank God!, for that matter).

"Some day you're gonna run out of cliches and lapse into a long, gloomy silence, Kevin."

"Bondage, Sean? But I must warn you—Deborah is a traitor."

"Everyone knows she blew her undercover story—"

They spotted me and with blinding smiles began the usual "Sterling darling, my eight o'clock died, can I have the night off?" and so forth; it's tough (yet highly gratifying) to be Boss. But beyond the standard daily clamor I felt caught in a mental thunderhead, unutterably fed up with "honest toil," and getting so fed up with the late twentieth century (including this studio and the hapless twerps it exploits, including me—*and* the fact that one is not supposed to *say* these things) that I was beginning to feel I'd been wrong. The "premonitions" were only a symptom of malaise caused by nerve gas, carbon monoxide, and the perils of modern living.

Something was troubling my mind. I've always prided myself on being able to fit in as the generations come and go, although God knows I'll never be a groupie—too many years

of hard, solo experience; too much suffering. The bottom line is, I'm a star, and what I do fascinates people but they don't really *like* me—not the way they like, say, Johnny File—and now, something about this Cox woman had made me feel distinctly out of my depth.

Johnny was involved in it too. Popular, reliable Johnny, who makes jokes on the order of "got a match? My dick and the Alaska pipeline" for which he is loved, honored, and accepted by all. His brain is fifty percent polyester but he teaches poetry at U.C., where he has been given tenure. But me? I'm not well-liked. I must grub for a living. Feared and respected, perhaps; liked and *accepted*, never.

Maybe I'm just jealous. Maybe I was merely upset because Johnny and Patsy hit it off right away.

Angst, angst.

The hell with it. Go home, Sterling darling; have yourself a good night's sleep.

The *merde* an innocent reader is forced to swallow.

Get a load of this.

"Her cameo profile seemed etched against the lights of the green-jewel swimming pool. The fever raced tumultuously through her blood as her lovely eyes, narrowed to mere slits, made her look feral, wanton. Her bare breasts heaved..."

Breakfast in bed: bacon and eggs, stack of golden toast, grape jam, strawberry jelly, three kinds of cheese and a pot of hot coffee, all courtesy of the hotel manager who is a very dear friend of mine. I skim the novel, turning pages swiftly as I nibble among the curtains and cushions, the accumulated treasures, the polished darkwood of my richly furnished, plush, spacious Edwardian parlor in the Drake Hotel.

"...the sweet, restless frenzy. She groaned and panted, unable to stop herself or to control her awful lust, draining the last drops, sucking in frenzy; already beginning to hate herself. In the street a lone siren came howling—"

Oh yeah? The rubes must have their spoon-fed lies, huh?

I read every vampire book that comes out (what a masochist), greedily hoping for some affinity. This one's better than most. Usually they have boring characters, wooden writing, and no ideas. Actually vampires are as human as anyone; in fact, more so. A vampire scratches her flea bites, worries about the job market and hopes some nice person will send her a valentine. But nobody wants to believe that there is none so monstrous it isn't her own mirror image.

I listen to the wind moaning round the old hotel and from my nest of pillows watch it ruffle Lake Michigan. The phone is ringing its head off but I don't feel like answering the beastly thing. So I don't.

The city is irritating, convulsive, surrealist, but it's luxuriously cozy here in my snug retreat. I read, and listen to the wind. Out opposite windows I watch it thrust overcoated lawyers and accountants and their secretaries, and their pushers, bookies, hairdressers, and bootblacks along Michigan Boulevard past our studio, across the street from the Drake where I live. I find it a bringdown living on Chicago's exclusive Gold Coast; I am alternately bored and appalled at this gimcrack civilization-- Who's crazy, me or them? (which is a direct quote from Einstein)... As I chew bacon, I skim along on wings of angst.

"Blood dripped from her dimpled chin onto Duncan Farnsworth's naked chest. A moan escaped the young heir's blue-tinged lips. He was perilously close to death, amid an overpowering animal stench..."

At least it has a refreshing Homeric bluntness.

The phone (that smug instrument of twentieth-century torture) shrilled on. I sipped coffee, pinkie curled, and ignored it.

"She was devastated. She wailed 'What have I done? O Duncan, speak to me, my dearest darling,' while hot tears brimmed from her eyes..."

Merde. Not as bad as *some* merde, of course, but still...What a slough this time period is. Even the biggies are banal. For my money, Camus' famous Meursault is a papier mâche Twinkie concocted by a guy who doesn't understand human nature in the least, which is probably why the Today People gave him so many prizes. They *love* papier mâche. They *fear* flesh and blood. Especially blood. Not that I'm putting Albert down, God forbid. I love him dearly, we met briefly at Cannes, I cried rivers when he was killed, but still...

I mean be honest, even Anna Karenina is rather poorly motivated. Tolstoy never shows Anna's love for Count Vronsky. He just tells about it. As if *he* doesn't know what "love" is any more than the average person does. Deep in my heart I feel that Leo was gay and was desperately in love with the dashing Count himself, but Society wouldn't let him write about it. Could this be true? Could Society be that cruel, that shortsighted? If so, no wonder he made Anna throw herself under a train at the end. Alas; but Tolstoy is still head, shoulders, torso, groin, and *ankles* above most writers these empty days; I mean heavens, even this crappy vampire thriller is the most vital novel I've read in months. Most of the junk is so wooden, so one-dimensional I can't bear it. Everything is jejune, pawkish, freeze-dried, predigested, but admittedly nicely packaged...

I should have put the phone in the fridge last night as usual — why didn't I? Ah, yes; because I was shaken up by that new teacher, Patsy Cox. But it's daylight now, and I'm wide awake, and I refuse to worry.

When critics say "New peaks of brilliance" they mean, "Prepare to die of boredom." And the s-f writers, alas! what babies, infested with a cant of materialism. Miseducation is a terrible thing, and how lucky I *never once* saw the inside of a school, but picked up all I know by tying in to the brain of Niels Bohr and some earlier first-class minds.

Thirty-two ringy-dingies! What persistence. Johnny's voice boomed out, "Sterling, get your ass down here immediately."

I made faces in the mirror, picturing my assistant (an ultra-groomed sophisticate who is *not* wearing a seersucker sportcoat, granny glasses and a sweater with a reindeer on it!). But like a good manager I chirped, "What's up? Something you can't handle, darling? Verses don't scan? Having trouble with a haiku or something?"

"'What you feared has come upon you.'"

I hate to be quoted by tenth-rate intellects, especially when they quote me quoting the book of Job. I was going to tell him to go suck an egg. But—an ancient instinct began to stir.

"Come on, just say it."

"Get down here."

"I'm tied up." I spread Port Salut on a piece of toast.

"This is serious."

"I'll get back to you—or tell me now."

"Not over the phone."

"The big bad wolf was dismembered early today when a bottle-bomb exploded in his Mercedes," I chewed.

"Don't be an ass; this is the real thing."

"Where are you?"

"Coffee shop."

"That's all very fine, but what will you tell your parole officer?"

"You're about as funny as—"

"Give me ten," I said and hung up.

And lay there for eight minutes or so, staring at a reflection on the ceiling. The reflection was shaped like a pitchfork. It had red tines.

I remembered my very first "real thing." The family and every servant had gone to the mountains, leaving me alone; so convenient.

It may sound silly that vampires pray, or at least they did in 1297. By the miracle of prayer or some damned thing, I squeezed through a rotten board in the wine-cellar floor and fled the Motherland, the beloved Romania.

At first I was despondent, very much the rejected exile, living abroad in outward conformity (a bit of panic does wonders for a deviant). I sold my pearls and spent a couple years traveling from country to country, after which I basked in the sun of a mellow Spanish landscape arranging an orderly, yet exciting, life for myself.

Without being aware of it I was inventing, and I mean *personally creating*, that baroque dramatization known as "the classical style." I wore yards of black lace. I spoke Spanish, kept bats in the tower, sucked in my cheeks to look hollow, and carried blazing candelabra up and down winding staircases. I slept in a canopied bed that any antique dealer would give me thirty thousand bucks for today, maybe more; it was hand carved. And I wouldn't trade all the conquests, narrow escapes while clouds scudded across the moon and all the rest of it, to be a welfare state protégé or bureaucrat or anything else you can offer; because life in that unplumbed castle in Spain was ideal.

But then, inevitably, my "sins" caught up with me. By the Beast! I've been shattered so many times I feel like an experimental windshield. And for what? For six ounces of blood. These turkeys protect their carcasses as if they were the Holy Grail wrapped in plutonium foil. Which makes me laugh, because in just a few years they die anyway, despite all that frantic "health care," and they die without ever having lived; and all that ruby blood pours into the undertaker's sink. This is called "going through channels." People seem to love it. It means they never have to think. Just follow the herd.

The saul-bellowing herd...

FOUR

Johnny was at our usual table with the usual pot of coffee. He wiped his lips and got right to the point.

"Do you know a guy named Armand von Saltza?"

I pretended not to be shaken, and said cagily, "Of course I know Armand. *Knew him.* We were married at one time. But that was at least fifty years ago."

"Heard from him recently?"

"Are you crazy? He's probably been dead for years. What the hell is this?"

"He's in town."

"Who?"

"Who are we talking about? Armand."

I was relieved. Johnny must be mistaken. Nothing to worry about. Just another false alarm.

Actually it was *Johnny* I was worried about. Old two-face. Always making sure he was approved by what he called "his peers." Why in God's name did I blab my inmost secrets to this man? I had stewed while getting dressed to come down here. Oh, sure, he was a Right Now bachelor with a USDA-approved body; the type that's known in the trade as "a heavy number," which in my book means a hairy Neanderthal or a mute, inglorious Kennedy with the expression pushed out of shape by the excesses, for which the crowd always forgives him; why, I'll never know. I don't trust him as far as I can throw him.

Bigmouth Sterling, I had fretted, hustling into body-sock, ruffled shirt and earrings. Am I a suicidal maniac or what? (sticking silver links monogrammed "S.O." into my cuffs); I shouldn't drink if I can't keep my big mouth shut. And how annoying that everyone tries to pair us off, in the compulsive way people have. "My boyfriend Johnny." Leon's always buzzes as we walk in together. What a couple! America's sweethearts. You've *got* to be half of a couple. If you're on your own, think of the deviltry you'll get into! Why, you might even learn to think for yourself, and then the whole system would collapse.

As the elevator dropped to the mezzanine, my paranoia also dropped away. Everything seemed so cozily normal and safe in the hushed arcade of specialty shops, very posh, very expensive. The pewter peacock told me it was 11:50 of a Wednesday morning, the eighth of October.

The lunch crowd had begun to overflow the coffee shop. The hotel manager gave me a dear-friend wink; a stray bellboy tugged his forelock, and the cashier, an ultra-classy serious-looking dame, threw me a kittenish wriggle in the best of taste...which *may* mean that I am *approved*, and am not a pariah, or it *may* mean that my hard assets include gold, oil wells, a hot portfolio, and 49% of this hotel — one never knows.

No, dear; not cynical; just realistic. But Johnny sat huffing and puffing.

"Sterling! Will you be honest for once? This is important. Important! Your life may depend on it. Have you been in touch with Armand?"

"If you call having three children together being 'in touch,' I might say 'yes.'"

Peculiar fact: if you're the most honest person in the world (like myself), every twerp will ipso facto consider you a sociopathic liar. At any rate, why fight it; Johnny was fabulously dressed in his gray wool suit, red shirt, and salmon tie, which may sound awful but which on him looks terrific. His massive shoulders were hunched. There was a scowl on his blunt features. Maybe I'm cruel, thinking of Johnny File as Og the cartoon caveman; after all, his incessant preening makes the Studio scads of money...and what the heck, *every* Today Person is afflicted by what I call the Wishy-Washy sickness. It's an epidemic; I can't blame Johnny for it; after all it's not *illegal* to wear pretty clothes, dance gorgeously and write tame-mouse poetry.

He'd just finished breakfast, but the plates hadn't been collected yet. Congealed egg with a dribble of ash is not my favorite, but what the heck.

"Three children? What happened to them?" he now asked.

"Expensive schools, good contacts, a bucket of credit and away they went...sad to say." And sad it was. Mansfield and Edgar, neither of whom inherited the Gene, both absorbed by Wall Street. Dierdre, the daughter, who *did* inherit it, blamed me for it and has been sulking in St. Tropez ever since. But: *tant pis.* No family lasts more than a few score years, and who the hell knows that better than I?

Johnny gulped coffee. "He's here, Sterling. In Chicago. Right now."

"Impossible."

"He was at the Studio an hour ago."

"If this is a practical joke I deplore your taste."

"I'm telling you, the man is Armand von Salzta. I got a fact sheet on him before I called you."

"From fellow pigs at the downtown precinct?"

"What else?" He scowled. "In *your* interest, Sterling."

I love it when people do things in my interest. It makes me go warm all over. There was about one chance in a hundred that Johnny really *had* seen Armand... but... my mouth had gone a little dry.

"Well, what did the old boy say? Did he talk tough, or what?"

I put it like this out of caution, so as not to blurt: "Where is he? Did he ask about me?" Or to tip off that, maybe it was the emotional jolt, but I was going into one of those unsettling, precognitive spasms, or whatever they were, that came over me so often recently.

But all Johnny did was give me an odd shrewd glance and say, "Disco lessons. That's what he wanted. Paid for a ten-week refresher course in advance."

"Oh my God." I snapped for the waitress to clear away the dishes; then unable to contain it any longer I asked nonchalantly, "Well, what was he like?"

To tell the truth I had but dim memories of Armand von Salzta. The person I saw in my mind was twenty-four years old, he was blond, healthy-looking, with a military bearing, but not at all stuffy. Fun to be around. In looks, a golden-boy type.

When you are a—how shall I put it?—a semi-mythological creature like myself, you are expected to act out a script written by others; one that ignores your true nature. This can be an explosive situation. But fortunately in my case I have a marvelous forgetter. Without it, my mind could easily turn into a black hole in the collapse phase. *With* it, "tragedy" occasionally becomes the funniest word in the English language. I sipped my coffee and kept my detachment.

Johnny was pushing the salt back and forth between his hairy paws. "You mean is he decrepit? Well, for an old bird he's in pretty good shape."

"You're an ageist pig, File, you know that?"

"I meant the guy's nicely preserved! that's all — What're you so touchy about?"

"It'll be interesting to meet Armand again. Certainly he can't mean me any harm."

"You're a terrific actress, Sterling. I never know when you're conning me."

Nothing in that called for an answer, so I waited until Johnny saw fit to continue.

"It appears von Salzta is an experienced intelligence officer."

"You don't say. Well I'm hardly shocked. Armand always wanted to be a spy. He wanted adventure, we drifted apart, so what? Are you implying that I know more about this than I'm telling?"

Johnny shoved the salt into its place and smiled. I guessed he believed me, at least for the moment. "His contacts are more widespread than you may realize."

"Didn't mention me?"

"Nope."

"He must know I'm here."

A shrug. "Sterling, your phone's bugged, I'm sure of it."

"All right, let's not lose our cool. I've been threatened by professionals."

"Don't think these are amateurs."

"Whatever his contacts, Armand is no threat."

Johnny was a little bent out of shape. His sense of importance was hurt. I do that to people. It's a paradox. I don't understand it. But it has to do with the survival factor. *I* survive. *They* go tits up, very quickly. I suppose they get eaten alive by this cannibal culture. The culture spits me out, but swallows Johnny. What does it mean? I don't know; he was really mad at me, though.

But with my bleak heritage, cut off from my nation and my language, addicted to the incomprehensible, I was bored with his problems. I stood up and told him to meet me later in my office.

Then, irritated by the false alarm, I stopped at the cashier and signed his breakfast tab with a cruel smile.

FIVE

reen. Preen. Preen. In my opinion, that about sums up the whole twentieth century.

For a while there, I was using my job to take my mind off my real problems. I who can remember sixteenth-century palaces; I who have seen the passing of countless heroes and beautiful people; who am growing slightly deaf from hearing too much rock and roll; my anguish and nostalgia could only be drowned in work. Not honest toil but civilized work, of the type known as "living on one's wits." Obsessive conniving. And the Max Arkoff Dance Studio fits the bill to perfection.

I'm at this studio ten or twelve hours a day, teaching, selling courses, managing, squeezing pennies, smoking an occasional joint in the can with one of the teachers, or playing psychiatrist. *Me*, playing shrink. If they only knew.

I'm attached to my job by an umbilical cord that stretches but never breaks. My boss Max Arkoff is a darling guy, a big movie star in Hollywood. The only time I get to see him is on TV specials, same as any ordinary mortal does.

Sure, I'd love to put Max under ever so discreetly and then shatter him (in my own mind at least) as man, as star, as "boss" and authority figure. I'd love to penetrate that divine, wholly unattainable throat and then slowly, ecstatically, establish mastery while feeding and feeding, *glutting* actually, on the slippery red water of existence, until I am satisfied. But...

Dream on, Sterling. You silly wretch.

As for the young lady teachers, they get jobs here so they can be made glamorous. And this is where our stylish, charismatic, and over-salaried O'Blivion steps in.

First I audition the applicant. If she has Quality, if she's Got What It Takes (that is, if she can be ripped off while believing she's ripping off Max Arkoff and company), I put her on salary immediately. Then I take her out and get the hair cranked, the makeup corrected, a few pounds lost or gained, whatever she needs. That done, I open charge accounts for her, all over town.

Now she's hooked. She no longer owns her own soul. She will do anything. And the fun begins.

We go to specialty shops where I help her select the most glamorous gowns—she goes out of her mind; it never fails. I've done miracles with some of these midwestern girls. That first week I introduced Patsy Cox to a hundred chic people and taught her a quasi-Transylvanian accent, which made her an instant sensation.

"Mina fötter ar hopplösa," she wept, kissing my hands in gratitude.

I call these my little spin-echo experiments on the human soul; they keep me from dying of regret and nostalgia. The girls go wild. They study themselves in the mirrors for an hour at a time. It's so easy to read their thoughts. "Can this be me? Crass, self-centered little me? Why, just look at me. What a gorgeous creature. How stunning from every angle. Look at the way I move, the swing of my low hips, my curving behind, my perfect bosom right out of a bra commercial—I'm falling in love! Yes, I am, and it's everything the poets ever said about it," etc. etc. etc.

As for me, I'm amazed and gratified anew; each time, I feel like Pygmalion. My next move is to supply the girl with plenty of male students. Immediately, her brain slips into high gear. She begins to figure. She buys a pocket calculator and sees for herself what an amount of cash she could rake in by going on commission instead of staying on salary.

She asks, "Sterling, darling, is it all right with you if I go on commission?"

"Of course, my pet," I answer sweetly.

So now she's off salary. The Studio breathes a sigh of relief. Right away I stop lining up all these students for her, and right away her next check turns out to be relatively small. But she's completely hooked by now; first because she is so utterly glamorous she can hardly stand it, and secondly because she owes bushels of money all over town, thanks to her good friend Sterling O'Blivion.

"Sell, sell, sell," I exhort the new teachers. "Put that pen in their hands! Get their signature on that line. *Homo homini lupus!*" quoting Dante, Cervantes, and Marcel Proust; giving pep talks, making charts, forcing them to compete with each other in a desperate frenzy; insisting that they spend every minute of their spare time collecting little bills and receipts for the IRS; or using their pocket calculator to figure capital gains breaks, health benefits, or retirement plans; or, if religious, quibbling with God; or, if not religious, polishing their teeth, curling their lashes, applying lacquer to their toenails, and preparing for wonderful, glossy dates with handsome closet cases who lift weights.

"This is the twentieth century," I encourage them earnestly. "We must fill our time with these activities so we won't ever need to think. If all else fails, stuff a Twinkie down your throat and go to a disco."

And I mean it. They don't suffer the same guilt I suffer; but in a way, what they must endure is far worse. Yet I wonder. Where can it end?

Perhaps I spend too many hours at the Studio. Between lessons we all mill around in libidinous frenzy, the women teachers and the men teachers and the students and myself, experiencing the same pulse of life that thrilled the poet Blake when he wrote the *Songs of Innocence,* or the painter Grünewald when he created his justly famous *Isenheim Altarpiece.* Everyone is in a mad rush, changing costume to a drumbeat in the back room, straining and complaining under the narcotic of ritual dancing, a skittery swampfire of thousand-year lost causes.

Patsy Cox takes down her strapless and switches bras right there in the thick of battle, proclaiming, "Now I gotta boogaloo with Mr. Glumfa of the big feet and bad breath who steers for the dark corners. *Faen! Helvete! Satan,*" and other medieval curse words I've taught her.

The male teachers all chatter at once: "Thinks she can dance and it's torture, talk about bondage my dear, but she's got megabucks and is generous. She likes me and I *love* hating myself," At which the bell rings and we all jump out and begin gyrating like the demons in a painting by Hieronymus Bosch.

Maybe I'm just jaded. I don't know. The haunting seems to be getting worse. A bleed-through from other times? I don't know.

Still, the dance biz is so agonizing it satisfies at least part of my craving for punishment.

At the first lesson you give your pupil a test to determine his dancing quotient, or D.Q. as we call it in the trade. This can be an enormously satisfying little exercise. You bounce him around to the music and you say,

"Well, Mr. Zilch, you certainly have a lot of potential. I'm going to give you a D-minus for what you actually know about dancing, which isn't much, but an A for your natural talent. Now tell me, do you think those are fair grades, darling?"

What can he say? He gobbles it up like popcorn. The point is, Mr. Zilch doesn't have a friend in the world, not really, or why else would he be here?

We sell graded courses in the form of brass, silver, and gold certificates, depending upon how many dances the student wants to learn. We have clever parties to build up competition between our branch studios. It costs a fortune to run a studio. You can't sit around trading baseball cards; you've got to *compete;* you've got to *hustle* in order to get ahead and stay ahead, and drown the funny things that are going through your mind.

The big dances are exciting. We hire a band and fix the hall up with streamers, confetti, gleaming punch bowls, sometimes even horns and hats. Everyone is showing off and suddenly the loudspeaker roars: "STOP THE MUSIC! STOP THE MUSIC!"

Then a hush falls. Nothing is heard but a few electronic crackles in the speaker itself. Then a deeply serious and important male voice (Johnny File's, usually) proclaims, "Lays and gentlemen, your attention please! Mr. B.J. Washout, whom most of you are lucky enough to know in person, has just signed up for a lifetime course of dance lessons. Come up and say a few words, Mr. Washout!"

The spotlights search frantically, locate B.J. Washout, and follow his silver head bobbing its way to the podium on a long drumroll.

Suddenly it's Born-Again time. A fervid silence falls. Mr. Washout, torn with emotion, staggers to the microphone, clutches it in his sweating hands, takes out his handkerchief and blows his nose, absolutely overcome, and finally gets the words out. "Yes! Yes! Miss Krantz has just signed me up for a lifetime course of dance lessons."

Pandemonium.

Cheers, applause, horns are tooted, streamers thrown. Mr. Washout raises his arms for silence (we must not forget that this is the high point of his entire life) and continues: "I spent my retirement savings, every last penny — "

Tremendous cheers. A honk, as Mr. Washout blows his nose onto the monogrammed hanky which he then carefully stuffs into his pocket and goes on,

"I'm so happy! So happy." (A long sigh from the audience, followed by scattered applause.) "I wish every one of you could sign up for a lifetime course. I wish the whole world could come to Max Arkoff and be as happy as I am!"

They help him off the stage. They leave him sobbing in a corner with his radiant teacher, who has just made a nice amount of money, depending on her contract.

It is the dance of life!, the mighty hunters cornering a woolly mammoth at cliff's edge. It is Cro-Magnon doing his brilliant wipeout job on poor dumb Neanderthal! But it takes my mind off a rush of giddiness, when for a moment I seem to be back in my beautiful Sibiu with its deer park and its vineyards, and golden sunsets, the air scented with apples and wood smoke...

Something is happening to me.

I hear Johnny's voice. "STOP THE MUSIC! STOP THE MUSIC! Lays and jelman, the senior Mrs. Nussbaum who is 82 years young" (applause, whistles, cheers) "has just signed up for 40 full years of dance lessons! Let this be an example of optimism to everyone here, because she sold her iron lung to do it!"

And Mrs. Nussbaum totters up gasping for air, gesticulates violently, and goes into convulsions, but the audience thinks this is some new dance step, and they applaud wildly.

Then everything is quiet, empty. Nothing but confetti, half-empty cups, and silence.

I had a sherry or two to pull myself together and looked over Armand's application, hoping he'd left a phone number or an address; but there was nothing. Just the blunt, honest-looking signature, in ballpoint, that I'd once known as well as my own: *Armand von Saltza.*

SIX

"**H**ave the conscience of a Viking," Ibsen encourages us.
One can but try. Like a Viking I love to bolt myself into my cave under the tower's western parapet, which juts slightly north for views of both lake and street, and order up goodies from room service: watercress soup; roast beef with Yorkshire pudding; mashed potatoes and gravy; a pint of Cabernet Sauvignon; an artichoke with plenty of melted butter; and a three-scoop hot fudge sundae for dessert. Blessed are the pure in soul, for they never get fat. I may wind up with a stake through the heart, but I will *never* have to have my jaw wired.

The Drake is a crumbling, medieval fortress for all that she sits foursquare on the "Boul' Mich" in this sophisticated city; and the texture of my life is rich and subtle, if somewhat cramped by foolish conventions. As I jot these words, the dinner hour is chiming. I don't have to be back in the goddamn rat race until seven. I'm feasting alone with my thoughts, having donned a purple robe (it is essential to wear purple when one eats the Artichoke, queen of all the Vegetables).

How good to eat and drink! How splendid just to be *alive*, here in my faintly sinister Edwardian flat, as the evils of the day fall away from me. I now hum an ancient troubadour ballad, pouring oil and vinegar on chilled lettuce and nasturtium leaves, adding a dash of Worcestershire and a dollop of sour cream — languid, crazy, romantic me! — a high-tempered person of oddities, with her own way of doing things.

So don't expect a discussion of "Vampirism as a Greatly Misunderstood Moral Activity" over dinner. Still, as an agent of destiny I'm willing to explode a few pernicious myths at this time. Like, talk about your food chain; some things are hard to explain, but, once I vampirized a famous Shakespearean actor whose name is a household word. I yanked open his dressing-room door and there the fellow stood, quaking in his Elizabethan boots; for as we all know, way down deep... one's fate springs from one's own character and actions.

Trembling, the actor held up a crucifix. I said, "You've got to be kidding, sweetheart," and gently took the item for my collection.

My collection has 947 crucifixes in it so far, plus 442 Stars of David, several obeah bags, a pile of wishbones, and a four-leaf clover embedded in plastic that says "I found it at Tahoe."

The ritual is beautiful; or as the Bible tells us, "In disorder is truth." First we paralyze the donor with an ancient command. Then we make two infinitesimal holes in his or her carotid, or subclavian, with our *very* slightly longer-than-normal, *very* slightly curving canine teeth. Then we lap (not suck, as jerks mistakenly believe) ever so delicately, like that most adorable of pets, the furry cuddly squeaky mousie-bat.

Afterwards we say the ritual prayer and depart in peace. I always feel very satisfied, unutterably fulfilled, and am not above pinning a tiny "I Gave Blood" button to the clothing of my donor. Sometimes I leave a few bucks on the bureau if he or she looks poor.

To *kill* while drawing blood would be a no-class act. But sometimes — very rarely — it does happen.

I comfort myself with the thought that it hardly matters. Most of the people you see walking around have been dead for years.

It's hard to believe that flamboyant Sterling with her clanking bracelets — Sterling, the compassionate aristocrat- brilliant physicist, inventor of the first functional "time-travel machine" [*sic*] (more on the ttm follows) — has been wanted for murder in two states!, her picture in the post office and everything.

Neither case was my fault. They were both heart attacks, brought on by bad press. Yellow journalism plus cheap cinema equals prosuicidal imaginations.

In the end, all charges against me were dropped. For I have the talents one associates, as a rule, with a P.T. Barnum (and I *don't* mean they let me into the top disco joints; of course they do — so what? I scorn all such twinkyhood).

I cling, in this blighted and smut-strewn culture, to one precious talisman. We called it *sânge* in the old country but you call it...blood. Human blood. Blood, the fiery liquor, the scalding, slippery jewel; red stream of eloquent fulfillment... The Ruby. On behalf of which, I often find myself in a mess of trouble.

Once I was condemned to death in absentia — in Poland, which figures.

But levity aside, this is a war of attrition; because if deprived of the Ruby I'd go into wracking convulsions, age rapidly, and become dust after a few weeks of mortal agony.

Other than that, I'm just an ordinary person. Just a twerp like yourself — possibly even slightly dumber. I don't want to build myself up as larger than life. Hell, I'm only a second-rate vampire; no Dracula I, climbing hand over hand up the Drake stonework, into the chamber of Sleeping Beauty at the topmost castellation, where posing bat-winged against the moon I take my six ounces of life eternal! No, not me; that would be doing it the hard way. Victims can be picked up anywhere; whereas most hotel windows can't be opened with a blackjack. If you *must* sneak into someone's hotel room, simply go and ask the desk clerk for the key. If you don't believe me, try it for yourself or ask any house dick to explain the facts of life.

Six skimpy ounces.

Less than they take at the blood bank.

Cheap, selfish bastards!... and for this I suffered the curse of excommunication and was enrolled among the damned.

Now I ask you — how can I take seriously this mob and its flimsy laws that are written on rice paper? Oh, sure, I'm fighting depression, if that's what these dreams are. "Stiff upper lip, for evolution is never in a straight line," I command myself. But now and again, in the cool of evening, I shriek at my soundproofed walls, "You morons! I hope somebody hurts you as much as you've hurt me," but of course I don't really mean it (I am not that cruel).

Now as I sat dabbling in the finger bowl, thoughts of Armand began nagging me. Soon I was opening the padlocked chest in my triple-locked closet.

A whiff of cedar memories...

On the top is a ponderous tome, my opus: the secrets of my

discoveries in the realm of matter, energy, space, and time. Under this Einstein-shattering work, I store my countless souvenirs: locks of hair of all shades, pictures in lockets, love letters tied with faded ribbons, children's drawings and report cards; old banknotes, once so important, now resembling Monopoly money; some old coins bearing the likenesses of forgotten kings... Each memento carries such an echo of travail that just thinking about that dear old cedar chest can make me burst into tears.

It's demonic to outlive 52 lovers! It's awful to endure the withering and dying of romance, excitement and mystery, desire, gas-lamps, the touch of a hand, the flow of starlight through an empty birdcage... Sometimes nostalgia chokes me so that I can hardly breathe. Other times I think it's absurd as hell, and I laugh cleansingly.

At the moment it was depressing to recall my ex-spouse Armand. A young man who loved crazy escapades; witty, Redford-looking, eager, passionate, devoted; I couldn't imagine that boyish sex object as a decrepit and rheumy old dotard. A retired spy! How perfectly dreadful.

I shuffled through albums, finding pictures of Armand and my former self and our cute little kids in their starched collars. There we all were; a nuclear family, smiling in a hay cart at Lake Geneva with some people whose faces I couldn't remember. And there was Armand, looking Beau-Gestey on a polo pony, as if longing for adventure, but stuck with a young family... A tear splashed onto the picture.

For a moment I sank back on my pillows and gave myself up to nostalgia, but of course, it wouldn't do. To wallow in distress is pointless. As Emerson says, we create that which happens to us, and are *not* victims of circumstance.

Besides, I had a lot to think about so I locked the albums away in my trunk, locked the closet door and sashayed into the parlor where I keep such marvels as a clavichord, a sixteenth-century astronomical globe, an astrolabe, and other scientific instruments of the Jules Verne era, including a telescope ornately inlaid with German silver. This telescope points down Michigan Avenue and at the front windows of the Arkoff Studio. (A voyeur? Not me. The tool once foiled a safecracker. It has often come in handy.)

Casually I cranked the rather overly large wheel and panned the side streets where I roam freely late at night. To the south, the dying sun laid a rosy glow over shafts of skyscrapers. Below, a bus stopped with groaning brakes; I watched as a flow of pedestrians crossed the street. A tiny old man scrambled onto the bus dragging a huge suitcase and I considered how, in all the thousands of people I see, almost never do I encounter the same face twice; and how unsanguine this is. The nervous system is not built for the assaulting influx of millions of strange faces. I was born in a feudal village, and I miss it desperately.

The light was ebbing. The studio lights hadn't been switched on yet. There was a shadowy private lesson going on, in a mirrored ballroom that had offices all along one side. I panned the alcove where a cabinet bulges with medals and cups, plaques, trophies, trumps and honors, each topped with a silly-looking dancing couple, and I thought: pity that which has been given an award, for it is thereby certified as junk food.

Just then came a break in the movement. I panned slowly downward and saw Johnny File. There was a woman with him.

I refocused, peering through the circle of glass that magnified every pore and hair. They talked earnestly; they linked arms, strolling to and fro in conversation. They approached the window.

The woman was—

Virginia Woolf.

Wait a minute. This was crazy. Were my eyes playing me false? Virginia Woolf, the famous author, died years ago. Tragically, she walked into a river and was mourned by millions.

I reached for *Britannica,* located the Ws, and read: "Mrs. Woolf drowned near Lewes, Sussex, March 28, 1941, and the coroner returned a verdict of suicide."

Was it a hoax? There she stood, gazing down at the traffic with an inexplicable look on her face: a sort of half-crazy grin that was very much out of place.

I didn't feel anything for a moment. Then… my "now" identity with all its props seemed to melt away. The past sprang alive and engulfed me.

SEVEN

I spent an hour with Virginia Woolf only once. It was in Paris, it was the spring of 1923; I was recovering from wounds suffered due to carelessness (jaw broken by a truck driver when I, mad for the Ruby and not having slept in three nights, foolishly tried to overpower him).

I'd gone to a reading of T.S. Eliot's thrilling new poem called "The Waste Land" by a soft-spoken young man, who seemed to empathize with what he read to such a degree that I was powerfully struck and could scarcely breathe, let alone endure a packed auditorium. So I crept off to the ladies room (of all absurd places) and was sitting before a mirror, trembling, trying to calm myself by gazing in awe at my own face.

And *she* walked in.

Virginia Woolf, who *was* London Society, just as I was... an obscure monster. That year V.W. was a celebrity; her book *Jacob's Room* was adored by the critics. She hadn't yet written *To the Lighthouse* or her science fiction classic (if I may call it that), *Orlando.*

I recognized her instantly. In some strange way, she recognized me too. Our eyes met in the mirror; met, riveted, and locked together, a knife-thrust glance. Thus we contemplated each other, and for a few moments were unable to look away.

Then I guess I made a silly remark, I don't know, perhaps it was a very profound one. What I said was, "Eliot is not for babies." Meaning that from this day forward, I would consider him the greatest of all poets.

And she understood. We left that place and for over an hour

we walked blindly in the park by the Seine, two fugitives in flight from their own natures; for it was at once obvious that, as much as I, she feared to reveal herself.

There was a smell of wet leaves, and a train whistle. Our shoes crunched gravel; but we spoke not a word. The night was so voluptuous and so heavy with nostalgia that I was in a fever.

We touched hands. Our bodies were close, occasionally stumbling into each other, flesh to flesh.

Once she rolled a cigarette and offered it to me. When I shook my head she lit it for herself.

After eons of time, she spoke: "Leonard has gone home. The others are waiting. Eliot is there. You're welcome to come."

"I can't," I croaked, meaning that I was on the edge of chaos and in no condition to meet anyone this night, Bloomsbury intelligentsia or otherwise. Leonard, I knew, was her husband, a formidable figure in his own right.

"Here then, tomorrow, three o'clock?"

I agreed, and she took flight. My last view of V.W.: retreating from me under the plane trees in a park in Paris, in the impersonal light of an ice-cold moon. Disappearing into a vast darkness, forever.

I was there promptly at three the next day, biting my fingers with nervousness. I pictured her striding up the path: charming, elegant, angular, with that long sweep of throat, the face a bit overfine, the eyes friendly but sad, as if focused on something far away.

Of course I knew all about V.W. — who didn't, in that season of her triumph? Her grandfather was Sir James and her father was Leslie Stephen, the distinguished scholar and lifelong friend of Oliver Wendell Holmes and James Russell Lowell; a man who was "honest, responsible, and sane." V.W. grew up in an atmosphere of books and intellectual discussions, surrounded by Huxleys and Thackerays. But me... No soft, gentle arms had sheltered my cradle. I had lived roughly, hand to mouth, surrounded by violence, and I often used street slang; she, always the refined language of the salon.

She had been accepted by her famous family. I had been rejected by mine. Now I envisioned her sweeping toward me, dignified and graceful. Her prettiness had been washed away by suffering but now she seemed beautiful, at once virginal and sensual, with green eyes that looked right through you.

Everyone knew that Virginia Woolf was sometimes unbalanced. I could understand and feel her suffering, the madness that would eventually destroy her, the inferno in which she lived; but I suspected I couldn't help.

Then, the brutal awakening.

I paced up and down for hours. I searched the face of every passing stranger. When she didn't come, I longed to jump into the Seine, or go to sleep in an empty carriage and never wake up. I trudged back home heartbroken. Years later I'd be grateful for that night in which no sensual act took place, nothing erotic happened; yet she left me with a fullness, a feeling of plenitude.

Like the rest of her public, I'd heard that V.W. was not always so agreeable. Indeed, she could be socially terrifying. She'd lead shallow people on to speak their minds and then with a calm, saintly expression, and in a very few words, would coolly puncture them with a death blow. The writer in me was fascinated by her staggering talent; but the woman was smitten. "Madly in love," I told myself. Later I would downgrade that passion as a schoolgirl crush, but at the time, the intensity of it was devastating.

It's true Virginia Woolf fired my imagination until I was exalted into an almost visionary state. I suppose it would have been a fatal mixture. But the fact remains: I did not fit into her life.

My unspoken plea remained just that.

A message in a bottle thrown out to sea.

EIGHT

Then it happened again. Against my will I crossed between present and past.

Springtime, a distant morning. I was out riding my bay filly Eurydice who I loved very much. Suddenly there were yells behind me. A band of peasants waving sickles came thundering across the meadow.

I looked to see what robber they were chasing, but nobody was in sight. They were after *me*.

A gang of them cut me off, shrieking, "Specter! Scum! Pervert! Scourge!"

The whole mob came pounding up. I was dragged off my horse; my hair was yanked back so they could get a better look. There were shouts, babbling voices. "Is that the gal?"

"It's her, all right," their faces prissy with self-righteousness.

I was manhandled and cuffed, but they soon quieted down, as a priest began praying in a monotonous roar about "evil things of the world" and "The children of the night" and all that familiar, horns-and-teeth bullshit. The priest glared, flicked holy water at me, said that I was a"demon of the lower air who sucks blood," said "Spirit be gone!" about ninety times (while I stood wondering how to oblige), and raised his crucifix.

I was scared witless, needless to say; but laughed boldly and explained that they were a pack of cretins.

"May you look in the mirror and see Nothing!" I howled, setting off a thrill among them.

"Devil's tricks!" -the superstitious priest could only pout and throw a tantrum. It must have been an absurd spectacle. Now four little girls, my pallbearers, stumbled up with a fresh-cut pine box that they could hardly carry. As the coffin fell, its lid clattered on some stones. Two old wives replaced the lid; upon it they carefully arranged a small wooden cross, a mallet, a wooden stake, and four candles. Nearby was an open pit, dug earlier.

But foolishly I still thought my deliciousness was enough protection. Then as now I had the tilted nose with the half-dozen cute freckles, the cleft chin, flashing eye, flowing hair, billowing bosom: everything which buys a safe passage through this Twinkie world of protected consumers. In addition, I have an honest, innocent, saintlike face. So naturally, I was trusting my looks to make the inner conflict of my tormentors so unbearable they'd let me go.

Ah, but... would they let me off the hook? Or not? A pot of tar was being heated up. Its noxious fumes were poisoning the air.

Clement the butcher's son now strolled over, wiping his boots on the turf. Clement gave me no sign of recognition, although I knew the idiot well. He wore a sly smile and swung the rope that was usually kept coiled on his pommel. His short, thick arms were covered with black hair. Clement was that grotesque automaton, the self-righteous clod. No conflicts for the butcher's son; he'd enjoy hanging me.

I listened to plenty of crazy gabble and some accusations (mostly false), as bumpkins of both sexes began jostling for the choicest view. Clement was stringing the rope over a convenient branch. He played to the crowd. The black hair was plastered down on his sloping forehead. I'd gone into a panic, because my horse had disappeared in all the pandemonium. But... I never saw Eurydice again. They drowned her because she was "a leech's horse."

Smacking his lips the whole time, Clement fitted the noose around my neck, then went off to stir the fire under the tar pot. I can still feel that heavy, stiff piece of hemp scraping my flesh. At least a hundred villagers were milling around, and troops of boys on ponies kept circling the whole mob; but I didn't spot one single person I'd ever taken blood from... no, there was one. Just one fat, little, trained rat: the clerk Roger in his wool smock, chewing a turnip and snickering, refusing to meet my eyes.

Their leader was a jowly farmer with a bristling, gray-streaked mustache. He pulled his enormous horse up short and gazed down at me, smelling about like you'd expect him to smell, and he meant business. He boomed, "Bloodsucker, you stink of Satan!"

I said something on the order of "Oh, don't be ridiculous, Maurice!" (Or my usual message to those in fear, which is: Calm down, Pierre. I wouldn't suck your diseased blood for a million francs.)

The leader wore the usual much-patched doublet, rough gloves, heavy sabots, had a wart on one eyelid, and, along with the stench from his mouth, he oozed an earnest, unintelligent pomposity that disgusted me beyond belief.

When I had the nerve to answer back, his jaw muscles went lumpy with injured self-importance; and he bawled out that I was vain, wicked, demonic, and a few other things, and added, "Repent, before you go to meet your maker!"

I explained that if I had a maker, and my maker made me like this, what was all the fuss about? At which the farmer called me a name.

I spat in his face — a tactical error.

Nothing changed in his sour mug. But the slap he delivered jerked my head around. My back was placed against a tree. They were going to hang me for sure, then tar my body to preserve it as a warning. I didn't know what the coffin was for.

But *still* I didn't believe they'd go through with it!- in spite of the countless tales I'd heard about what they did to vampires. I even watched them boil one alive (and later sell the fat), but I never believed it could happen to me.

A pale young draper, a "very dear friend" of mine, a lonely queen I'd befriended for years, now glided up out of breath. Keeping his head lowered, he tied my wrists firmly behind my back.

"What am I charged with? What's my crime?" I kept asking, with as much dignity as I could muster. Actually the draper's eyes were not without pity, but what could he do? If he tried to help me they'd rip him apart. And, in any case, in spite of our friendship, his fear of "the supernatural" was making his eyes pop. He paid attention only to the ropes, jerking and tying them just right, and not answering me.

And then— rescue! Or so it appeared, as a party of cavaliers came galloping toward us. My heart leaped; I'd be saved, now, and always, because I am a survivor, a creature of mythology, indestructible, not to be killed by these stinking swine! For am

I not part of their very fantasies? And as such, death can never touch me.

But— my measure was not yet filled up.

One of the cavaliers leaned down, drew his sword, grabbed me by the hair, hacked, and spurred after his buddies: cloak billowing, my cut-off mane brandished high in triumph. (In those days, they braided watch fobs out of vampire hair for talismans. Such pieces bring horrible luck, but the poor brutes didn't know it.)

I was undone. My illusion-bubble had burst. But it was an intoxication, a sensual pleasure to discover that when death comes running at the speed of light, time slows to a crawl. Here is my freeze-frame of deepest inner concentration:

The man on the shaggy horse, who bent over me. The sweat was no longer rolling down his nose. The mob (some in jerkins and tights, some robed, others caught in the act of rubbing their codpieces) were so many foolish statues on trampled earth. The unknown law I had evoked was this: Only a fool sets out to kill any living creature. You don't know what forces you are releasing.

They hustled me up onto my coffin. The pine box had been flopped onto its open side, below the hanging-branch, all set to be yanked from under my kicking feet by these clowns (who were sealing their own doom), as soon as they all gave a hearty pull on the rope. It was majority rule at its finest.

But I had entered the place beyond fear and was able to freeze time again, and now my powers blossomed— exactly like the "flowers of the night" the foolish priest had babbled his prayers about. In this vision of wild joy, I felt pity for all fools everywhere who want to be flattered and called "right" no matter what crimes they commit; and yet— in the interest of personal survival, I was forced to lay a rather strange curse on the whole idiotic species.

Then, a carriage came rumbling up. I expected nothing (especially after that psycho horseman had cut my hair off), and I was in a trance, hardly feeling my cuts, abrasions, and broken ribs. There was a slow clatter of hooves. A dry creaking of wood and metal. And oddly enough, my tormentors suddenly vanished.

An aristocrat jumped down, a certain duke of the area whom I knew by sight only. He was tall and gaunt, middle-aged according to the standards of the day, wearing a well-cut blue coat and side whiskers, and the sun was reflected twice in his spectacles. He said: "Get into the carriage" (which I did, with great pain and effort). Then he said, "Have some brandy" (stripping off my blood-soaked clothing), and, "Wear this blanket. We'll see the doctor now."

In the Duke's mansion, I had access to the most splendid library since Alexandria. It was here that I began the work of a lifetime. Perhaps the shock of the lynching had released tremendous powers in me; I don't know; but in my ignorance I began freely experimenting with ideas of relativity (400 years before Newton, mind you!), interdimensional jumps, chronon-splitting, or "temporal translation of matter" or whatever the hell you want to call it in this culture's confused terms.

And never a month went by, but that some hideous fate happened to one of the men of that posse. First the leader was drawn and quartered, after a supernatural experience had driven him partly crazy. Then Clement got himself hanged, his hairy arms lashed to his sides; my draper friend died (not as pretty any more) of the pox; Roger's fat head was cut off by the executioner; the others were hanged one by one, or badly crippled by falls or disease, except for the cavalier who hacked off my hair.

This fool turned out to be my brother-in-law and a prince of the realm. He apologized to me on bended knee and was then whipped and drummed out of his regiment.

My endowments are, as Poe points out, but little susceptible of analysis.

But during my years with the Duke, I knew real love; and I knew the flow of long, graceful, monotonous afternoons under black-beamed ceilings, with our tumbling cubs at play on the sweeping lawns, which we glimpsed through leaded casements.

On the other hand... how can you "prove" an old memory? What if all this is a fantasy and what really happened was that those brutes hanged me, drove the stake through my heart, and buried me, and later— a hundred years later— some science-oriented twerp pulled the stake out, and here I am?

But what I *remember* (I think), is that one soul-shattering day my Duke died of old age. He passed away into the shadow; while I, alone again, stayed young and darling as always.

Either way, O gracious lords and ladies, it was a roaring *bitch* of a lousy experience.

NINE

On the other hand... how many husbands can a woman bury and still take it all seriously?

It's one thing to bid a tender goodbye to your brave lover in his suit of armor; and quite another to catch a glimpse of him a few minutes later through the trees, crying, his spear bent, being chased by a wild baby pig.

These mishaps can shake a person up for the rest of her goddamned life. I was still looking for a logical explanation; like they say about angel dust, *bang,* when you least expect it, you're in the middle of a bad trip. But I was no doper. This was real. I had the urgent feeling... that I was walking into the propeller.

Virginia Woolf, here, in Chicago?

The woman I'd worshipped from afar in 1923? No way. She'd always been a visionary on the wing; but unless she possessed legendary gifts to match my own...

I tried to read her lips, but I have no skill at it. How beautiful she looked, back from the dead, uninjured by time... Johnny knows of this telescope; he borrows it to check up on goldbricking teachers. Maybe the routine across the street was being enacted for my benefit.

To make me jealous?

What a rat my assistant is.

Or maybe the rat was trying to warn me. But of what?

I sat drumming my fingers on the vintage eyepiece and worrying. I wished for a directional mike so I could pick up what they saying. But soon the figures walked across the plateau of dance floor, to the far end of the studio, which stretched beyond my field of vision.

Faugh! I cast off the purple robe and began to pace naked, struggling with paranoia. Woolf, alive, undiminished! Whatever this unholy pair were pulling, it was essential for me to get my head together and dump all feelings of envy. Not that envy isn't justified; of course I'm jealous. Jealous of anyone who hasn't suffered as I have suffered, who doesn't need the lights on to fall asleep, who hasn't been persecuted and stigmatized. Not to mention kicked, spat at, lacerated and despised! Yes, I'm jealous of everyone who isn't stuck with the complexes and inhibitions that I've picked up over the years. Of everyone who doesn't remember being on the run: half-frozen, chased into alleys, across rooftops, sick, starving, with the scabies, the crabs, the rats, the insults... the sore feet... By the Bulbous-bodied Pax! But my life has been one long war: Sterling O'Blivion versus the rest of the human race!

On the other hand, if there's anything I hate, it's self-pity. It was time to think carefully, without bitterness or anger. What was the significant factor here? I had a pretty good idea.

Long ago, I attended a country fair in Wales at which a juggler performed an interesting trick. I was struck by this exhibition, which shattered once and for all the narrow view of reality I'd held up to that day. All the juggler did was pass a ring through negative space and materialize the object again, *next to itself*, a few seconds in the future, or so it appeared; but hoax or real, I flashed on the basis for a workable ttm (or time-travel machine).

Now if some physics department putz should happen to read this account (and you know who you are!, petty monopolist who wouldn't acknowledge me or give advice or help through those early, messy workshop experiments of mine), just remember: it took centuries for me to unravel the Minotaur thread and outstrip your much-adored fundees and grantees. So don't smile your superior little smile when I tell you that you've got nothing going for you today but *jargon*, carefully arranged, like a plate of stale noodles, around a colossal chunk of emptiness... But me? I solved the unified field mystery alone in that unheated workshop. And why not? After all, I was standing on the shoulders of giants! Giant squids, to be sure, but giants all the same.

And now it's my turn to torment *you*, you miseducated little degree snob. "Big Bang?" Don't be an ass; the radio emission is left over from the Little Whimper (all good things start that way). "Time"? A change of location in space; no more, no less. "Time" is a substructure of the dream manifold, and although the manifold geometry can get pretty complicated, "time" is at best a self-gravitating fluid, existing solely to provide an event horizon upon which we perform our adiabatic idiocies.

But no system can be observed without perturbing it. Here was Virginia Woolf come back to life. I still had the hots for her; no question about it, I was warm for her form. And here was Armand von Saltza of the CIA, returning to the family bosom after all these decades. Could the government be thinking of using vampires for biological warfare? Were those generals several degrees more paranoid than I had assumed? Or had my probable-universe experiments been paralleled, somehow tapped into, by a person or persons unknown?

I wondered if Virginia Woolf (the original? A double? How could I tell?) was working for Armand's office. But if she was, where did Johnny File fit in?

Well: only one way to find out. It was still early but I dressed myself in basic black, with a sapphire cross at the throat, and wrapped myself in my floor-length black velvet cape. Then I turned off the lights, opened the door, and slipped out.

I have always envied creatures that crawl and are poisonous.

Crossing with the light, I kept thinking, "Perhaps I'm being led into a trap." Even so, I took no steps to protect myself. The elevator came down; I got into it, I went up, I got off at the Max Arkoff floor... not yet realizing I was about to have one of the strangest experiences of my life.

Johnny was sitting in my office. He was working at the oaken desk. He didn't look up or speak.

I tossed my cape at the rack. "What's new?"

"Not much," he grunted.

I sneaked a peek over his shoulder and read:

Womblike horns, traffic whistles
I gently withdrew and she bit my ear.
Gathering dust on the TV lies my love,
A victim to society's stolen pie
Dancing my pulsating organ to sleep

A knot on a sea of pink coral.

I refrained from saying "God protect us! God defend the memory of Eliot, Pound, Joyce, Dylan Thomas and even e.e. cummings, now and in the forthcoming Years of Slop."

Johnny yawned and said, "Your friend Armand will be around tomorrow afternoon."

"Is that the whole message?"

"You expecting more?" He leaned back in the chair, eyebrows raised. He picked lint off a cuff, looking everywhere but in my direction. He was in love with me!, how horrible.

I said, "Not necessarily. I thought you might have something to tell me."

"After the way you brushed me off this morning? No chance."

"Exactly what do you want?"

"Apparently more than you're willing to give," And the niggling martinet pursed his mouth primly. Johnny's clothes are smashing, his awards are piling up, and his mind is an illegally parked Pinto. I threw up my hands and left him to get over his sulk—or not; I didn't give a damn either way. I went striding across the empty dance floor and into the ladies room.

Virginia Woolf was in there.

I guessed that she'd showered and was now struggling into her clothes. Wet hair snarled, she had put the brassiere on backwards, and was trying to leap into the panties.

Was the woman insane? She glanced up with a jolly grin, wiping her mouth on her forearm.

I said, "Excuse *me*," and whirled to make a tactful exit.

"Hey!" she roared.

Before I could get out, Virginia Woolf shot forward and blocked the door. She grabbed my elbow. I wrenched away. We struggled, ridiculously, toward the washbasins.

"Stop this," I ground between clenched teeth.

"Sterling O'Blivion," Woolf bawled. Slipping into a crouch, she tried to get me in a half nelson. I threw haymakers, loving the sound they made when they landed, and she bellowed, "Hey!" several times; but what else could I do, drawn as I was into a perfectly mad situation over which I had very little control?

Woolf pivoted, crashing her shoulder into mine. Her wet hair lashed my eyeball. That eye began an agonized watering as, legs pressed against the plumbing, I gripped the bottom of a stall door and refused to let go.

Next thing I knew, Woolf was peeling me off the wall and thundering.

"Let's have a little talk, sweetheart!"

"Take your paws off me, you grotesque," I stage-whispered, hoping we couldn't be heard outside the restroom.

I was confused by the onslaught, but managed to heave the woman's bulk off me, hoping that no student would enter and see this disgraceful exhibition. Woolf ignored my words; her head shot forward. I felt the impact of her flying leap and dropped sideways, trying to gain a little purchase. But this was not my day for acquiring glory in battle. I found myself trampling and kicking, then flopping, floundering, and clutching. By the time I got her by the throat and was bumping her head on the tiles, I could have murdered the dizzy bitch for all the humiliation she'd caused me.

"EE-ha," Woolf yodeled between taps of her head on the floor. "Looks like the inmates have taken over the asylum!"

At that, she threw me. I sprang up and grabbed her again, but in a moment was floundering on the tiles, where I did more twisting and panting, and clawed at the hand dryer; but the struggle was unequal. Woolf had the magnificent strength of the deranged. Worse, I was psychologically stuck in 1920 when she was the big cheese and I was a social climber, or Bloomsbury Bunny, albeit a shabby-genteel one with a lot of old lost money and all that. (True I had a letter of protection from King Philip II of Spain, but by then it was of historical interest only.)

"This is one swell brawl," brayed the madwoman.

A click of high heels approached the door but, thank God, they went on by.

I panted, "Let me up and I won't press charges."

"Your mother wears army shoes," she said with a wink.

I do not know if "telepathy" is an electromagnetic force or merely clever observation, the picking up of subtle clues, and so forth; but as I say, I have some skill at it. So, throwing myself into the spirit of my rival, I questioned if she was the high-strung, neurotic, desirable Virginia Woolf that I had known. Could it be possible? But what about her prodigious strength? And her terrible glee, the glee of insanity? And what about the variations in her expressions? She used her face like a rubber mask; as if untaught to follow the familiar patterns, all of our common expressions, from which one must never deviate, upon pain of being thought to ridicule Humanity.

We sat on the floor, me licking my bashed lips; I sensed that she was trying to communicate on my level, and it was quite a struggle for her.

"O'Blivion, your help is needed."

Woolf's mouth hung open, and her brow was furrowed, but I felt she had no truly hostile intentions— otherwise I'd have been thrown out the window by now. As for me, my heart was racing. This was not a Today Person; this was a live, flesh-and-blood woman, not a robot, and she took my breath away. I threw out a question or two, and she answered,

"Transcend yourself and understand," or words to that effect. I suggested we discuss it in my office, then tidied myself and helped the great author zip, buckle, and hook. She seemed to have little idea about how clothing went on. She didn't care a rap about her appearance. How refreshing, from the days of the snooty, fashionable Mrs. Woolf, celebrated by hordes of admiring meatheads.

Once in my familiar office, the plum carpeting sinking beneath our feet, my confidence began seeping back, although the assault had left me feeling vulnerable. Woolf, for her part, was completely at ease. Her eyes devoured the room. Those eyes were exactly as I remembered them: as liquid, brooding, and intelligent as ever.

I went around the desk and sat down.

"This is bigger than any mere war," Woolf began.

Chewing a toothpick, she straddled her chair backwards and said:

"You can keep your trap shut."

"No argument."

"But it's a mournful life you've got going here," she said. "Our studies show that your thrilling tragedy is about due for a big change, Vampire. The first human to sense it, of course, is yourself; the quintessential, most advanced, and by far the oldest bat on this planet. You've been screened by me personally for a great and holy task: that of restoring order to the chaos of your world."

I looked at her suspiciously. "Where does Johnny File fit into this?"

For answer she took a shiny object that looked like a laser gun from a zippered pocket and spun the chamber. Out in the ballroom, the music was starting with its bass-pedal banzai, but she paid no attention.

"See this?"

I had to confess that I saw the laser gun.

"It's an H-2 unit."

"How interesting," I smiled.

"It's designed to freeze a being into a body. A fate worse than death."

I said nothing. Woolf continued, "That happened to me once. Then I was given a release and immunity. Now, I'm foreseeing a day when you try to destroy me with this. I'm asking you not to do it. You'll destroy yourself, not me."

I never argue with screwballs carrying laser guns. "What is it you want? Make yourself comfortable and let's talk. Put that thing away and sit down, for God's sake; you're driving me crazy."

Woolf had begun circling my office the way a beast prowls its cage. "You are more fortunate than you know, because the laws of compensation are working in your favor. Each time you almost get lynched, you become more powerful. But at the same time, as you grow more powerful you attract attention." She paused; then,

"Look at all those stars out there. It would be absolutely insane to believe you're the only sentient species in the universe."

I was fascinated and enthralled by her, but flatly refused to show it, asking in bored tones, "And who are you?"

She straddled the chair again and said,

"Don't you know? I think you do. Let me put it like this. Some people here are desperate to expand. They say they need more room, and some new kinds of buffalo to exterminate, and some fresh alien species to kill off while they take over and exploit their planet. Only one trouble. We're here to see you discover a way to make yourselves sane, before you start expanding out into the universe."

She advised us to study the pathology of social customs and not only that, but change them. I let out a whoop of laughter.

"Impossible," I jeered.

"It can be done. And by humans themselves, working full time at it. Other beings can't bring you peace, sanity, and wisdom; you've got to do that for yourselves."

"And if we won't?"

"Then you're a race that must stay in its own solar system, may even need euthanasia. Psychosis is contagious. Can't let it spread."

I listened, fingering my sapphire cross. "Is that the bottom line?"

She pointed the toothpick at me. "Don't bottom-line *me*, you old bat. The human race cast you out, and don't forget it. But me, I'm your friend. My name is Benaroya, I hail from a planet called Rysemus, and here's me at home; take a look at that."

She riffled through her wallet, took out a battered photo and threw it on my desk. It was a snapshot of a sea pig or fat dolphin, incredibly ugly; all flippers and bloated neck. I licked my lips, faintly nauseated.

"That's me, all right. The body's built like that to fit a heavy-water environment, so don't go getting critical." She snatched the photo out of my hands and stuffed it back into the wallet. "I'm here to study your tiny little sweet human souls, which you think are superior to animal souls but aren't. I'm an anthropologist, testing to see if you can't get over that one big hang-up. See: you are a part of nature, not 'above' it. As a vampire you know this instinctively, but the Today People reject it."

No, she wasn't the "real" Virginia Woolf.

"We analyzed your entire output of books, comics, films, newscasts, and found out what you like, how you think, what scares you; the whole armor of false beliefs in which people wrap themselves," she yelled over the strains of Travolta Lust. "Now, every damn one-a-ya must have 'a wholesale revision of the personality,' as Kierkegaard says."

She really spoke my language... a little too well. I played along, curious to see what would develop. "I plan to preserve my lifestyle no matter who says what."

"Surprises are coming."

"Why don't you let people know you're here?"

"What for? The place has always been full of aliens. Humans have never recognized it and never will, not even if they spend a hundred billion dollars trying to pick up one whisper from

Arcturus."

I grinned. "And how will we know when we're 'sane' according to your standards?"

"When one person, just one person, stands up and says 'Hey. Wait a minute. Why are we acting like psychotics?'"

My cynical sneer was lost on her. "Your naiveté is incredible." I chuckled.

"Yeah? Your science fiction stories of Trekkies going out into space with their old caveman mentalities and *winning* are baloney. Too many surprises in store. Nobody's planning to let you nitwits 'colonize the galaxy.' And believe me, no superior race is gonna travel way out here in the boondocks and kiss your feet and play lovely spooky music for you. Are you kidding? No other race is even gonna let you know they exist, until you grow up. They're around, sure; always have been and always will be, but you ain't gonna know it, ya jerks!"

She said that our fates were linked, hers and mine. She said that all the old structures were coming down and the old framework would soon lie in wreckage.

"Can you face psychosis and lick it? That's the test."

"Why pick me?" My confidence was all on the surface.

"You are one of the few humans who has begun to understand that the physical universe, or P.U. as we call it, is far less solid than your post-Einsteinians suspect. It's an agreement, emanated by you. But with humans unable to look or to have, you need a self-propagating chain reaction of sanity and you need it *now*."

"And?"

"You think like an immortal, to some degree, yet you're human. That's the link we need." Woolf stuck the shiny gun in her belt and went on, "A guy who's after something, a grant, an award, a political office or whatever, is never gonna be trustworthy. He can be corrupted. But you, you've lived long enough to know better. Now don't get me wrong; the loathsome flesh you devour is atrocious, and you're as commercially debased as the worst of them, and crazy as a bean besides" (the music stopped and started again, boom boom boom) "but get past all that and you're very old, very wise, and not only a damned good theoretical physicist but a square shooter."

I looked over my shoulder. "Who, me? Nah. Not hardly," thrilled and captivated but too well trained to show it. "So you want my help," I stalled. "For what?"

"Research, of course."

"Along what lines?"

Then Woolf (or "Benaroya," as her sea-pig name was) expressed admiration for a part of my work that is so secret I hardly even let myself think about it in public. She made an oblique reference to antimatter that gave me gooseflesh; then, "...scared they'll skid right out of this space-time continuum," was the expression she used.

So my worst fears were true. My experiments *had* been paralleled, at least to the educated-guess stage. I felt very upset and said, "How come you waited so long? I really needed you, back in 1295."

"You need me now far more. Something has gone wrong. Just about everyone on Earth is aware of that fact, it's so obvious."

There was a musical ripple, a pause, then Johnny's voice on the P.A., rapping out instructions. A smooth, reasonable voice with an echo chamber effect. When the violent throb of drums began, the noise actually sounded good; I said, "I've got to get out on the floor."

"Meet later?"

"Yeah, sure, why not," I said as I locked the door behind us with that self-satisfied smile that says "It's *your* idea, not mine."

TEN

Favored by Nature's gifts as I am, the trendy hype of the Arkoff Studio is a piece of cake for me. I can shut everything out and go drown myself in details, many of which are so absurd, labyrinthine, yet sanguine, that they satisfy a person completely.

For instance, suppose one of your students gets to thinking he's too good a dancer already and he can quit taking lessons. Now it's obvious that if you're a survivor like me, you can't let that happen, right? So what do you do? You start giving that student more trouble than he can handle. You get him out on the dance floor and you don't cooperate. And you say,

"What's the trouble, Mr. Zilch? Aren't you practicing enough at home? You'll have to come down more often so I can give you some special lessons."

Or you can say, "I'll tell you what. You can switch off and dance with Miss Bloom for a while," and then you signal Miss Bloom to give him the same treatment. After half an hour of this torment you return and say, "You mustn't get discouraged, Mr. Zilch! We all reach this point. We call it 'the learning plateau.' You go and talk to Mr. Sleazy. He will help you plan your future achievement. We must all plan ahead and set a goal, you know!"

It's like walking a tightrope. You're on stage all the time. In every three-hour lesson, Mr. Zilch spends an hour and a half being guided around the floor and another hour and a half reviewing his charts, signing new contracts, and absorbing the "success is just over the horizon" treatment.

All this calls for plenty of strategy, timing, and polish on the part of the teacher. You've got to graph Mr. Zilch's achievement, using lots and lots and *lots* of paper; each graph bristling with red marks and blue checks, and apt comments, neither too up, nor too down; plus pictures, diagrams, gold stars, dotted lines, initials, flags, signatures, and seals.

I'm fond of this routine, if only because it's the mirror image of our entire civilization. Everyone gets the same shuffle in college; without it, people wouldn't take "education" seriously. What would they do? Life would be boring. Life would be empty.

But the Studio galvanizes us. By late night we're all half crazy with the overwhelm of tattered nerves. It's a fascinating line of work. Let's say that Mr. Zilch decides to give you a little more trouble. Perhaps he hasn't had enough attention. There are various ways of dealing with him. It's important to remember that his teacher is the only one who cares about him in the entire world; if anyone else cared about him, he wouldn't be here.

So, we get him out on the floor, and we put a spotlight on him.

All the Studio execs are seated at the long table, watching him. He is the center of attention!, the cynosure of all eyes. Then the program director asks his teacher, "What courses has Mr. Zilch studied?"

"Well, he's learned the Latin Swing, the L.A. Hustle, the Fish, the Fox-Trot, and the Tango," you say.

"Can he run through a step without any music?"

"He certainly can."

"And did he learn the Cha-cha-cha? No? Well, the first test dance will be the Cha-cha-cha."

So they turn off the music, and Mr. Zilch is really sweating. Everyone is watching him sweat it out under the spotlight. If he passes this test, the reward is, he can sign up for more courses.

And his dance teacher is being very encouraging. She is his Only Friend in All the World; all of the others are against him, but she is with him, she is on his side. "Come on," she whispers. "I know you can do it!"

Then they start doing the dance together — and she louses him up completely. He's shattered! He's depending on her to see him through. What can be wrong? "You and me," she whispered, and now they're stumbling around under the spotlight…

It's miserable. I don't deny that. But it's human nature. It's basic. Otherwise people would have nothing in their lives;

nothing, nothing, *nothing*. So it's terribly important to give them a lot of emotion and trauma and agony, and awards, and tests, and degrees, and razzle-dazzle, just to make life exciting. And anyway tomorrow Mr. Zilch will be on top of the world again, bouncing around, trying to peek down the front of Miss Bloom's dress, trying to back her into a corner... The only dress he ever got to look down before was his mother's, and he was too young to take proper advantage of the opportunity, which was a limited-time offer only.

So, the entire staff is seated at the long table, watching: very noncommittal, grimly silent, faintly sneering. All Studio business has stopped. Only the metallic beat roars on. All the teachers and all the students Mr. Zilch has ever known in all his days at the Studio have all trooped in and found chairs and are watching.

So after about an hour of this painful performance, the executives say, "Well, we'll have to look this over and come to some sort of a decision. H'mm... We'll have to talk among ourselves. If you'll just step out into the lobby for a few moments, Mr. Zilch...?"

It's magnificent! It is the way every human has been broken to the whim of the mass, since society began. Actually we could overcome Russia, or whoever we happen to be fighting at the moment, with this remarkable technique. We'd make them dance around under a spotlight with all their friends watching.

At any rate, they let Mr. Zilch stew out in the lobby for an hour and a half, while they sit in the office and drink coffee and tell jokes. Finally, Mr. Zilch is called in.

There's a rubber stamp on the manager's desk; one side says FAIL, the other side says PASS. The FAIL side has been turned upward. This is the first thing Mr. Zilch sees when he walks into the office. So they give him a few minutes to absorb it.

Meanwhile they've lined up his papers and charts and everything he's ever signed (which is plenty) on the manager's desk. Mr. Zilch is experiencing internal contractions, you can tell by his expression, and no doubt there is an icy tingle chasing itself along the curve of his buttocks.

THEN—They open up his folder, and the word PASS has been stamped inside the front cover.

"Well!" they say. "Mr. Zilch, we want you to realize that this has been a very difficult decision. But on the recommendation of your teacher, we've decided to pass you. If you think this is a fair grade, sign here."

A pen is placed in Mr. Zilch's trembling fingers.

And what do you think he does?

He nearly breaks his wrist signing that contract.

Then they all smile radiantly, because they've each just made $800 or $2,400 or $48,000, and his teacher gives him a great big kiss, because now she can pay off some of these bills she's piled up. She might even give him a free supplementary half-hour and build him up big, make him dance beautifully for a change, to stifle his buyer's remorse and show him that everything is going to be just dandy in his life now that he's signed this agreement.

And so together they plan a whole new course of lessons, this time beginning with the Cha-cha.

O tempora! O mores! O, E Pluribus Unum! Oh well. No wonder I have an occasional depressive jag in which I lock myself in my rooms and play my two favorite records: one of applause, the other of people laughing. Other times I light the fire and stretch out on the chaise, candles blazing all around, stark naked under my floor-length black velvet cape "in the grand tradition," as I get up the nerve to go out and pinch a little blood — and I don't plan to be "reformed" by any brainwashing or drugs or scoldings or punishment or any damned thing at all. I either want to be left alone, or accepted wholly as I am, not as some law-loving sneak thinks I "ought" to be.

Yes, I'm a heel; but Virginia Woolf (or Benaroya, as she called herself) had said I was a "square shooter." I couldn't get the lovely compliment out of my mind. People seldom say nice things about a person like me, especially things that are true. A square shooter. An absurd, old-fashioned phrase, which could easily make a sucker out of me, I supposed — along with the fact that the new Woolf was titanic, Valkyrian, and sexy; a prodigy of jovial splendor, and I could hardly wait to see her again.

Leon's is the glossy bar below the studio where we relax after a hard night's work. We hold staff meetings there. We nurse bruised feet and egos there; we carry on our romances there… In a distant booth I glimpsed Johnny and Patsy sitting together, but made like I didn't see them.

I had agreed to meet Woolf at Leon's and was already late, making my way past friends with a salute at this table and a word at that, until I caught sight of my own overwrought face in the bar mirror. Next to it was the pale, impassive face of this hypothetical spacewoman, Virginia Woolf.

I saw her tonight as a wild animal; one with large velvety eyes full of dark mysteries, a little chilling, perhaps tantalizing, but always haunting, fascinating… the edge of something.

The edge of what? What was I telling myself?

The charm of the unhuman. And the *fear*… lifting my imagination above the Earth. This was as close as I was willing to come — for the moment.

She said, "Watch," pointing to the TV over the bar, where a commercial was in progress. I'd seen it many times before, but had paid little attention. Now I watched carefully as the expensively scored and mounted puffery, labeled a "public service announcement," revealed a cartoon god stepping out of a cloud. He grinned rather sadly and said,

"Hi, good buddies! My name's Scaulzo and I think you're great," at which he shot a jagged little bolt of lightning off-screen. He had the smug, practiced concern of a darling bear or curly-headed Indian asking people to please not start forest fires, but test themselves for cancer instead. I chuckled as he continued,

"How many think this is a gimmick to announce an upcoming product? Get those hands up… Well shucks, this is better than a new product. I'm a Sajorian, which means *good people,* and I'll be coming around to help you solve a few problems now and then. But first, listen close."

He glanced from side to side, lowered his voice and confided, "You've got to be on your toes, friends. Don't let them take you by surprise. Who do I mean? Why, the Rysemians, that's who. They may show up in your neighborhood any day now, so watch out. They *look* like people, but they're really ugly fish who'll try to poison your minds against me. But you be smart, y'hear, good buddies? and don't listen to their tale of woe."

Thwang; another lightning bolt and a sad, boyish smile. "Because what they say is not right. The Sajorians love ya and don't you forget it. Remember — Scaulzo Loves You!" Then some explosions in the distance, "But I hear my people calling. I'll see you later, so long for now," and he pulled the cloud over himself and was gone as another voice, a caressing voice, said, "This message has been engraved on your synapses and will restimulate every zomma-one-twenty."

Then back to the ballgame.

I ordered a drink and asked, "What was that all about?"

"Star wars. The real thing; not some cutesy-poo Earthie version made to show how morally superior you jabeeps are. It's like *Hamlet*. Any psychotic can pour any kind of poison in your ear, and if you complain he'll sue you for character damage."

Our eyes met in the mirror. She seemed mad about something. "You know how many humans disappear every month, without a trace? Thousands. You know what happens to them?"

"Never thought about it."

"The Sajorians pick them up and sell them to bidders around the Bright Lights Worlds, where I come from. It's called slave-trading. No big deal; just a game with them."

"That's quite a hunk of fiction."

"Yeah, so unbelievable nobody complains. But I'm afraid *we* introduced our enemies to TV. They follow us and make wreckage of our work. We did a TV study. Used stuffed, battery-operated football teams, the freaky giants audiences prefer, with the rounded buttocks the men get off on while saying they don't. The games were so enormously popular they swept the ratings. They sold literally *tons* of useless crap: cheap drinks, cheap books and films, shaving cream, genital enlargers, and so on. The teams played the same games over and over, with slight variations so that rubes could 'bet on the outcome' while announcers squawked out scores, hour after weary hour— a meticulously perfect waste of time. The Sajorians found out about it, and needless to say, they loved it. You see the results."

"Scaulzo called you an ugly fish."

The insult upset me more than it did her. "We've got the real Scaulzo aboard ship, frozen into an Earthie body, poor devil. His second in command, a creep named Sylvester Beel, is backing these commercials. It's aberrative material but very popular; we don't know why. What we do know is that the Sajorians are a higher harmonic of the Earth mentality. They are what you'll evolve into, unless a conversion takes place."

I laughed. "You can't change human nature. Don't think it hasn't been tried."

"Incorrect. For the first time in the history of your world, evolution is going to be psychic and is going to be based on conscious choice. It won't be for everyone, needless to say; but you can expect 'reality' to start changing drastically, beginning with your personal life."

I let out a guffaw. "Are you serious?"

"Deadly so." Woolf said they were testing Scaulzo to determine "the basic components of evil." It seems he hotwired all the nuclear tactical weapons on Earth; all of our atomic weapons could be detonated from Sajor with radio waves, or what she called "blinnies." Meanwhile the Rysemians ("the good guys," was how she referred to her people) wanted to help responsive humans evolve. As for those who refused—

"Change or croak. Is that the idea you're entertaining?"

Her eyes flashed. "I didn't really *entertain* that idea, I just gave it a glass of Perrier and some stale Muenster."

"So we live or die at your command, right?"

"Did you climb down from the trees without some kind of kick in the butt? What do you think evolution is, an armchair journey through the Paleolithic?"

"So you're the superior alien who knows it all." I sneered.

Woolf shook her head. "There are no aliens. Your help is needed," and she put out such a calming, flattering radiation that I found myself revealing more than I'd intended, and launched into a complaint about my waking nightmares, at which she looked grim and said:

"That's the Agony Organ. The contents of the dominant mass mind are picked up and hurled back as a weapon. And they launch the attack every time we zero in on an individual."

"How do I fight it?"

"Don't fight it, you'll really get stuck. Just don't send out evil thought waves and they won't magnify and swamp you."

I failed to see how this applied, and she said, "Take your own case, for example. What's vampirism but a variation of a materialist fixation, huh? And you revel in all the bad things that have been done to you, and this attracts more bad things, and it all gets heavier and heavier--"

I was outraged. Attacking a person's uniqueness, her contribution, her very *raison d'être*, and on quasi-religious grounds at that! It was the worst affront I had ever swallowed. But, B. was so captivating I couldn't stay angry for long, so I downed my boilermaker and wiped my lips, saying,

"A cute theory, but it has absolutely no basis in fact. Come on, this is a *hardware* planet. We want ideas that *clank,* not a lot of lurid mysticism," and was still arguing the case as we entered the ladies room (why is it that V.W. and I are always winding up in some john or other?) which is tucked at the back of Leon's. But then as we were returning to our seats, a most peculiar event took place. A man jumped out at us, a typical street gorilla. I dodged away by reflex but my companion reached out in a most casual way, and before I knew what was happening, she had turned our attacker's head around backwards.

Then quickly she tucked the still-twitching body into the nearest trash can. Its postmortem grin would send me shrieking, later, in dreams; I couldn't quite remember the sequence— I'd been saying in dogmatic tones, "There is no life beyond the undertaker. I'm a vampire, and when I die that's it," and she'd been about to answer, when the thing happened. Or at least it *appeared* that it happened; of course it couldn't have happened. Woolf put the top on the can and we returned to our barstools. I noticed that it was getting late. But I was three sheets to the wind and had begun telling my life story.

"Yeah, I've lived all over the damn world, and over the years I've pretty well seen it all, and I'm here to tell you: things were better before the Inquisition." I blew my nose. "We lived a slow, exquisite, *classical* life and people appreciated me. They knew I was a vampire and they *respected* me for it; not like today. My very existence made life fabulous for them. In summer in a full moon they would lie shivering in their beds, hoping, fearing, praying that I'd swoop down and give them the thrill of a lifetime... it was delicious!

"But now what have we got? Blood banks, sitcoms, watered tomato juice; Big Brother— you go 40 in a 30-mile zone and some uniformed twerp lays a *ticket* on you. So you can bet all our vested interests need new, inexperienced people to sell their stereotypes and their junk to" (catching the bartender's eye, ordering two more),"because what wise old sage would go into hock for ten tons of useless crap including cars, roller skates, makeup, rotten food and hideous music?"

"I'll drink to that," Woolf roared, and we did. On the other hand... her story fascinated me, but how much of it was believable? I'd read about 'lesbian experiences,' but this was beyond calculating.

I was intrigued, frightened, amused. Something magical was happening, but I was beset with indefinable emotions, as if lost in a strange fantasy...

The Rysemians, said my delightful drinking companion, had learned everything they knew about humans from old novels and movies. They grew their bodies on shipboard. Tomorrow I'd meet some of her friends (out came the wallet, as she slapped Polaroid snaps on the bar)— General Patton, Dirty Harry, Guillaume Apollinaire, and the James boys, Henry, William, and Jesse.

"Very nice folks. You'll meet a few of 'em. This here is Boolabung, our captain, wearing the carc of your General George S. Patton; you'll like George; he's hard on you but he's as straight a shooter as you'll find anywhere."

She ordered us each a boilermaker and said, "We know all about you. A missing link who can only live a few years in any one place, then must move along; hated and feared, confused as to your own basic identity, and feeling no loyalty to the human species that has caused you such untold misery."

"You said it," I agreed with great feeling.

She made an expansive gesture. "But you gotta remember that just because billions of people believe in a thing doesn't mean it's real or right, or normal or healthful."

"No, no, no," I chanted. People were staring at us, but that happens to me a lot, with or without company... By now we had our arms around one another's shoulders. Woolf hoisted her drink:

"Down the ole mousehole," she bellowed, and kissed me on the lips, saying,

"You're a successful manager for that Arkoff franchise. We admire that. Business is the hot number here. Fits in with research plans, talk to you about it. Learn a lot. You an' me. Any ideas?"

I hiccupped. "Good bet is hot tubs, accommodate thirty adults standing up. Ha, ha, picture it? Or how about... roller skate rentals. Swell leisure time activity, rent skates by the hour. Wait, I got it: a gigantic insurance swindle. Nah, on second thought, market's crowded with them already."

Woolf nuzzled my cheek, egging me on. By now I was madly in love; her earthy sensuality was making my pulses pound, as I bragged on. "Chimney sweep service. Or recycling; everyone hot for it. Wait: a pet cemetery, there ya go. Part of booming industry.

Great potential absentee-owner business," my lips brushing hers tenderly. "Pizza!, or tennis club can't miss— hold on. I got it. We take over the government."

"What government," she sighed, eyes closing.

"Any government. Most lucrative confidence game on record. Why I've known people..."

Her caresses had a most calming effect on me, as did her flattery; she knew how to do it so well. She spoke my language so perfectly. I never thought that she could pick my mind, whispering nuggets like, "Ezra Pound warned us, remember, my darling? 'They all think the public has to be apologized to for the existence of genius in any form.' Remember Ezra?"

"Wait a minute." Looking into her eyes was like looking into the Bermuda Triangle. Just possibly, you might never find your way out. I pulled back and asked, "Where is all this leading?"

"Revenge."

"What are you talking about?"

"Revenge! That's what I'm offering you, Sterling. Not only a deep and abiding love, but revenge."

When it finally got through to me what the woman was saying, I cracked up. Revenge! It was the funniest thing I'd ever heard in my life. Revenge. Getting back at all those sadistic bastards. Making them suffer as I had suffered. Sweet revenge!, what an exhilarating prize.

She wiped the foam from her lips. "The planet Earth will be all yours, Sterling O'Blivion. You will own it, every mountain, ocean, factory, person; and you can do *exactly* as you like with it."

"Oh boy." I wiped away a tear. "What a Mother's Day present."

Benaroya was a gift of fate, coming to me from across unimaginable vastnesses; and although horribly frightened, I was also wildly in love. Thus we went arm in arm into the barren streets: a bold Rysemian; a drunken, confused, and sentimental vampire.

At Woolf's request we prowled restlessly here and there. Although the wind was sharp, we paused to investigate more than one garbage can. I felt gloriously free, like an alley cat; it was thrilling to be with Benaroya in the dead of night, examining grapefruit rinds and coffee grounds, wandering in alleys behind elaborate hotels, when everything was hushed and dark, and we saw but one or two lights in the rooms of restless travelers.

In due course we headed for the Drake Hotel. On the way, we sang bawdy songs, and yelled "Give 'im a banana!" at the few passers-by.

A cop car pulled up beside us and the driver, who looked about fifteen, asked, "Are you ladies drunk?"

Woolf said, "Sure we tossed down a little booze, so what?"

"So nothing," he said and pulled away in haste.

ELEVEN

I didn't know how long I'd been asleep, but the bedlam was awful. I longed for quiet, but the voices droned on… evil spirits from other worlds:

"Big trouble. A dangerous gamble. The situation is delicate, risky operation; hostile ships. We have no choice."

There was a turned-around head in a garbage can, its lips mouthing the words, "She's dead on schedule!"

At which Sterling gives a mighty jerk and wakes up, one foot in each world. Belonging nowhere.

I had been drunk as a skunk. Now it was hangover time. But it beat that awful dream. Bleary, I fell into Levis and an Indian cotton shirt and striped weskit, and crossed the boulevard.

In the elevator my gut took a bounce trip to Universe Twelve, where Patsy Cox got on board. She lit her cigarette with a fiery supernova. Her smile alone could have blinded me. She remarked that the morning was good. No mention was made of her last night's date with Johnny. I crossed myself.

At the water cooler my skull redshifted painfully, each cranial nerve enlisting for a flight through a black hole, in spite of which I drank like a walrus, then had to spit the water out— ptooey! Abominable stuff; unbelievably horrible-tasting— as my stomach passed through a Kerr singularity into antigravity.

Yet despite the discomfort I was happy, happy, happy!, dodging between exquisitely barbered males who polished their waltzes with the Studio's prettiest teachers. I recognized a couple of hit-men swirling gracefully across the ballroom. After all, this *is* Chicago. And my head *is* an object collapsed to zero volume under awful pressures. I sat at my desk with the icepack and the V-8, and thought tender thoughts of Virginia Woolf, whom I'd left sweetly asleep after our most gorgeous of nights.

...Or was it? Listening to Johann Strauss, an attack of dread seized me.

Expendable. Is that what I was? I popped several aspirins with the V-8, and wondered what web she was spinning. When she rang up, I refused to take the call. But five minutes later came a knock at the door; and in a moment Woolf was straddling a chair backwards as she boomed around the toothpick in her lips, "You didn't tell me you got nasty in the morning."

"I'm sick. That should be obvious," fumbling in the drawer for shades.

"Remember what I promised?"

"No!" Found a pair, put them on; things looked slightly better.

"Ya ready to take off into the stratosphere and beyond?"

Again I felt that dichotomized weariness, as the tales she'd told last night came crashing back to oppress me. "We're visiting my ship immediately. Omark and the crew want to meet you."

Had I made promises? We'd fought like demons, that was for sure; even amid the joy of finding blissful rapport, she had infuriated me. I was "a spiritual creature" and should evolve beyond savagery. Mad stuff about turning me into a magician: "There is a serenity that exists beyond time. You can be in touch with many lives at once. You can change the past as well as the future; can have, be, or do anything you want; can be a hundred percent spontaneous, uninhibited, loving and good—"

"Vicious, malicious!" I had howled. "You're belittling me. Sneering at my ancient glory."

"Do not heed or obey the conventions of Man. Follow your star! Paradoxically, this is the only hope for the human race, including yourself."

Indignant and insulted, I was screaming, "This is my life. Don't minimize it," as we entered the Drake lobby (what would the doorman think of me now? How humiliating this was: I'll never, never drink again), her guffaws maddening me.

She said,

"Heyyy, don't get bent all outta shape. I didn't mean to insult your life-style, or your body, which is nothing but meat, ya jerk;

your life doesn't depend on it."

The woman was infuriating. She kept saying,

"You're a test case, so don't panic. If you can't break the A-O spell, who can?" and trying to jolly me through some heavy stuff. But worst of all, she was a natural murderer. Or at least a careless, gross animal— a fish, for Godsake! I was having an affair with a *fish.* How could I be "in love" with this demon from hell? Was I out of my mind? (Answers: I could, I was. I didn't care. I wished I'd never met her. On the other hand, I was so in love I couldn't stand it... But was it "love," or a demonic mesmerism?...)

"How does one ever know?" she asked.

She gave me a present, a pair of cufflinks: plain, small, old-fashioned gold ovals inset with a three-carat diamond. I'd have sworn they were the links I lost down the drainpipe in 1902. But maybe not. She said, "If your body is shot out from under you and you need another one, these'll help you make the leap with no trouble at all."

I didn't want to take such an expensive gift after only one date but she insisted, so I replaced my old silver links with these nice diamond ones.

What other "facts" had this mad, monumental Amazon used to bedazzle me? The Mousehole: that was an expressway between star systems. Heidi's Grandfather: her leader's code name. The nixons: ship's stewards, around fifty in number, identical replicas of what Woolf called "a minor twentieth-century president." And her boyfriend Omark— God, but I was jealous of that Hercules-type hero!, reportedly off to trap the archfiend Beel in South America.

Not to mention the morbid hallucinations. About "Earthies" being kidnapped and shipped, kicking and screaming, to remote galaxies.

And for me... revenge, sweet revenge.

Ah yes: now I remembered everything.

The *Vonderra,* an organically grown diamond, alive, filthy, seething, encrusted with space moss and barnacles, could not be told from a battered meteor. "The ultimate disguise," Woolf boasted.

The ship was in orbit several hundred kilometers above Earth. Patton captained her; I didn't have to meet him if I didn't want to.

Vonderra had paragravity drive, was over five thousand years old, and hummed through the ether with a sound like an enormous and soothing OMMmmmm...

"And this is our honeymoon suite," Woolf warbled, flinging open the door of a fleabag hotel room of the 1980s complete with cheap prints, peeling wallpaper, rattly pipes, and sink in one corner.

"It's lovely," I said in mounting excitement (despite my better judgment).

The shade flapped. We were on the third floor gazing down on grubby neon signs and wires. Across the way were brick storefronts, a water tower, train tracks, warehouses, the smoggy skyline of what appeared to be a smallish American city.

Up the street the garbage men were burning nixons in a trasher. These used-up stewards were being replaced by the trendier ronald reagan robots. It was regrettable to see hair and clothing afire and flesh bubbling and mouths working, and so forth, while a score of other nixons shuffled and wept in line; but as Woolf explained, "Obsolesence *is* Earth's most important product and we've got to be as precise as possible."

She squeezed my hand. "No tears, my precious. We can make jillions of these meat bodies."

Turning, I noticed that a skinny, coarse, uncouth old lady was sprawled on the bed in silk pajamas. A siren howled by in front; the woman gave an explosion of flatulence, rolled over and went on snoring.

"You didn't tell me you were bringing your mother," I said irritably.

Woolf was bouncing around turning up thermostats, flushing the john, fiddling with the lock and so forth, the way guests do in hotel rooms. Personally, I was so spaced out with culture shock that my head was spinning. Our door opened onto a shabby corridor; various guests, along with reagans bearing room-service trays, kept tramping past.

"What is it, a convention?"

"Just an ordinary day in a cheapo hotel," Woolf burbled. "I want to work with the crowd. Go into the audience. Feel the life-style. I want to know in my very *bones* why Earthies are insane! But first let's cure that hangover of yours, my dearest one."

A maid banged in, pushing a cart loaded with brooms and

supplies; seeing us, she snarled and banged out again, all very usual. But in the hall I caught sight of Mr. Spock, the Vulcan of *Star Trek* fame, who was no doubt going where no man had gone before. Wretched as I was, I still wanted to run after Spock and sign him up for a course of dance lessons or at least get his autograph but Woolf had other plans; she said,

"We can flush out that mortal coil of yours in a jiffy, my angel, if you don't mind wearing one of mine. Rub your cufflinks."

I said "Sure" and touched the links.

Then an uncanny thing happened. I don't recall the exact sequence, but there was a sort of mental slither, and I found myself (now this may sound crazy but I'm simply reporting what happened, as accurately as possible) *inside* the Spock body looking out the eyes, gaping at my hands and my tunic, that famous tunic, the Federation uniform worn aboard the old *Enterprise*...

I was really Spock! I *was* the emotionless, green-skinned logician, Spock with the pointed ears, who had the magical appeal of the nonterrestrial.

"I'll buy it," I yipped in a booming baritone.

Now it may seem peculiar that such a fantastical enchantment could feel entirely natural, but so it did; a perfect fit, no complaints. I stood marveling as two of the reagans loaded my own body onto a trolley and wheeled it away, the mouth gaping, the eyes half shut, in a stranger's awful grimace.

Woolf said I would now enjoy The Tour, after which my own Sterling O'Blivion carcass would be feeling up to par.

"In at ten, clean and starched by eleven!"

"No hurry," I insisted, exploring the Spock head and ears, working the fingers and otherwise experimenting with this new temple of my spirit.

Profound philosophical changes had already begun. For the first time in my life I was in nonvampire form; how did it differ from my ordinary condition? How-- why— a hundred questions came welling up; but what happened next was what often happens when you are a visitor at the home of a friend. Instead of leaving you free to indulge the new sensations, they rush you off on The Tour, as if trying to show off their entire house, patio, garage, and stainless steel flatware before you can stop to ask about any rumored skeletons in closets.

"Microcosms," Woolf had explained. "We build anything you

need. We can build the state of Rhode Island, or your parents and friends and childhood home in Romania— but not today, my love, for this is orientation day."

These wonderworlds were in no way bogus sets; they were the true actualities, she warned.

"So keep on your toes. A person could get lost, and I mean permanently, in one of these manufactured realities. Actually that's what has already happened to Earthies, but we can't stop and discuss that now."

I stuck close by my friend, as uneasy as Dante being guided by Virgil through Purgatory... no, worse; this was incredibly more of a strain, and harder to assimilate.

"Please accept that matter's an emanation of mind. The sooner your scientists accept that, the better. You manufacture everything that happens to you. There is no 'reality' aside from what we all create. The next evolutionary step is for your species to become fully aware of this."

"Well basically, as a theoretical paradigm," I trembled... but Woolf brushed my tension aside with a giggle.

"Tee hee. Take a look at my silly old boss grinding away," she whispered, cracking open a door.

Abraham Lincoln dipped into an inkhorn, signing papers at his desk in the Oval Office. He wore a gold lamé gown with a slit up one leg. He looked much svelter in drag than one would expect.

"Out of the closet after all these years," she whispered, and closed the door.

"Does that mean— anarchy? We can do anything, despite consequences?"

"In a pig's valise!" Woolf gave a demure wink. "Mersoid's a Council Chief, feminine but hardboiled. I don't wanna lose my cadet stripes, whaddaya think?"

"I think yes, baby."

"You're such a dashing outlaw," Woolf murmured, snuggling against me. How seductive she was... I snuck glances at that aquiline profile I'd swooned over in Bloomsbury days, desiring her madly, yet squeamish with apprehension. We walked hand in hand that way down a slanty-walled hall, where rows of bodies reclined, each in its own transparent coffin. Some were hung by the ankles— to equalize the flow of blood, I presumed. Many were people I recognized; from Elizabeth I and Janis Joplin to F. Scott Fitzgerald and Jimmy Hoffa. All were stark naked. It bothered Woolf not in the least that a few had suffered some mischance and were rotting away; she ignored it when I gagged in revulsion. Above us ran a balcony lined with prehuman monsters, dreadful experiments better not looked at, so as to avoid dreaming about them.

Woolf was very tactful about all this, but my mind balked at most of it. I wouldn't accept that the *Vonderra*, Benaroya's home-away-from-home, was anything but an outrageously costly Hollywood set; a waxworks, or museum; I could not take it seriously... particularly when we toured "the carcass shop" where the bodies were grown and repaired.

This mile-wide, weird-smelling plant produced a cataclysmic dizziness in me. Senses reeling and mind vapor-locked, my entire psyche was wrenched out of its comfortable socket. I'm describing this just as it happened, before I got any perspective on it. "The carc shop—" She tossed off those words so casually... But I'll dwell no more on that place of horrors, it being a true paradox, which gets in the way of what happened next.

Charles Jennison blocked our path. I recognized this man Omark from the snapshot Woolf carried next to her heart. He lounged contemptuously, arms folded.

I felt Woolf go tense as he said: "Well, look who's Spock."

Jennison wore a pair of notched revolvers, tight sweaty jeans and buffalo-hide shirt bulging with muscle. He had a good twenty pounds on me. Before I could answer, he spat a jet of tobacco juice on my starship insignia.

"Listen!" Woolf yelped.

The gunfighter ignored her and gave me an elbow in the ribs, grinning sourly. Hardly thinking, I shoved back; at which his fist exploded in my face, with the far-off crackle of a mast splintering.

"You broke her goddamn nose, you goddamn gorilla," Woolf was howling.

In agony I clutched my ruined face; I writhed on the ground, blood pouring between fingers; then I scrambled to my knees, crazy to get up and massacre Woolf's taunting boyfriend.

She kicked and flailed at him in a blind rage. Omark blocked nearly all of these blows, his mouth twisted, giving her a few backhanded cuffs. Two Ayatollahs trotted up with my Sterling body; they loaded the bleeding Spock onto the trolley after the switch was made. Nothing to it. Like shedding your old skin. But the switch didn't cool Jennison off in the least. When he saw Woolf throw herself into my arms and hold me tight, the gunfighter became even more crazy-jealous... Screw him.

It's not easy shifting gears into a totally new frame of reference. What were they gabbling about? It hardly made sense. We had grabbed a yellow cab back to our hotel room, me in the middle and the two of them arguing around me like a couple of demented fishwives; Woolf sobbing, "I can't live this way! I can't!" and the cowboy folding his arms and replying, "I'm sorry, sweetheart; I tried to warn you."

"You have no evidence of sabotage," she wept. She had a slightly bloodied nose and was stanching it with a greasy Kleenex. I trembled between them because the woman I loved had been abused, but Omark, disdainful, ignored me.

"I had my men drag the river," he said grimly. "They found a wonderful little restaurant that serves cheese dishes."

"Sterling, how the hell are you?" Woolf suddenly bawled in my ear. "Is your hangover any better?"

I wouldn't answer, but then after a moment, "The seeds of tragedy have been planted," I said in the most ominous tones I could muster— at which Jennison gave me a withering look of amused scorn.

The cowboy paid the pimply cabdriver; then he whispered something in private to Woolf.

"That burns me up," Woolf hollered.

"You think she doesn't operate her own defense system?" he yelled. And when he turned to me and growled, "Virginia learns what to say from reading your mind— what else? We're praxiological anthropologists following the logic of the situation; how many times must that be explained to you?" I had a feeling that someone walked over my grave. For an instant I actually forgot who I was or how I got here.

During this interval, there was more whispering and Woolf snapped, "Cheese it or I'll lop off your franking privileges" as her rough-hewn boyfriend followed us upstairs, yawning and tugging at his crotch.

I felt chilled and oddly lonely in their company. "Human

warmth" was missing, but the action rushed right along. On the stroke of ten Woolf and I would return to Earth together, dine in Seattle several years in the future (because there were helpful force-lines at those coordinates), and explore whatever possibilities were open to us. It would be a time of worldwide depression and unrest, and we'd roll with that.

Meanwhile Jennison was assuming the body of the snoring female upon the bed. He was operating both bodies at once and was kind of nervous, Woolf said.

"He's not really your enemy," she whispered, her lips tickling my ear. "Just coaching you to maintain a stoic calm while you're working with us... or as Camus says, 'When you have accepted death, the problem of God will be solved, and not the reverse,' sweetheart."

When the woman had roused herself, dressed, and began walking about with mincing steps, she looked positively regal. Omark tucked her wisps of gray hair neatly under a stylish tan hat. The lady was the bossy, meddlesome Mary Worth of the comics.

Mrs. Worth offered me her hand with a sweet smile.

"It was absolutely lovely meeting you, my dear," she simpered.

I stopped off at the studio and found a letter, heavily sealed with wax, atop the in-basket. The letter was from Armand. Just the heft of it told me something was wrong. I slit it open and read:

My beloved Sterling,
By the time you read this I will be dead. Unless a miracle intervenes.

A group of highly placed people plan for you to join me swiftly unless immediate action is taken. Your "secrets," highly marketable as they are, have imperiled you and although I don't entirely know what's involved, I've glimpsed you from a distance; you didn't see me; you are unchanged after all these lonely decades, and I still care as much as ever.

You are quite right to fear John File. Originally employed by a European secret service agency, he's now fronting for the group I mentioned. The woman (photo enclosed) works closely with them. I don't know what more to say. Except that if you have any slight impulse to mourn me, don't. I'm an old man at the end of his bankroll, I've lived my life, and have no regrets, except the one you suspect. But time runs out and I must break off.

In haste,

Armand.

I shook out two photographs. One was of Johnny; a sinister mug shot I hadn't seen before. Quite different from the 8 x 10 glossy on the billboard downstairs.

The other was a snap of Patsy Cox in green fatigues, cradling a tommy gun.

TWELVE

"Why the devil did you hire Patsy Cox?"

"She said she was broke and needed the money. I couldn't say no."

"Well, there's plenty to arrange," Woolf said, her gorgeous eyes sparkling with excitement. "Better suspend judgment until we find out who and what is involved."

"In the meantime, I'll be wiped out and so will Armand."

"Bullpucky. You'll be invisible; and we will consign all those dated, boring spy plots to the garbage can where they belong" — with a lingering kiss that sold me.

Again, the worst of my fears were calmed. I put out of my mind the fact (was it a fact?) (of course it wasn't a fact!) that Woolf was working on me for purposes of her own. And that she was tremendously magnetic to everyone, could do as she liked with any person who crossed her path, and was carefully striving to drag me "upward" on a gradient of her own devising.

All of this would have made me despondent; but Woolf said, "Horseturds! Your skull is a necropolis! We're gonna have *fun*, kiddo."

But then: I cannot even discover the motives of people I know well, let alone a...foreigner (she hates the word "alien," saying "nothing alien is alien to me," misquoting the ancient Roman author Terence's "*humani nihil a me alienum puto*").

Next day we backpacked into the heart of the Olympic Mountains, collecting our energies for the task that lay ahead. We needed a change of scene, somewhere quiet where we could discuss plans. I had seen Benaroya's rooted environment; now

I wanted her to see mine— my beloved, adopted country, the U.S.A. — or what was left of it.

The Olympics are a snowcapped, jagged range in America's last bit of trackless wilderness, in the far corner of Washington State. My playful comrade called the scenery "a staggering creation" and "an amazing example of multilayered realism," as she skipped stones on a glassy trout stream.

We crossed marshes on drift logs until the stream became a torrent, which we followed upward into dense forest. After an hour's climb, a stupendous view opened up; of mountains and valleys, fir jungles on gloomy steeps, with a breeze pouring down, and the sun all twinkly in the trees.

"Fine artisans have been at work here," exclaimed Woolf in the tones of a society lady about to buy a clever model of the world.

Then over the hills at a good trot, striking out for some haven of seclusion where we'd throw off our clothes and swim. In the churning river I knew at once that she was no human but a sea beast, a tantalizing one who said: "I'll teach you how to kiss under water, my vampire."

And so we made love "out of our species," perfectly nested in translucent green, until Woolf's honey mouth and shiny hair combined with the pine fragrances of a fabulous dream...

The snow owl woke us. And life was a benefaction! After 700 years of being choked and smothered by human "morals" (what a joke *that* is), I could at last live for pure, wild joy, skyrocketing to a peak of exhilaration as we roughhoused, climbed like cougars, declared eternal love, wrestled, kissed, and zinged stones at targets. My life had been empty of such pleasures. Just being in Woolf's presence was such a keen delight that I feared no treachery, in spite of what Scaulzo had said in the commercial — which I was convinced was a lie.

We kept up a vigorous conversation while foraging after firewood. I asked the same question over and over. "But what should we *do*?"

"Pattern yourselves on the noble heroes of history. Live like a champion, shun dishonesty, and never complain."

"That should be easy once we get the hang of it." I whooped. "You say we'll evolve like the Sajorians, but what makes them evil? What do they do all day long?"

"Sue each other," she giggled. "Live like bees or ants in

statewide metal cities all crawling with security guards. Make their surroundings as ugly and oppressive as possible, and blame each other for it, as if they couldn't have anything in the galaxy they wanted. Lots of them cling to one body and gloat over its illness. Others get into power positions on planets like Earth and grind down the dominant race, saying they are 'helping' or 'doing good' by suppressing people. They're the ultimate groupies, loving strange entertainments and concerts in which 'aliens' are dismembered to music; all that kind of stuff. Evil is boring. Same thing over and over."

"How can we avoid becoming that?"

"Dump your laws. They are unworkable. The Ten Commandments didn't work for shit, so you passed a billion more laws which work even less."

"But what about poverty?"

"Is that a joke, or what?" She slapped the ground. "We're sitting on the wealthiest planet in the Sector. You could build ten Rolls Royces for every human and never miss the outlay."

"Enemy attacks? Armies?"

"You've got superweapons to last forever and a day. A single Brownie Scout can destroy any country in a second. What do you need armies for? To collect pensions? To look tough and dramatic in the movies? To fight the Civil War over again?"

"But the government—"

"The government grows out of the character of the people."

With that she threw herself on top of me as if to show that the conversation was ended.

I held her body pressed against mine, and murmured, "What you don't seem to comprehend is, you can get most anybody to accept any degrading thing, but you can't drag them to heaven."

"Snakes can slough off their old skin... the process has already begun... You are more than the sum of your parts," as we exchanged the most thrilling kisses I'd ever known.

But like a fool, I asked the same question over and over. "What should we do?"

"You don't need me for that. Go to your sages; you won't listen to them either. The answers are always there; ridiculed and distorted, certainly, but always available. Take Confucius. He's become a big joke. Ha, ha. He said, 'Lead the people by laws and then by penalties, and the people will try to keep out of jail, but will have no sense of self-worth. Lead the people by virtue and restrain them by the rules of decorum, and the people will have a sense of self-worth, and moreover will become good.' You take that, distort it beyond recognition, then teach it in a college course— and now you're begging 'someone from a superior race' to teach you how to live? Wise up. Or take Jesus, who said 'Don't build rich churches to me; simply live as I live, and that's the whole message' — which got distorted into rich churches and slimy lives. Go back to square one!"

"How?"

"Keep clear of the mob, and *evolve*. Insanity is a contagious disease."

I said: "You should take over a TV station and perform some miracles. You know— show them your stone tablets, so they'll *know* you're from an advanced race and are here to help people."

"What can I tell people who want to be in a trance from cradle to grave, and when they die, go out like a candle, and not hafta take responsibility for the future because they won't be there? If I admit they create their environment and live forever they'll tune me out. Nathaniel Hawthorne said it all, a few years back: 'Should some phenomenon of nature or providence transcend their system, they will not recognize it, even if it come to pass under their very noses.'"

Then we ate some berries and replenished the fire as Woolf told stories of her homeland— which sounded so alien and weird I tuned most of it out.

But we also had work to do. "Better buckle on our harness!"... My beautiful sea-lady chewed a blade of grass, frowning into the flames. "The point is, not only are you on the verge of space travel, but the Mousehole is changing the picture drastically. We've *got* to introduce you to conscious evolution. This is a moral imperative."

"Meaning what?"

"First off, we need a research project to clarify what you call 'human emotions,' which seem to go on a progression (not unlike the keys of a piano) from deathlike gloom to radiant joy. And in between are all these emotions like sneaky anger, which you hide, and embarrassment, terror, blazing anger and a few others. And I want to tie this in to our pressing question, *how* can we Rysemians reach humans as effectively as the Sajorians do, but to bring them upscale and not degrade them?"

I thought a minute, then said, "Well, after selling thousands of dance courses, if there's anything I know it's marketing. This may come as a shock but here's your answer. I'm going to tell you how any product, from a dance course to a religion, is sold.

"My only aim is to make customers buy that product. I must have no concern for what their real needs are, or what's best for society or anything like that; already you can see how the Sajorians fit neatly into this and you don't."

She looked puzzled, so I clarified as best I could.

"The customer is looking for *approval,* above everything else. He sees the people in the commercial getting lots of approval and he wants some too, and we use that against him. We hint that love and friendship will be given as soon as he buys the right brand of jeans or mouthwash, see? And so the customer buys our product, and of course doesn't get any approval, and he thinks: 'It's just because I haven't conformed enough,' so he conforms more, and buys more products hoping to find the 'right' one, and never gets what he needs, and it becomes a dwindling spiral.

"And by the time anyone gets old enough to realize 'I've been cheated!' it's too late. They've got their whole soul invested in the lie, so they've got to approve of it. And everything conspires together. The educational system teaches them not to think, not to trust themselves. And society insists, 'This is pro-survival. We can't exist unless you conform this way, even if you don't get love and approval,' and that is a lie. See how it works?"

Woolf looked solemn. "We gotta teach people how to be happy. It takes no more effort to be happy than to be miserable; you just say 'I am happy!' and picture yourself doing what you want to do."

"Yeah... but how do you sell people on that idea? It would be strange to sell them the truth instead of a lie for a change. 'You only feel powerless because you talked yourself into it. The world is in the business of convincing you it's true, because they think it's easier to deal with people who are powerless. But it's not easier; look around you; it's a mess. So quit agreeing with it.'"

"Yippee," Woolf said, jumping up for more wood.

"Wait: the master-planner is getting an idea," half game-playing with her and half serious. "In mass advertising, you never meet your audience in person. You don't know or care anything about them. You've got to have a ruthless attitude toward them or you can't plan an effective campaign, right? They're statistics, nothing but a lot of greedy hands; so how about an effective grass-roots campaign that takes your message directly to their homes? See each one on an individual basis, meaning face-to-face and in person, so you can *really* gauge what results you're getting?"

"I like it," she crooned. "And how about we aim it at women, the masters of the future of humanity, huh? Can they be changed and brought upscale, and if so, *how*? Of course this must be just a simple, preliminary test—"

"Maybe use a questionnaire. Simple stuff: 'Would you like to be happier? Are you worried? Would you like to be more successful and get your way more?' Or maybe a little harder questions, such as 'Do you need a leader? Why?'... Wait. Here's one I'd really like to ask. Let me frame it right... 'Now that you've banished *The Catcher in the Rye* from every library, and replaced it with shelf after shelf of inane drivel, and seen to it that J.D. Salinger is no longer writing, do you consider yourself a better, finer, more moral person? Or should you be banished to a remote planet for being an enemy of the people?' "

"Not bad, but what do we base it on? What product, I mean?" she asked me.

"What product? H'm." I thought for a minute, and said, "How about a Sperm-of-the-Month Club? Could be directed primarily at women. Talk about research: this would get you right into their home for a direct, personal contact. What do the mothers of future generations secretly desire for that future? Where are they, in your emotional scale?... With the right questionnaire, coupled with their choices, you could determine what emotional band they're in, and from there how to manipulate them into ever higher bands. You could advertise in *Vogue, Women's Wear Daily,* the chic European magazines... With a slick Package, no one would ever guess you were anything but just another 'creative entrepreneur' out to make a bundle."

"Telegenesis," Woolf mused. "Genetics at a distance. We could sure give it a try."

"And speaking of making a bundle, I bet we will."

"We don't care about that,"

"But it's how you keep score."

Woolf put both arms around me and leaned her head on my shoulder. "It's not how we keep score," she said.

THIRTEEN

Thus we schemed and daydreamed in the last sunshine. Nothing the *Vonderra* could offer (I was sure) could be more beautiful than this uncharted bit of American soil. And Woolf's presence synthesized it all for me; my ancient grief was mellowing into joy, as she stroked my hair in silence, counting stars, pointing out where her homeland was, far up there in the Milky Way.

This childishly simple, trusting person seemed poles apart from the real Virginia Woolf; and yet...

"What worries you, Vampire?"

"I don't know. Nothing."

Certainly no food ever tasted better than our berries and ash-roasted potatoes, washed down with crystal spring water. Shadows came creeping up the mountain, and the wind blew more strongly as Woolf, tenderly drowsy, was saying: "Well, I'm worried about Omark. He's sneaking into a Sajorian compound as Mary Worth, I'll bet, and with no weapons except a couple of little Earthie revolvers. He can't conceal an H-2 unit. They'd spot it, and then—" She shrugged.

"Omark is a mountebank." Jealousy had flooded me; after the smashed nose he gave me as Spock, they could smash his head for all I cared.

"Don't harbor those thoughts, my dashing lover. Omark is my clone sister."

I let out a guffaw at this notion.

Woolf was breathtaking when she was mad, saying at a pitch of intensity, "Don't knock it! Rysemians are sexless in your terms. We used cloning until recently; you jabeeps might be better off with this method. Take the nucleus from any body-cell and the nucleus from an egg cell, then place the body cell nucleus into the egg cell, and grow a new body identical to the first; or a hundred of them— and not inside some other body to be jolted, x-rayed, poisoned by your miseducated doctors, or warped by evil thought waves, but in a safe, quiet flask, which guarantees no birth defects. And I hope this removes the last of your fears about my clone sister!"

"I only hate his guts."

"He doesn't like that role either; being macho, wearing tight pants, having to avenge insults all the time; so don't be jealous, because *you* are exotic. A genuine 100% bona fide *Homo sapiens...* Wow, it's a thrill to know you, O'Blivion."

And she made me forget I'd ever been jealous of Omark.

The fire was dying. I smiled to think we were several years futurized, having disengaged from the temporal; yet how little it mattered what the date might be. We looked up into trees, as snugly entwined as any two cavewomen in the cradle of the Past. Woolf was murmuring,

"My promise holds. Earth is yours if you want it. You can turn the planet into whatever you like."

But still I was insecure enough to importune: "Tell me the truth, O love of my life. If things get touchy... under circumstances we can't foresee... will I be liquidated, if the others are?"

"Do you believe in the transforming power of Destiny?"

"I don't know yet."

She chucked a pinecone at the fire and sighed. "Let's vamoose to Seattle" was all she'd say.

Power is intoxicating.

Also terrifying.

I'd been given carte blanche— but felt numb and empty each time I realized that the Rysemians had an infinite supply of "money"; mortgages weren't required; the family jewels didn't need to be sold; I could requisition anything I needed or wanted.

Meanwhile I still wore the cufflinks Woolf had given me, although they scared me so badly I put them into a plastic bubble so I wouldn't rub them without thinking about it and be catapulted off my body, lost in space, or God-knows-what. By so doing, I could put that aspect out of my mind and go ahead and arrange the basics; after which Woolf in person would train a go-get-'em sales team. The work went quickly as we ironed out details. We'd gather data and plot curves: Where was humanity *really* heading? What type individual would dominate Earth's future: a Buddha, or a Scaulzo, or something not yet imagined? Would the species require termination, or laissez faire, or radical change; and what would be the cogent way to implement decrees?

We needed two crews: One to sell the Package, on an installment plan, to women with good credit histories. The basic pitch would be, "Why have children by that miserable pauper, loser, and all-around grouch, your husband? Why not have John Travolta's glamorous baby instead? Think of it: yours, to have and to hold — for only pennies a week!"

Crew Number Two would collect sperm from famous men. Every male celebrity on Earth would be offered the bait of wealth and power, in exchange for a flask of healthy, microscopic tail lashers.

Celebs of other ages could be propositioned through judicious use of my ttm (not a "machine," merely two chips and a dandelion puff). Once the kinks were ironed out, a specially drilled squad would be dispatched to collect sperm from heroes of the past. We made lists: Washington, Napoleon, Caesar, Dostoevsky, Valentino, Lord Byron, Elvis Presley, Euripides, Alexander the Great, Tutankhamen, other kings, emperors, writers, actors... also religious figures. That might be tricky, but I was confident that a highly trained agent could secure samples from Mohammed, Zoroaster, St. Sebastian, Buddha, the various apostles, and so forth... In the meantime, polls could be taken to find out which donors were more popular with our customers.

Woolf laughed at my worries about the cufflinks. "You don't hafta stick to that carcass like a blind bat. Carcasses croak, but you're an eternal, deathless being. Fer cryin' out loud, you don't need to go pant-pant-pant after creature comforts; see, we're trying to cure the death-birth cycle that afflicts humans. We're doin' our best; we learned West Virginia accents from your TV shows — we're tryin', good buddy."

I told her not to speak to me like that, or our emotional and physical bond would be weakened. "I've got enough to cope with," I explained. Woolf worried about my attitude, but otherwise, she was exuberant about what we were doing and still seemed to think we could solve all the puzzles with this program.

"Wow, I'll explore a suppressive society, with no holds barred! I'll watch all the phases: the rampant moral decay, all studded with generalizations and clichés, and a 'politics-will-solve-it' mood; then disillusionment, as nothing gets solved and energy is pissed away in trivialities; then an increase of banal kitsch, as mediocrity is highly rewarded; quickly followed by a resurgence of suspicion, witch-hunts, and anger, as the pendulum swings, and you get the extreme violence that always follows suppression. Next, an amazed sadness, a self-pitying and dramatic 'Where did we go wrong?' and guilt-trips everywhere; and finally back to the beginning again: rampant moral decay.

"Oh, how lovely the Earthie pendulum is! Oh, what fun we're going to have," she burbled.

We incorporated, hoping to go public and sell stock to whip up interest. We found an abandoned bowling alley and fitted it with floor-to-ceiling freezers, installing a generator system in case the city power failed. Nothing must go wrong. The sperm must be kept frozen. When all was installed and double-checked, I felt satisfied. This old bowling alley was going to be the center of the biggest economic boom in history.

"We need a final okay from the Chief," Woolf said.

She never let me forget that her people were here to study *us*: a primitive species, absorbed in what Lévi-Strauss calls "the cruel game of prestige and domination." But what did she really, really, *really* think of *me*?, a lonely outcast; insecure and beset with inner struggles; always hoping I wouldn't disgrace myself. Did I have the wits to keep up with her?...

Mersoid appeared in his basic form, or a holographic image of same. I was again shaken by how hideously ugly the Rysemians really are. The Chief had temporarily stored his Lincoln body. He was off duty, swimming lazily among the crystal stalagmites of the *Vonderra*'s vast simulation of their homeland. I saw only a grizzled, dowager-like cetacean, ugly as a mud fence, relaxing in soiled water; but Woolf had actually begun to sniffle with homesickness. I put my arm around her.

"Humans are up three points on the Exchange," the ugly whale informed us. "Beel's busily picking up slaves to work the lutso mines."

"We're moving as fast as we can." Woolf dried her eyes and

showed him the suite of offices we'd leased on the forty-seventh
floor of the Seafirst Building, with a view of snowcapped Olympics
(so that whatever happened, we'd always remember our day
there). She displayed the switchboard and newly installed battery
of telephones, saying, "The FMTC will soon be the city's number-
one firm. Famous Men's Telegenesis Corporation— like that
name? Sperm-of-the-Month Club; doesn't it have an impressive
ring to it?"

I couldn't read an expression on the blunt, slobbery features,
but Mersoid seemed to register skepticism. He obviously thought
my FMTC venture was quixotic. Standing there in his presence,
I almost believed it was. Woolf asked, "Please give us your go-
ahead, boss."

"It's a crapshoot of a plan. Did *she* dream it up?" He jerked his
whiskers at me.

Woolf was patient but obstinate. "Look, Earthies *drool* over
sales pitches. It's all they really understand. We can pick up data
by testing this market and, best of all, we can introduce a bit of
genetic manipulation."

"A gimmicky scheme, which may invite untold suffering,"
was Mersoid's judgment.

"No it won't," Woolf argued. "O'Blivion says it's just an
ordinary, everyday business deal—"

His shrewd eyes glowered in my direction. "Can the vampire
speak for herself?"

I straightened, cleared my throat and began, "I know my fellow
man—"

"Then you know the Flying Dutchman." Impolitely, he blinked
the gleaming plates that were his eyes in their nest of fat. The
old gentleman was in the act of disrobing, or maybe cleaning his
fins; there was a glimpse of plump pinkness, and a weird, rotund
gleam at which my eyes bugged out.

"Uh." I swallowed. "It's true people buy what seems to flatter
them and appear to dislike the truth in any form. I understand
your concern about safety, but—" Was this really how my beloved
Woolf looked in her original, native body? I felt slightly dizzy and
more than a little sick. "Most people take it for granted that these
defects cannot be changed; it's considered in bad taste to even
suggest the possibility—"

"You're begging the question," the Chief snapped.

"We're setting the experiment five years in the future. There's your safety factor right there. And I'm your comm link, so show a little respect," I responded.

It seemed clear that if I spoke with arrogance, he (she?) would accept it much as a human would; even though a Rysemian could read any thoughts of mine that I didn't deliberately shield. Woolf was looking at me with admiration.

Her Chief asked, "Do *you* understand these people, Vampire?"

Sadly I admitted, "Not very well."

He gave a nauseating ripple of the purplish gills. "In any case, it's immaterial. The Bureau of Missing Persons has a list so long they keep it hidden. You two clowns can't make the Earth situation much worse than it is."

To Woolf he barked, "You're pushing into the unknown! These savages can't tell good from bad. Scaulzo's commercials are sweeping the field; they match the local tone-level exactly, so don't let your freeze-immunity make you too cocky. Anything can happen."

After Mersoid vanished, I said a great many aves and paternosters under my breath, and persuaded myself that all was as it should be. Under stress, even a Hermetic Master like myself will cling to old, familiar rituals. But they didn't help.

Why did I go on kidding myself? Woolf had as much as confessed that just to know her was the Kiss of Death. "They follow us, they kidnap our friends," she'd told me; I kept trying to forget it, but the Agony Organ was a prelude... and on another level, the sense of wrongness had been intensified by Armand's letter; yet by comparison, a mere death threat was nothing.

The paranoia nibbled away at my mind. Who was Virginia Woolf? However charismatic, she— it— was an alien life form!, who had bewitched me into loving her. And love her I did!, but where could it go? I was moonstruck. The last few days had been so frenetic I barely had time to analyze my emotions.

On the other hand, soon I'd have to get my nerve up, go out, and take care of my vampire needs in the old familiar way; but...

But what?

I shook off these final doubts. They were too dreadful to confront.

As for Woolf, she gazed dreamily at the Olympics across the

Sound, where we'd shared a stolen day. Her next step would be to place an ad in the employment column of the *Seattle Times* and see what sort of people would show up in this office to have their lives warped beyond recognition.

She sharpened a pencil and began: "*Are you ambitious? Sincere? Want to help others?...*"

Then reaching for my hand, she murmured,

"I'm gonna select two typical humans, a male and a female, and... hot diggety! I'm gonna plumb the depths of the human soul." There was a pause. Then: "The only trouble is—"

"What, my dearest?"

"I just hope I'm not sending them to an unspeakably hideous, lingering death in some Sajorian lab," she sighed.

FOURTEEN

Are you ambitious? Sincere? Want to help others?
New research program. Interesting work, opp. advance;
guar. $120 day, up to $6,000 mo. to start.
Hurry! Box XYZ, Times.

Vicki Bauer saw Benaroya's ad in the *Seattle Times* on Thursday.

Vicki had been out of work for sixteen months. She'd had this good job in the secretarial pool at Boeing, reading the *Enquirer* and doing crossword puzzles for eight hours a day, but suddenly thousands of people had been laid off, for no good reason, including Vicki.

It was almost worth it, going down and collecting your Minimum Income check once a week, to see those former executives standing in line. Even old blue-haired Betty Badoo, head of the secretarial department. Even old George Stone the supervisor. And all those conceited pricks of draftsmen, automated out. It was almost worth being out of work to see those dudes squirm. Especially the ones who used to bring briefs in for her to type "in a hurry." They all collected Minimum, of course, but they also all had big houses, a car or two, a boat, a ski cabin, and a pile of unpaid bills.

A lot of them must feel like jumping off a bridge. Especially the jokers with kids to support. Thank God for abortion! Vicki had only herself to support.

But Christ, how could she pay her share of this lovely apartment on Minimum Income? What a crock! The whole thing was unfair: her roommate Ronnell had finally landed a job as a topless-bottomless. A no-cover dancer. It was unfair that Vicki was dumpy and ugly. When she stripped, guys broke a leg running away. Why should she be stuck with this blobby body? How come a zuts like Ronnell was at least okay-looking, even if meaner than shit and dumb, dumb, dumb? It wasn't fair!

Vicki decided to stay in bed again today. Why get up? For what? Life was a peeled zero. All those grabby, nasty zutses, all putting her down. Just thinking about it made the tears come in floods. Here she was, twenty-one, already four years over the hill. It was *shit* to be born ugly and ambitious!

Thank Christ her boobs were big, even if they were flabby. Actually they'd pass with a good bra. Men seemed to like her boobs. The problem was her butt. She hated to think about her butt. It was— what did her brat brother call it: three baseball bats across. And nothing helped. Exercise didn't help. Chemical girdles didn't help. It was bad genes. Her mother had an even fatter ass, if possible, than Vicki's.

People could laugh, but it wasn't funny! The pillow was drenched with tears. Life sucked. Even Ronnell's bragged-about job was no thrill. Shaking your bare ass and tits up and down a crummy runway. For about four dumb males. Big deal. Ronnell worked at the Iron Bull on 45th Street. Together, they'd met these Krishna Youth dudes who hung around that corner. The Krishnas were strict as hell, putting everybody down and saying only *their* bunch had all the answers.

Vicki started going to their meetings with Ronnell. What else was there to do? What other excitement was there? None at all. Everybody around here was embalmed. The Krishna Youth were at least breathing, if you could call it that. They lived in a commune near the Iron Bull. They didn't take drugs. They didn't even sleep together. They took cold showers instead. They were flippy. They weren't normal. They smelled funny. They were like tape recorders. They were always smiley-faced, talking about Inner Peace. If you said something was bad, they'd say, "Krishna provides for everything. The way of Krishna is the right way. You shouldn't trouble yourself with worries such as that."

This apartment was too nice to lose. It was a swinging singles with a big pool and lots of bachelors and it cost $950 a month. If the girls couldn't come up with the rent money, the fun would be over. Ronnell had the dancing job; Vicki had been doing some baby-sitting but the bills were piling up and she was flat broke.

There wasn't anything to read around here. And TV stunk even worse; only creeps watched it anymore. But maybe things would get better. She'd seen in the *Enquirer* where they programmed a computer to write books. Science fiction, spy stories, romance, everything but classics. The computer invented real good plots and characters. It could make up a book like *The Hobbit* in fifteen minutes. It was coming up with some good reading, they said. Nothing to scare or change people, just good reading to make you feel good. It wrote 20 years of a really good soap opera in twenty minutes.

Vicki'd only had one really exciting night since she moved in. Lots of men lived here, but half were gay and the other half were in love with Queen Zuts herself, Ronnell. But there was this very handsome black dude who had a street bike, a big hairy Harley with gobs of chrome all over it. His name was Herman, a dumb name, but he was just up from Texas and making plenty as a carpenter. She could hardly understand what he said. He talked Ubangi, or maybe it was Texan. He took her for a long ride, and that night they made out at his place. But the next time he saw her, he acted like he didn't know her. It wasn't right. But she pushed painful memories like that to the back of her mind. Otherwise she'd be crying twenty-four hours a day.

Oh God what a SHUCK life was! Vicki punched her tearstained pillow in misery. In one way, the Krishnas were right. It would be wonderful never to think!, just be ordered around, and have everything taken care of. But on the other hand, Vicki knew there was tons of money around and she wanted to get her hands on some of it. Why not? This was still a capitalist country, wasn't it? That was the name of the game— money! She'd mentioned this to her dad once and he'd called her a pig. Pig, huh? She'd show him. Up his!

She sure as hell wouldn't try asking Ronnell for a loan. She wouldn't give her that satisfaction. One thing she'd thought about. That was, going down on First Avenue and hustling. Why not? It sure beat losing your apartment. She wasn't much interested in sex, so hustling was something she could just *do,* and pocket the cash and put it out of her mind.

Sometimes when she walked along Pike Street or First Avenue

at night, there would be these women standing around, eyeballing everybody in a smooth way; she knew they were professionals. What would it be like, to be one of them? You could make a hundred bucks a trick, often more. But, no... She couldn't do that. Never! Because— well— not one of those professionals had an ass as fat as hers!

Vicki ground her face into the pillow, sobbing heartbrokenly. It was disgusting! The only thing that stopped her from becoming a whore was fear of ridicule! Some john might make a nasty comment about the size of her keester, and she couldn't take it... Oh shit... Anyway there wasn't that much money in prostitution. She wanted to be rich. *Really* rich.

The frightening thing was... Vicki's debts were outstripping her Minimum, but fast. In another couple of weeks she could either starve, rob a bank, or become a hooker. She wasn't the kind of girl to sit around and do nothing. She had ambition. What was wrong with that? Those smiley-faced punks the Krishnas didn't have anything better. All they could do was wear their yellow robes and chant, and shave their heads and recruit a million runaways. And to think they were the only bunch around who had any organization or did *anything* that was the least bit exciting!

Vicki got up and put on a bathrobe, moving to the front windows so she could look down at 1-5. A gray day with a little drizzle. To the west was the Space Needle, its top poking out of mist. She liked the way it looked. To her, it spelled success, good clothes and wealth and a glamorous, emerald-studded life. A *meaningful* life; not this blah nothing everyone else seemed happy to settle for.

Some day Vicki Bauer would *have* a glamorous life— in spades.

She just *knew* it would happen. Once she'd even been dumb enough to mention it to Ronnell.

"I've got a feeling," she'd said, all kind of breathless: half scared to tell, but dying to communicate her dream to somebody. "It's so strong I know it's real. I'm going to have scads of money and an international playboy husband who's madly in love with me! Ronnell, this is so real I can taste it."

Ronnell had been washing her hair at the time, standing at the sink in bra and panties— how Vicki had envied those shapely hips! But it was Ronnell's expression that really cut her to shreds.

Pity. And humor. Ronnell actually thought it was *funny.*

Vicki had turned around and walked out, red with embarrassment, and never mentioned it again. From that moment on, she hated Ronnell.

Pulling her robe tight, she sneaked downstairs to get the mail and the *Times.* She didn't want anybody to see her looking like this, frowsy-haired, bleary-eyed and all. But there was nothing but the usual junk mail and two bills.

She made herself a cup of coffee and turned to the "Help Wanted" column. Same old crap. Employment agencies advertising jobs that didn't exist, as a come-on. A few jobs for no-cover dancers, baby-sitters, housekeepers; otherwise nothing.

Funny item. Doctors found that women who got frequent exams for cancer got the most cancer. They said it was hypnotic or something. Funny as a crutch.

Politicians. Same old baloney.

Then she spotted Benaroya's blind ad under the compelling headline: ARE YOU AMBITIOUS? SINCERE? WANT TO HELP OTHERS?

It sounded too good to be true. They probably had a thousand replies already. But, what could she lose but a stamp?

"Research program." Did that mean they wanted to experiment on you? But the ad said "Help others" so it must be safe.

Vicki began to write out her resume, telling a few white lies to make herself look good. She *had* to get this job! It seemed like her last chance.

FIFTEEN

B lake Reardon was too bombed to drive home. Today had been Minimum Checky–day. Ring-a-ding! You line up with the other fired Boeing draftsmen and the Tooth Fairy hands you a piece of paper worth 200 beans. Then it's a five-martini lunch at Little Athens and on to the Fog Cutter Bar to get wiped out.

Once a week.

Blake tried like blazes to sort it out. He asked himself questions, "What's the point? Is manhood obsolete? What are people for?" and "*Is* there a life after high school?" He wondered why the U.S., which when he was a kid had been presented to him as "the greatest country in the world," was full of apathy cases like himself.

Minimum Wages.

He felt not only insulted, but spat upon, kicked in the gut and left to rot by an aimless System which was committing suicide faster than you can say Internal Revenue Service.

Maybe it was his own fault. A man with integrity would take to the hills. He'd eat giggleweeds. He'd shotgun down any sonofabitch who dared come near his cabin. He'd shotgun the whole FBI, CIA, KGB and Marines if they came near his cabin. He *never* should have let his mother enroll him in kindergarten! It started right there! The bastards sucked him in. They sucked him into their precious "society" and turned him into a Muscovy Duck like the rest of them.

Yeah. In the early seventies, everybody wanted to be an engineer. So little Blakey Reardon wanted to be an engineer. See Blakey run! See him study drafting at the kitchen table.

Good thing his folks didn't have the dough to send him to college. That really sank you. Engineering was a brown-nosed job. It was all based on making suckpoints with the boss, like school. You didn't need talent— they hated talent! You were supposed to "fit in" and glide along on other people's brains. *Dead* people's brains.

See Blake get his first drafting job.

In any big company, a drafting room is a sham. It's a complete lie! Hypocrisy in motion! You sit and draw pla-pla. Pretend to draw something that might work. Act busy. Then along comes the engineer supervisor. He takes ten minutes and redesigns the whole thing you've been working on for six months. Correction: he doesn't redesign it; he copies it out of the book. Didn't the old Romans design a thumbscrew pretty much like this one? But the point is, Boeing has got to hire ten thousand bodies, because the government says ten thousand people must work on the project, or else money won't be funneled into the Seattle plant.

It's a nuthouse! Nicely run by that head bureaucrat, the Tooth Fairy.

The bartender was giving him looks. So what. One time Blake had to draw a connection for a bridge. It took ten days to complete. If he finished it in *nine* days, that would be terrible. The Tooth Fairy allotted exactly ten days for this job. The connection was nothing important; just a way to stick a gusset in so the corner wouldn't fly apart. So in exactly ten days the Supervisor came by, opened his Structural Designer's Bible, found the God-given way to put the gusset in, changed Blake's drawing completely in five minutes, and the job was done.

Blake had drawn it all to painstaking scale, all the pretty little nuts and bolts drawn in correctly, hexagonal template and all. The Supervisor scribbled the correction on a piece of scratch paper, even unto the correct clearance. He could have done it at any time because he had access to the information, which Blake did not. But, they needed thirty people in that department. Two workers and twenty-eight seatwarmers.

Muscovy Ducks.

How did honest Blake Reardon get into a mess like this? Easy. Slid in, feet first. Wanted to be an engineer with a capital E. Glamorous Masterbuilder, pipe in face, Texas Instrument in pocket, pride in job, handling big pieces of steel. Structural, mechanical drafting. Took courses in the Army. In trade school.

By correspondence. Working little brain to bone, ten-twelve hours a day, really *frying* in the good old Judeo-Christian way. Falling into one job and another, always trying to be a hard worker. Same with his best friend at Boeing, Good Old Jimmy Fitz. Jim was at Lockheed now, but they'd had a ball together at Boeing.

He remembered one day, in the middle of one of those spells when Boeing was threatening to lay off ten thousand people. Their Glorious Leader wanted to keep all his people together, to make his kingdom look good. Empire-building, they called it at Boeing. Jimmy and Blake were bored out of their minds; they had to look busy, so Glorious Leader gave them little jobs, but it was all make-work because there was nothing to do. That was the great plague of Boeing. Thousands of people with nothing to do, trying to look busy.

By the very act of forcing Muscovy Ducks to get up at 4 A.M., you scramble their brains. Sensible people don't even have a *pulse* until eleven!, if the Tooth Fairy only knew it. But according to her, the early bird gets the worm. Honesty is the best policy. A penny saved is a penny earned. What a lie all those cute old sayings are. So half a million dummies leap out of bed before dawn and rush off to the Plant— because that's the way they did it in World War II, everybody's favorite war. But now, there was nothing. No Krauts, no Nips, no Jerries, nothing. Nothing! No exciting war. No big beautiful Cause everybody could stand behind and wave flags. Nothing but boredom, ego, pretty toys, and bills for same.

But they had some crazy times at Boeing. Like Wall Measuring Day.

Jimmy and Blake, wearing their Tool Designer badges, went down to the shop and ordered everybody out of Section Ten. Sternly they approached the Supervisor, tape measure and reference book in hand, and said their Leader wanted special measurements taken; all personnel and machinery must clear the area immediately!

(Their Leader was not interested in measurements, but he liked it when his men looked busy.)

Anyway, there were twelve Muscovy Ducks who worked in Section Ten, among bins used for storing scrap metal and other garbage. Jimmy and Blake moved all of these Muscovy Ducks. Then they requisitioned a forklift and moved all the storage bins. Next they had to move the Machine. This Machine that the Muscovy Ducks worshipped resembled a lathe; Blake didn't know what it was called, but to move it presented an interesting engineering problem.

When that problem was solved, they had a conference, standing with folded arms in this enormous building that had walls a hundred feet high. (The Muscovy Ducks moved lunar modules and jet planes around in here. To watch was always a shot in the arm. Blake loved the surrealism of watching ducks move jet planes and lunar modules.) Problem: to measure the wall to the nearest microboron. For are we not problem-solving animals?

Jimmy and Blake measured, scribbled on clipboards, measured this way, conferred, measured the other way, scribbled, crisp and frowning; efficient. Texas Instrument in and out of pocket every ten seconds. See the engineers compute! Twelve people stood around drinking coffee, watching the Engineers at work. Their Supervisor was mystified. He kept trying to look over Blake's shoulder and see what Blake was scribbling. When he did this, Blake would jerk the clipboard away with a professional's indignant look. How dare this layman question an Engineer? That was tantamount to checking the work of a Surgeon! *Nobody* questioned the work of a Surgeon! And this job, it was even more important. It was Top Secret! The lives of millions depended on this job. Perhaps a security check should be run on this Supervisor. His phone should definitely be tapped if that hadn't been done already.

They kept measuring that frigging wall all afternoon. They'd take an arbitrary dot, a flyspeck, a tomato seed from somebody's lunch, and measure up and down from it. Three point ninety-six! Four, eleven and three-eighths over stat! Dropping lots of technical terms. "The lift." "Draft over drag." "Lift exceeding drag cuts our thermal pressure." "But the space-heat ratio—" If anybody tried to listen, they would glare, and fall into a cold silence. Everything at Boeing was secret. It was all part of Status. And Status was Everything.

They'd make a pencil mark, then move up or down four feet. The reference work was Crane's Plumbing Catalog and a tattered copy of *Howl* in a plain wrapper. Shuffling back and forth, measuring, scribbling, frowning.

Finally they said, "All right!" and glared. Snapped everything shut. Clipped and stowed pencils. A curt nod to the Supervisor.

"You'll be hearing from us!" And marched out muttering.

What a strange way to make a living. Blake didn't understand it. How could doing this produce food on the table for the wife and kids? Yet it *did*. And the married guys had to take it seriously and act their parts right, or they'd go insane. And he was a married guy.

Blake sipped drinky. Bartender was busy with others. Boeing had been a lot of fun, though, and he missed the old place, strange as it was.

Boeing. They all believed in the Tooth Fairy. Every man looking over his shoulder, afraid of being Found Out. And what was there to Find Out? Ah, there was the question! You could never pinpoint it. The only thing you could pinpoint, with deadly accuracy, was Quitting Time. A precise moment: Quitting Time. Everybody put their coats on. The Muscovy Duck stands at the edge of its drawing board, lunchbox in one hand, thermos in the other. The bell rings! Stampede!, at a fast walk; to run was beneath the dignity of an Engineer. It was a status symbol to be the first one out. It was a status symbol to be the last one out.

Favorite game, having a name paged over the P.A. system. Broadcast over the entire plant. One day the Lakers basketball team was paged, player by player, all morning. Another day the innocent speaker kept blabbing "Calling Buster Hymen, Calling Buster Hymen" for eight hours.

Oh God how we miss Viet Nam! And hell, we'd give our left ball for World War II.

War gives meaning to our lives. Now we have only elaborate practical jokes that take all day to set up. The plastic spider on invisible thread, strung with great care on overhead lights, so as to hit as many people as possible in one day. Slowly, slowly, it lowers over a drawing board. It hovers. It drops! and the engineer goes over backward screaming; always gets a big laugh. Or the two-way sticky tape that tapes all his pencils and tools to his board, when he goes to the can. Or the googly extension cords: lights flash, fans blast, radios howl, and the electric erasers go on and off...

Those were the days. And now what? Now what? If they took away the Minimum Wage, would he starve, or would he develop some guts? Susie the wife, with the little hack job, would she starve? And the two kids who spent their days with a baby-sitter?

What's missing? Something is seriously missing here. What if Boeing starts hiring again, and Jimmy Fitz gets tired of California, and Blake's whole department files back to their boards again?

It would be business as usual.

The Empire would flourish. When the Glorious Leader needed two men, he'd hire thirty and keep them all on their toes with layoff threats. Payday would be jackpot day. If you had seniority you'd reap the rewards. This little tidbit; a percentage off this or that; hockey games, basketball tickets, a show or two; Wednesday off to go skiing; and if the boss liked you he'd punch your timecard for you.

Blake lit a cigarette, signaled for a refill. There was only one slight problem. After a few years in that cozy womb, you've had it. You are *terrified* of the outside world. Boeing's a snug prison. You miss the familiar cell, your buddies, your enemies, the guards, the brass, the rules, the orderly little world. After Boeing, it's mind-blowing trying to get another job. Where is the Tooth Fairy and her gravy? Where are the fringe benefits, the sick pay; this plan, that policy, those bonds, the credit union at a discount? They told him it was a World War II technique. A system of rewards from when guys had to work all night. But now, no purpose to it. Where is our war? Things *move* in wartime. Things make *sense*. A war is what brings us together. Is *war* what it means to be alive on this screaming-mad planet? Is *war* our glorious goal and heritage?

Was bartender ignoring him? Blake banged his glass down. I'm getting maudlin. I'm a hamster in a shoebox. Fouling my nest, like people everywhere. Undisciplined, meaningless. Cleaning my whiskers and dreaming hamster dreams.

The newsboy brought papers in, tossed them on the bar. Blake opened to "Employment." Forget engineering, look for what else. He read Benaroya's ad: ARE YOU AMBITIOUS? SINCERE? WANT TO HELP OTHERS?

Weren't people damned fools? He tore the ad out. Tomorrow he'd write a cute letter. "I'm terribly ambitious, and oh, how I long to help others. I'm just *crazy* about others. Also you will be delighted at how *sincere* I am," etc. etc.

Right now he'd crawl home and tell Susie how sorry he was to be such an underarm, or underachiever, or whatever.

Take bus home, leave car in lot. Unlawful to drive while bombed.

SIXTEEN

Vicki Bauer was excited when she got the letter inviting her to a reception at the Seafirst on Saturday. She dressed carefully, scrambling through her wardrobe to find something that might make her look less blimpy. $120 a day! Oh God. She *had* to get this job. She applied eye makeup, which took the curse off her blonde lashes; it helped a little but she still loathed her appearance.

"So what?" she snapped at her reflection. "You're no gargoyle and you've got brains, which is more than Ronnell can say. Maybe for once they're not hiring on looks."

She took the bus, cheering up as she entered the massive glass-and-stone building. At least this was better than crying in bed all day long. The elevators were jammed. Was it competition? Two hundred zutses applying for the same job? That was bad news.

At the forty-seventh floor, right where you get off the elevator, a woman stood welcoming applicants. "My name is Virginia Woolf," she said in ringing tones. Vicki was impressed. Virginia Woolf, wasn't that a former movie star? Of course. Liz Taylor played her part on a Late Show. Vicki was *very* impressed. Wow. And the actress was wearing old tennis shoes. No jewelry, no earrings, no nothing. But she had real class.

She certainly knew how to relate to people. Took Vicki's hand, smiled directly into her eyes. It was the warmest reception Vicki'd ever had. The woman's clothes were doggy, but then she was a pacesetter type: ahead of her time. She could easily be a *Vogue* layout from four or five years in the future. A real cool Image. Something Vicki'd always yearned for. When she wrote what she called "her real name" on the blackboard it turned out to be one of those super-hip, single names that a European film star might have: Benaroya. And such a kindhearted personality! She seemed generous, frank, and spontaneous, and Vicki was half in love with her already.

"I'm an anthropologist from Rysemus and I am older than the hills" she said, turning from the blackboard. Which was bull; she was young and darling, saying with lots of peppy enthusiasm,

"Holy Moses, but I love ya! What a thrill to be here. Boy. You all look so *nice* in your absurd stylish getups. Haw, haw, haw! Dressed-up carnivores, that's a hot one," grinning merrily.

Woolf bounced forward, combing her messy hair with a piece of chalk. The crowd had fallen silent. They were wary as she leaped to the podium and began to address them.

"Come right in, you bushwhackers! Sit down and take a load off your feet. Welcome, a thousand welcomes, you uglies who live out here on a spiral arm away from everything that matters! But cheer up; you've come to the right place."

At this, the whispering and rustling stopped dead. Not a foot shuffled, not a cough was coughed. Woolf danced along the podium, her arms waving joyously.

"Welcome down from the trees! What took you so long? Haw haw that's a joke, we all *know* you won't be down for another thousand years. Come along to the front, you twerps in the back! Don't be shy."

More people kept pouring into the room until it was uncomfortably packed. Woolf seated them deftly. She could sure handle a crowd. She had a pair of twin brothers busily unstacking chairs. They looked a lot like Ronald Reagan. Vicki watched the routine intently. She'd never admired anyone as much as this energetic, outspoken Virginia Woolf. Did that mean she was in for a disappointment? Maybe Woolf was the champion moray eel of all times. Out to exploit helpless job seekers. You'd be dying for a hand-squeeze from her, then she'd turn around and stab you in the back. But she seemed very good-natured, saying,

"Are ya ready for something new?... You're a gang of bush-league Emperors, surrounded by flatterers. Your ads flatter you. Your books flatter you. Nothing gets published that doesn't flatter you. That's why you never learn or grow," with a broad wink.

"Now! Do you think I, a superior being, consider you a bunch of hysterical monkeys wallowing in false praise? Well I sure as heck don't! I am an infinite being, but so are you. You can reach my level and beyond." She beamed.

An angry muttering had begun. Some people in the back were boiling mad. Vicki thought it was terrific. The speaker didn't mind making a fool out of herself, getting people mad at her. She raised her voice and went on,

"Yes; in fact, you are hypnotized gods (so to speak) and I'm here to deprogram you, un-hypnotize you, and restore you to your long lost power. Not all of you, of course; just the receptive ones. The others, who in my opinion are total imbeciles, may stand up and clear out of here on the double. On your feet! Pronto!"

A porky lady in fake fur and too much makeup suddenly arose, shrilling, "The attorney general will hear about this!"

"Uh-huh, you betcha, if you got a spare month with nothing to do but leave messages on his jam-packed little recorder," Woolf agreed sweetly. "Now! As you depart, my dears, one of the reagans will hand each of you a hundred dollar bill just for showing up. So vamoose outta here *quick* because I'm gonna get much more insulting in a minute."

Five or six people left in great haste. Vicki could hardly believe her eyes and ears. She'd never heard anything remotely like all this. Woolf said,

"Now, dear friends, I'm gonna prove that your desires are controlled by corporate groups, and that there is *never* any shortage of *anything.* You've been conditioned to think there is. You have been brainwashed. But I'm going to break that conditioning. Each of you who sticks with me will be a millionaire within a month. Of course you must each detach yourself, as quickly as possible, from Mass Thought… Question, sir?"

A copper-faced man stood up just behind Vicki, twisting his hat in his long yellow fingers.

"I've been lied to all my life! One fancy sales talk after another!" he shouted. "We all know these things are true! So what! Prove you're not as big a liar as anybody!"

Woolf hitched up her jeans. "You'll have your proof, sir, in due course; meanwhile for everyone who sticks around, it's a free lunch and free beer. Now who's with me? Huh? Get those cute little paws up."

A few score hands shot up, including Vicki's. The speaker

counted them, using her chalk as a pointer, and wrote the number on the blackboard. "Now listen carefully, you jabeeps. My company, known as the Famous Men's Telegenesis Corp., is about to launch an all-out sales campaign. First let me explain telegenesis." She turned and scrawled the word in big letters on the blackboard. "It means parenthood at a distance."

There was a silence as Woolf looked from face to face; then she continued,

"The fact that our plan will upgrade the human race is incidental. Basically, we're going to train sales crews to go door-to-door, calling on housewives, selling them a bundle from heaven, which we call the Famous Men's Sperm Kit."

Vicki's jaw dropped. There wasn't a sound in the room.

"And now!" Woolf trumpeted, "I wanna introduce my friend Sterling O'Blivion, longtime vampire and mastermind of sales pitches, who'll tell ya all about it."

There was scattered applause as a bespectacled, monklike person in dirty jeans, who'd be pretty if she cleaned herself up, but looked like she was in the middle of a nervous breakdown, stood up and said,

"How very nice. How very, very *nice* that your ignorance and barbarism will soon be a thing of the past, as my dear Virginia Woolf has just informed you. And now to business.

"You, our shock troops, our sales crew, will be taken to a promising neighborhood, where you will knock on doors. You will give a cheerful little speech: 'Good morning, ma'am! I'm from the FMTC. We're taking a survey of what people are thinking, in regard to crowding, overpopulation, and other problems. Yessirree-bob, here's a chance for you to state your opinions without any backtalk!'

"Then chuckle a friendly chuckle, whip out a questionnaire and begin,

"'How many children do you have?'

"Write down her answer carefully. Say, 'Madam, I'd like you to be as frank with me as I'm being with you. If this question is none of my business, please tell me so and we'll skip it.' Smile disarmingly. Be sympathetic! Sympathy is of the essence. If she's angry, excuse yourself and leave; but if she's receptive, spring the all-important question.

"Before I tell you what it is, here's one last chance. If you want to leave, do so immediately, and collect your hundred dollars at the door."

Nobody moved. Sterling went on. "So now you ask the qualifying question: 'Do you want more children?'

"If she says 'no,' excuse yourself politely and rush to the next house. If she says 'yes,' scrape your feet on the mat, lower your head, and push on into the parlor. Expert door-to-door salespersons will train you to get in without an argument.

"Once inside, flit over and turn down the TV with an engaging smile, saying, 'Goodness me!, I can't compete with professionals.' Then plop onto the couch all relaxed and cheery, and invite her to sit next to you. When she's comfortable, snap open your questionnaire and ask:

'In your opinion, what is the ideal size for a family?' Write down her answer and then ask, 'Should population be limited by law? Should people need a license to have children? What is your stand on abortion?' Whatever she says, write it down and tell her it's a very good answer; then proceed to your final questions. 'How big should a city be? Should cities be designed, or just grow?' and so forth.

"At first she may appear shocked, but if you remain warm and friendly she will loosen up. When she is approximately goose-loose, throw your bombshell.

"'Madam, have you heard of the Sperm-of-the-Month Club?' Chances are she will say no, but she will be hanging on your every word.

"Open your briefcase. Whip out this big broadside." O'Blivion opened a folded sheet of heavy paper on which was printed:

WOULD YOU LIKE TO HAVE A BRILLIANT CHILD?

—along with a picture of some strikingly calm and thoughtful preschoolers playing with an electron microscope and a two-hundred-inch telescope. She pinned these items on the board, continuing:

"Check off the prospect's answer, *yes* or *no*. Then flash your next broadside."

WOULD YOU CHOOSE A HANDSOME SON...
OR A STUNNING DAUGHTER?

—with photos of several gorgeous toddlers.

The next broadside featured glossies of sports stars, headed:

WANT TO BE THE MOM OF A TOP CHAMPION?

Followed by:

OR WOULD YOU PREFER YOUR CHILD TO HAVE A POTENTIAL FOR VERY SPECIAL TALENT?

—with pictures of an opera star, sculptor, French chef, test pilot, Supreme Court justice, tightrope walker, and so forth.

"In this way, you focus her deepest hopes and dreams," O'Blivion told them. "Suppose the client confesses she'd like to have a strikingly handsome child. Open your section on Handsome Daddies. Flip the pages. When you come to her favorite star (let us assume he is Jomo Delp, the newest disco sensation) she will stop you with a shy gesture, and she will confess, Yes!, she'd like her baby to resemble Jomo Delp as closely as possible.

"Here is where the sale is made. Now you swing into your close. Tell her she can have Jomo Delp's son or daughter for as little as thirty dollars a month. She will be astounded and will ask, 'How?' You will be reassuring as you say, 'Simple! Our company will furnish a kit that contains this movie star's frozen sperm, along with easy-to-understand instructions.' She will keep the sperm in its plain wrapper in the freezing compartment of her refrigerator. As a built-in bonus, its very presence will lend a dreamlike dazzle to simple desserts such as homemade ice cream."

You could have heard a pin drop.

O'Blivion smiled gently and lowered her voice to a whisper.

"Your client will insert the sperm (or ask her lover's assistance, as she chooses, using a syringe that we include absolutely free) at the precisely indicated time of the month. Nine months later she will produce the infant of her dreams, to cherish, rock, nag, diaper or Pamper at her discretion, and love forever. If she fails to get pregnant, the company furnishes additional sperm kits at *no extra cost* until pregnancy is assured. She can choose either boy or girl, and all for the amazing price of $30 down, $30 per month for 48 months, at a cut-rate 9% on the diminishing balance, which is an unheard-of interest rate in today's market.

"And now I'll turn you back to Ms. Woolf for a brief question period."

The audience went bonkers. They started asking so many questions Woolf couldn't hear herself think.

"Is this legal?"

"Absolutely. We've got the top talent in the country on our law team."

"How can you do it?"

"We buy sperm from celebrated men, paying an agreed-upon sum averaging fifty thousand dollars, with a bonus for refills if necessary. Each sperm sample can be cut a million ways, to fertilize a million women."

"How can you preselect the sex?"

Woolf explained about X and Y chromosomes, how they can be separated by centrifuge because Xs are heavier. "The male determines the sex of the child, as you all know. An X produces a girl; a Y, which is really a malformed X, produces a boy. Now suppose that your client would like another woman to be the father of her child. This is easy to do. We simply shrink and be-tail egg cells, turning them into sperm; or we use body cells."

"Since when can they do that?"

Woolf smiled her warm smile. "It would probably upset the bejeezus out of your parents, poor old cavefolk; but reproduction can be done lots of ways. The public is not told everything, because the public tends to fly into hysteria and upset the stock market. Questions?"

A hand waved frantically.

"Can't the women sue these males for nonsupport? After all, they're the fathers of their children."

"Every customer will sign a release, stating that the donor has no further obligation to her. In exchange, she gets a handsomely engraved and framed certificate signed by the donor, guaranteeing he's the biological father of her child. And that's a lot more than most kids have, you gotta admit."

"What if the client's husband objects?"

"We call that 'The Husband Objection.' Simply depart before he reaches for the shotgun, and run to the next house as fast as your little legs can carry you."

A lankhaired youth in chinos and windbreaker leaped up.

"What famous men are you using?"

Woolf rattled off a list of famous names. "And we're enlisting more every day. This morning we signed up Robert Bly the poet; Rod Stewart the rock star; Vito Corleone the Mafia chief; and Barry Malzberg the science fiction writer. More questions?"

"When do I start?" Vicki heard her own voice trilling from the front row.

"Right now. Let's get to work."

A livid, bearded man jumped to his feet, trembling with fury. "Do you have the nerve to believe these celebrated men are going to be party to such a cheap, smutty scheme?"

"Darling, you're forgetting the money we offer is a considerable sum. Also, we sell the gentlemen on the notion that they are upgrading the human race. What male won't believe that *his* children are superior to all others? Also, the donor gets more publicity than a nude centerfold. We've booked dozens of our donors on the *Tonight Show*. And think of the ego gratification. Even Moses would be flattered to think there'd be a million little Mosae lining up at the Pizza Hut next generation. And now, my friends: Who is willing to give it the old college try?"

Four dozen hands shot up. The last few protesters left, muttering about filth, crime, unnatural acts, and complaints to the Better Business Bureau. In an hour Woolf had the live wires galvanized with orgiastic zeal. They were given free sandwiches with unusual but delicious pickles and frosty steins of milk or beer. Next to each platter was a free kazoo. Woolf bounced among the diners, giving everyone a delightful surge of well-being by her very presence.

Sterling O'Blivion and Virginia Woolf seemed to be having an argument; they stood in the doorway holding hands. Just before Sterling left, they kissed. Vicki was deeply shocked. Could the two be... lesbians? She hated to even *think* of the terrible word; but of course they weren't; they were just good business chums. (Nevertheless, she wondered what it would be "like," and what they "really did" and all those terrible things. Then she put it out of her mind and ate another sandwich.)

When she had gorged until she burped, Vicki went into the bathroom and splashed cold water on her face. She tootled a soft note or two on her kazoo. She emerged a few minutes later, vowing to see this exciting business through to the end.

Break over, the crowd gathered once again in the briefing room to hear Woolf say:

"Your five-day training program begins immediately. No longer will you be poor, washed-out ghosts, living empty non-lives! No longer will you be guilt-ridden sickies drowning in despair, sitcoms, and heaps of say-nothing books!" The troops, she said, would quickly learn to be triumphant conquerors rather than drab, brainwashed jabeeps. Each session was a religious revival filled with dazzle and mystical unity. They marched and played their kazoos; there was plenty of chanting.

"Are we spreading the word?"

"Yes!"

"Are we spreading the word?"

"Yes!"

"Do we create reality?"

"Yooo-betcha!" (Kazoo tootle.)

"Do we create reality?"

"I said 'Yoooooo-betcha'!"

"Are we boomin' ahead?"

"Boomin' ahead!"

"Thank you, Mother Nature!"

"Amen!"

"Thank you Mother Nature!"

"Aaa-men!"

Doing a snake dance, the troops thrilled to their own bubbling power. Virginia Woolf explained that inflation, wars, unemployment, and boring novels were all symptoms of a disease called mass psychosis; and they were now unhypnotizing themselves from the compulsive vibes of the Mass Mind. Vicki Bauer's rapture was complete. Here was something to live for at last!

Woolf was cuter than anything, saying, "Bounce, and tootle that kazoo! Bounce above the Bureaucracy!, for the happy woman is king! You don't hafta creep like a bunch of snails and manipulate each other like crazy, under the dopey illusion that to get ahead of some other poor little snail is 'success.' What good is that kind of 'success' if the other little snail is sad and unhappy and is gonna *die* in *a* few years anyway? Nosirree, you deserve a happy life and not a sad one," and Woolf embraced the troops with that grin which could get her elected President in about ten seconds — Shit, if Vicki could be *half* that great!...

After the second session, Vicki screwed up courage and went and stood by Woolf's desk.

"I- I'd like to ask a favor," Vicki gulped.

Woolf put out a probe. Bauer, Vicki. A human who felt she was destined for something better than twentieth-century life in a sardine can. She was in chronic despair: rejected, belittled, teased, ridiculed, coaxed to buy things, then burdened with bills; upset about her body's *looks,* of all silly things; helpless and hopeless like so many others... It could make you cry.

"Shoot," said Woolf.

"I know I'm being trained for direct sales. But, well, I'd much rather be a sperm collector. I mean, I think... that I have natural talent along those lines."

Woolf tossed the hair from her forehead in a gesture everyone seemed to go ape about. Funny how Earthies had a core of goodness that didn't show up on the mass level. Funny how the media turned everything into little heaps of plastic poopoo, but in person, people weren't that way at all. She took both of Vicki's hands in hers, nodding thoughtfully.

"That's fine with me. You're getting in on the ground floor of something really big. You'll personally hand each donor fifty thousand or more, so naturally he'll love ya; and you'll also get a ten thousand dollar finder's fee, plus expenses. How does that grab you?"

"I- I—" Vicki was dumbfounded. Her brain had slipped out of gear. "Oh Benaroya, you're so terrific. You're warm, and real, and beautiful and noble and proud and elegant and, oh, you're the most wonderful person I've ever known." And she fled in tears.

Alone, Woolf yawned and stretched, making the bones in her shoulders crack. It had been a great session; but she was worried about Sterling O'Blivion. The vampire had run back home, five years into the past and 2,000 miles eastward, and wouldn't answer the phone. She'd locked herself into her apartment, where she did nothing but play records of people laughing and people applauding.

"Don't call me, I'll call you!" Sterling had insisted. "Leave me alone until I get my head together."

Sterling's ex-husband Armand had been found shot twice through the chest, and his body had been stuffed into the negative space of a Henry Moore at the Art Institute. Sterling was devastated, of course; but on top of that, she was suffering from acute culture shock. Going aboard the *Vonderra* had been too much for her.

"Saints protect me!" she had cried with great drama. "I, a good Catholic, have made love out of my species!" and she flung her cape tightly around herself.

Holy Moses. And worse, "I've got to go out and drink blood but my nerve is all shot," Sterling had wept. Woolf said there was tons of blood aboard ship, but Sterling said no, that was goat blood and had the wrong chemical composition and besides it was the *tradition* that counted.

"You've screwed me up," she wailed.

Wow.

Earth was sure a cold, lonely planet without that darling vampire, Woolf mused, gazing at the melancholy rain that lashed the chill waters of Puget Sound.

SEVENTEEN

Blake Reardon raced down I-5 in his green Turbo TX33C. He was doing 80, watching the rearview mirror for the state patrol, because he was late. Overslept. Knocked off a six-pack last night in front of the TV. After his more serious daytime drinking. Did that mean... what the commercials said it meant? Or was he just avoiding dry rot? Anyway, he had a nice invitation in his pocket. Printed on creamy, expensive paper. With *FMTC* embossed in real gold. Very impressive, but no clue as to what FMTC stood for.

There was a number, so Blake had phoned first.

"What kind of research is it?"

"A Foundation project," the buttery voice told him. "Everything will be explained at the meeting."

"Is the 120 bucks a day for real?"

"It's the guarantee. Actually you'll make a lot more than that."

Blake had visions of a gang of Marine recruits being sent down a mine shaft, like canaries, to test the lethal power of some new nerve gas. More likely it was a come on for some outfit that hustled aluminum siding. Or cookware. But for $120 a day, what was there to lose? The reception was at ten. It was now half past. He kept the go-pedal floored.

Beautiful day, cool and sunny, with a stiff breeze ruffling Lake Union. Lucky dogs in cruisers running with the breeze. How did they get so rich? Minimum wage didn't begin to cover Blake's bills. He had too many hostages to fortune. Too many goodies. His boat, for starters, and his camper, parked at his suburban home, along with a wife and two small popsicle-eaters. Clincher: if he couldn't raise three Gs by the first, the bank would repo the boat. Susie didn't know that yet. She loved the boat. It was their ticket to paradise. It cost fifteen Gs last spring, arranged in balloon payments, before Blake was told he was going to be laid off.

At least they'd had one beautiful summer: tooling to the San Juan Islands on weekends, anchoring in some little harbor, where you didn't see a human face for two days. Nothing but four Reardons in salt spray and a forest of conifers. And now, Big Daddy had blown the whole thing.

Sun bounced off the Space Needle as he flew by. Job hunting was *kaput.* He'd combed the whole town. Yet there was money around. Three TVs in every house, plenty of gas, cash registers jingling while everybody wailed about a recession. Susie took a checkout job at Safeway, which was a bringdown but kept her feeling productive. Small wonder Blake was hitting the sauce. No income, no prospects, nothing but the unpromising card in his pocket.

Something terrible is going to happen.

Now hold it right there. No DTs, buddy. No pink elephants. No sinking into shady fears. He'd popped a decongestant tablet for the sniffles and it was doing warpy things to his head. Complete *episodes* kept flashing through. Some of them, but not all, were memories. Realer than this steering wheel in his hands. Right now, he was 17, working as a dockhand on a party boat. A friend of his Dad's had a 40-foot diesel on San Pablo Bay so Blake was shipped down for the summer. He was overjoyed. He got to sleep on the boat. He was watchman. Night, stars, and waves rocking you to sleep. Mornings he felt like Sinbad the Sailor padding around in cutoffs cleaning her up, getting ready for the day. Making coffee on a hibachi. Smell it and taste it. Customers started piling in about eight. Businessmen. Still drowsy but excited as a bunch of kids at a picnic. One of them brought his wife and the others were mad; leave the little woman at home, they told him, and catch yourself a man-sized fish.

And the bait! He could smell the bait, real as real. Beautiful smell, on his hands right now. San Francisco Bay shrimp frozen in little plastic bags, cost 35c, very good for sturgeon. The bait smell mixed with coffee and diesel fuel. Boss revved her up, took the wheel, Blake untied the line, gave it a shove, jumped aboard at the last second, grandstand play that drew a gasp from the dude's wife. Passengers huddling in the cabin. One or two jocks in the prow, eyes weeping in cold raw fishy wind, gulls screaming all around.

Christ, being back there was so good! He didn't want to leave it. Seventeen was the only age worth living. They'd pull around slowly and fish. And when you hooked a sturgeon! You'd fight him for half an hour, sweating and trembling and keeping the line taut without quite breaking it. Blake was in top shape as a kid but still it hurt all over to reel in a five-foot sturgeon. And then the hero's reward. He could feel the whole thing. It was happening *now*. Somebody jams a cigarette in your face, the others pound your back like crazy-time. Afterward, crouching on the hatch cover, arms heavier than marble, stunned and sweating like a young Greek after a fantastic victory— why couldn't he earn a living like that today? What was wrong with this constipated, mousy red-tape world? Christ! If it weren't for the family he could be a deckhand again, or a ski bum, but it was too late now. Too late. Much too late. Muscles going to flab. In another year he'd be 35. Thirty-five! Pretty soon old age, poverty. An ego-beating he had to avoid at all costs. He *had* to pull his head together and figure a way out of this trap.

Maybe this job would be it.

Blake had gone to work after two years of college. That was a point on his side. An excess of college fried the brains. Millions of rubber stamps marching off with degrees, getting locked into one narrow field, and when that field blew away in the morning breeze— goodbye, little specialist! But Blake was flexible. He'd pull ahead in time. Sure he would. He used to envy the PhDs from MIT but not any more. They'd been preset, like goddamn hardboiled eggs. But the future was calling for gnomes and mavericks and ESP-y practical jokers.

Why was humanity stuck in a sewer? Hard to imagine that whole Boeing complex lying idle. All those hundred-foot-tall rooms gathering dust... Oh how he missed Boeing. And all because Boeing missed a missile-launcher contract worth fifty billion, because the public was dead set against it. Wanted no more war stuff. He agreed, but why couldn't they tool up for mass transit or something positive like that? Why just close up shop? *Why?*

Maybe there were too many half-asleep people demanding good jobs with big pay. Wanting "good conditions" furnished by somebody else. Forgetting you have to snatch every ounce of meat out of God's deepfreeze. Everybody was covered with baby fat! Birdies in a nest, waiting to be fed! But it's time to snap out of the trance. Become a brave and clever wildcat. Shut your mouth, open your ears, and when something big stirs in the bushes, pounce on it.

He always expected "something big" to show up. Was that dumbness, or the only thing that kept you alive? Was "something big" just around the corner? Or was Draftsman Reardon a tiny ant hauling dung like everybody else?

Football interview on the radio. He snapped it off. "Only yesterday" he'd been crushed because of not being big enough to rate a football scholarship. One more close miss! Now he saw what a bad trip it would have been: five years of having his fundament kissed, then fifty years of being a has-been. Maybe Earth was a prison planet. A very slow torture chamber for damned souls? Now where in the world did *that idea* come from? But what other explanation made sense?...

The FMTC suite was crowded. Blake sat in the back row. The woman doing the speaking was not bad-looking. Matter of fact, she was a knockout. But next to Reardon sat a scabrous lady wearing a button that said "YOUR smoking may be dangerous to MY health" — she kept frowning, shaking her head; didn't agree with what the speaker, Virginia Woolf, was saying. She looked leprous. HER skin condition was probably dangerous to BLAKE'S health so he moved away, sticking a cigarette into his mouth as he went.

Woolf scrawled figures on the board, writing like a second-grader; but when she moved, when she spoke... she really made the pulses race. Projected a sensation of power — more here than meets the eye. Blake sucked in his breath. She was different. Not even well-groomed. Nails not polished, hair slightly unkempt. But very alive. Almost too much so. Terrific cleavage. A wild and beautiful critter. Didn't seem at all conceited about it. Not a snob. Was she a trained con artist? Whoever trained her did a great job. She seemed to be running the show... Blake began to feel twinges of married guilt. For long minutes, he was so knocked out by the impact of Woolf's presence that he forgot to listen to her words.

Then it finally came through.

She was telling these people to go out and sell *sperm*.

He almost fell off his chair. Had he heard right? She was describing how the women of Seattle were *longing* to buy a Package of fatherhood from their favorite politician or hydroplane racer.

This was the most inane idea Blake had ever heard.

Yet there was certainly a feel of money in the air; you could almost hear the coins clinking into an invisible cashbox. He thought— Hot damn, why not? Maybe this FMTC has keyed into some big new market. Could be like real estate in the seventies. Or conglomerates in the sixties. Or advertising in the fifties, weapons in the forties. Sparks were flying here. The gung-ho excitement was in the air. You could feel it.

Blake listened carefully as Benaroya outlined the program. Yes, the 120 bucks a day was guaranteed to everyone who qualified. "Qualified," always an interesting word. The pitch was door-to-door; he disliked that part. And yet, why not? Grass roots; that's where the business is. A provocative item, sold to the housewife in a personal interview in her own home. Why not?

It had possibilities. Woolf said there was plenty of room for advancement; he'd be getting in on the ground floor. He looked around to see how the audience was taking this. Some looked very grumpy. Others had already clumped out. The rest were hanging on Woolf's every word.

When she asked for volunteers to stay for training, Blake stayed. He spent a heavy afternoon going through what was called "the door setup." This was just an ordinary door in a frame. You'd knock on that door. A tough snotty girl, trained earlier, would fling it open and say "Well? What do *you* want?" in a typically nasty and irritable way.

"We're visiting the parents—" Blake would begin.

"Not interested," and she'd slam the door in his face.

"Every slam is a bucket of gold!" the wide-eyed Woolf told her students. "Who cares about rejection? It means nothing. Just float with a smile to the next house." Or, "If ya can't stand rejection ya can't stand life! Turn again, Whittington, Lord Mayor of London," she would proclaim, standing cross-legged on a desktop... He liked the way she handled things.

So try again. "We're visiting the parents—"

"I'm not a parent," with a shy look.

"Do you plan to be a parent some day?"

Zappo. This time the "prospect" let him in and he went through the pitch, reading from the typed copy in his hand. He could memorize it tonight in front of the rec room mirror. What would Susie say? Maybe he shouldn't mention it to her. What if *she* wanted to buy a Package? He'd go out and cut his wrists... Or would he? Did it matter if Japheth begat Shem, or if they all hatched out of ostrich eggs? Oh balls, no use borrowing trouble. Stick to business.

That night Blake went home, locked himself in the rec room and practiced the pitch into the mirror until he had it cold. Susie could sense he was onto something so she left him alone. She was always good about that. Blake was a quick study; he had the whole thing to perfection by the time work started next morning.

Benaroya ran the crew out to a North End suburb. She chauffeured eight people in an air-conditioned limo, explaining that she'd leave one on each corner at nine in the morning, would pick them up for lunch, have them back on their corners by one, and collect them again at five. She drove the way she spoke: much too fast, but with a fluid *chutzpah* and the skill of a flat-track racer.

She said, "Each of you will make a few hundred bucks today. We pay $250 per sale. Some of you will sell three or four or more.

"These women are sitting out there *waiting* for you. This is the most glamorous day of their lives! What a reception you'll get! This generation grew up revering the Beatles or Mick Jagger or John Kennedy or the Dallas Cowboys. Can you imagine the *thrill* and the *delight* you will stir in their hearts this morning?"

Blake glanced at his fellow passengers. All down-and-outers like himself; until now. Now, they were all turned on by this crash-bang-sunrise talk of Woolf's. Would the pitch really work? He felt excited, standing alone at the end of a long block of tract homes.

Now was the moment. Slowly the gung-ho feeling ebbed away. He stood and hefted the sales kit, thinking, How did I get talked into this? Have I gone crazy?... Head a little funny, from time to time, but he shrugged it off.

Lawns. Chimneys. Dogs and cats. TV-antenna jungle. Tricycles abandoned on the nine o'clock sidewalk.

Well, here goes nothing.

He knocked at the first door.

Nobody home. Sigh of relief.

He went to the next house. A man in shorts opened the door. Blake gave him the brush-off pitch they were supposed to give men: contacting people for a later survey, will follow next week, sorry. He went to the next house and knocked. It was a woman.

"Good morning, Madam! We're contacting the parents—"

"I'm not a parent." She shut the door.

Blake shrugged and went to the next house. Knocky-knock. "Good morning, Madam; we're contacting the parents—"

She opened the door wider and looked him directly in the eye as he talked. Blake felt stage fright. Real fear. Woolf had said that was natural. When a person enters somebody else's territory he feels that fear. It's a relic of the cave days. Beware the stranger! But with four billion people in the world you can't afford cave reactions. Blake forced a smile, deliberately made his muscles loosen.

He kept talking; saying the words he'd memorized, asking all the questions. This woman was interested. She was really interested! They sat on the couch; he finished the questionnaire. She was in her twenties. Two preschoolers played with Blake's shoelaces. The woman was attractive, long brown hair, hazel eyes. The furniture wasn't new, but they weren't poor either.

By the time he reached the selections, she was very nervous.

"What will I tell Don?" she kept asking.

Blake reeled it off: "That, you must decide for yourself. You can tell him, or not tell him, as you think best. If you believe he has valid objections, don't do it. But you must examine your own conscience. If you think this is the right thing to do— then go through with it. Don't let anything stand in your way."

He pulled out a sheet of paper and showed her the figures.

"Thirty down. Thirty a month for forty-eight months. Just put your name right here," marking an X and handing her the pen. "If there's any problem, let us know within forty-eight hours and we'll gladly refund your down payment. You have nothing to lose and everything to gain."

Her face flushed; she was agonizing over this, going through an emotional turmoil. He could almost see the years of bored conformity warring with the lust for a glamorous, wider life. Should she do it? Should she not do it? There was no way to resist.

"Sign me up. I might just keep that little vial for a souvenir... not use it at all... but here goes. Is Elvis Presley available? I'll take Elvis Presley."

"Elvis Presley," Blake said briskly, checking the required forms. "An excellent selection; your child should be talented and attractive, to say the least. Let's see now. Can you give me two credit references? Where do you bank?"

He took the information, then asked, "Will it be a boy or a girl?"

"You mean I get a choice?"

He explained about X and Y chromosomes having a difference in weight, and about FMTC's centrifuge that separated girl-maker cells from boy-maker cells. Yes, she certainly had a choice. She was a little incredulous, but he explained that the procedure was simple. After a moment's hesitation, she chose a boy.

When it was over, and the signed contract with attached thirty-dollar check were snug in Blake's sales kit, he went out and leaned against a tree. He felt drained. Stunned with victory. He'd just landed a five-foot sturgeon. Zappo! Hero time again!

He ran to the next house. The woman let him in and listened in silence to his presentation. When he was halfway through, she said she wanted her girlfriend to hear this. She made a phone call. The girlfriend, whose name was Sharon, made it across the street in two minutes.

The young women listened avidly. They kept giggling at each other; Blake got the distinct feeling they'd talked about something like this already. They snatched the contracts from him and each one gave him a check. He finished the forms, inserting their choices. The Shah of Iran, girl. Jerry Brown, boy.

"Can we change our minds later about the choices?"

"Yes, if you let us know within four days, which is when the Packages will be delivered. What's the best time to make delivery? How about eleven o'clock Monday? We want you to be here, because the Package must be transferred immediately to the freezing compartment of your refrigerator."

He finished up and left. It was almost noon, so he went to his corner to wait.

Seven hundred and fifty dollars.

He'd just made 750 clams, in one morning.

Three giant sturgeons. He could hardly believe it.

The limo slid to a stop. All the windows were down and people leaned out waving and screaming, brandishing orders.

"How many did you close, Reardon?"

"Three."

"You win the Bullshooter Award! Martha sold two, Dave sold two, everybody scored but Ray, who's gonna score this afternoon," was how the clamor went.

Blake could see that Woolf was pleased. Eleven deals in one morning. That was really spreading the gospel. They went to Crawford's for smorgasbord lunch and Woolf radiated that tingling voltage as they ate; being with her was the best thing that had ever happened. Her charisma was a shot of superlife, galvanizing the whole crew. She was an airwalker who rejoiced,

"Press the key that says HAPPY and that's all there is to it. There *is* no other consideration."

Or she'd say: "Rely on your inner senses. What you call 'reality' is a mask; it deludes you."

Blake refused to swallow this stuff whole. By now he felt tired and grumpy, asking, "What the hell's that supposed to mean? Not that I haven't heard it before, from pie-in-the-sky religious types."

"You extend yourselves in the wrong direction. Go *in*, where the real riches are, instead of *out* towards fool's gold."

"Does not compute."

"Ever feel out of touch with reality?" (Yes! Blake had been very much in-and-out, recently, but no sense belaboring the point.) "What you call 'reality' is created by you, who are more wonderful than you want to take responsibility for. You create fabulous artworks while you sleep."

Somebody brought up the subject of death, and she said, "Of course you survive physical death but forget it every time, the way you forget your infancy."

Again Blake wanted to bring up the realistic hallucinations he'd been having, but didn't. What Woolf said was interesting but he felt disturbed. She attracted him too strongly. This had never happened before; he loved Susie and wanted to be faithful to Susie for life. He grabbed the crossword section of the P-I and started doing the puzzle, keying Woolf out.

That afternoon Blake closed two more deals. By five o'clock the crew had scored sixteen sales. A little fast arithmetic told Blake that FMTC wasn't doing too badly with this operation. That night he told Susie the whole story; she was excited by the novelty, already planning to give notice at Safeway so she could sell for FMTC and start making some real money.

Next morning Benaroya dropped the sales crew off as usual. When she and Blake were alone she said, "I'd like to talk to you. How about coffee?"

"Fine," he said.

Zappo. His heart was pounding. This woman made him nervous. She was too high-powered. He'd promised himself not to get involved with her. Since his marriage to Susie he hadn't even thought about another woman. Woolf was too damned attractive, with a dash and elan nobody else possessed; and how could he say no to the boss? This might be very bad.

When they were seated across a table from each other, she said,

"You're a great human being. You're alive, not a zombie." She tossed back the lock of hair, gazing at him with respect and affection, as Blake poured half a bottle of sugar into his coffee. Woolf went on,

"I need a manager to take crews out and train other managers for other cities. FMTC will spread all over the world. Can you handle it? I'll guarantee $200,000 a year minimum, plus your personal production, of course."

Blake was speechless. He knew he must look a complete jackass, but the whole show had somehow gone out of his control. One week ago he'd been on the dole, lining up for a handout with thousands of other losers. Now (how had everything gotten away from him? Couldn't be antihistamine; nor booze; was it a dream?) he was trainer, manager, executive, making two hundred thousand a year.

Their heads were close together. He looked into her eyes.

"I-I—"

"Good! Here are the keys to the limo." She tossed him the keys and stood up. "You know where to find everybody, right? Say I grabbed a cab to the airport. Back in three days.

Please check in at the office, and if Sterling O'Blivion calls tell her I must see her right away, it's *urgent*. Oh, and here's a hundred thousand on account" — handing him ten crackly green bills, with a picture of Salmon P. Chase on each one — "in case you run up a few expenses."

EIGHTEEN

Virginia Woolf, President
FMTC Hq.
4700 Seafirst Bldg.
Seattle, WA 98101

My cool, shining sea-lady,

Your forlorn O'Blivion is scared out of her wits. Mine has been a life of storm and shipwreck; but our tumultuous love affair, *plus* my present troubles, along with the threat of being snatched away by Something Else— No!, I don't wish to see you again, my fish, until all ends well.

My simple nature can't cope with such complexity.

Armand has been destroyed by hired assassins (whose law of beak and talon I despise) and my own life is in constant jeopardy. Just now they took a shot at me. By "they" I mean a sniper on the hotel roof. Missed my head by inches. Was it a true miss? Or just a warning? I ran up and searched the area but found nothing, only an oily Q-tip and some knee prints in the dust.

The slug had embedded itself in Leon's door jamb under the studio. I pried it out. It matches exactly the slug taken from poor Armand's heart, forever stilled. Here, I omit much; but want you to hurry and investigate a group called Inner Core, described as "post-terrorist, international, recently formed, Latin American-based." And the worst of it is, the bastards appear to know my every (repeat: *every* — even our Seattle setup of the future) move.

These are not stage tricks. I've always been separated from

the rest of mankind by my daring crimes, it is true; but have also been "saddened with heavenly doubts" as Milton so sorely laments. And what is it that plagues me beyond endurance? Only the secret, the hidden part of myself: that fearful Presence which bursts forth when least expected.

Quickly now, I must confess that I've destroyed two warm, throbbing human lives in the past 24 hours. One was my protégé Patsy Cox (foremost among the *jeunes filles en fleurs* at the Studio); the other was an innocent, albeit twerpy, insurance salesman.

These murders would not upset *you*, my divinity, in the slightest. You don't believe in the sanctity of human life (any more than *we* believe in the sanctity of *animal* life). You'd say "Well, gosh-whiz, look what I went and done; clumsy old me," and continue cracking your gum.

I killed Patsy in self-defense, thank God. But the ill-fated insurance man, with the wife and three kids in Cincinnati... guilt wracks me.

Will I, perforce, share Armand's hard fate? Do I deserve such cruel punishment? Is it my fault that I'm driven by a senseless mechanism, and have always dreaded the day when, in the grip of an overpowering lust for raw blood, I would lose control? Well, sure enough, it happened. "What I feared has come upon me" as Job so woefully wails. I blame the lapse 100% upon culture shock. An aftereffect of our archetypal meeting and of my experiences aboard your ship. (Turning into Spock, being beaten by Omark, etc.) Now don't think I'm blaming *you*, my Valkyrie, in the least! But in my opinion, love is love the universe over, and if you say you love me, you must mean it with all your might. How? By helping me expunge my guilt. "Our honor is precisely in proportion to our passion," as Ruskin so pungently puts it.

I keep thinking of your words when you said... "Ya jerks, longing for somebody from 'Outer Space' to come along and take the place of your God, who you say is dead, and then when we finally show up, boy, do you hate it. Your ego gets all shook— even when we're being *nice!* and bending over backwards to communicate on your level." I guess you meant me; I feel so inadequate I can't stand it.

And then when you told me about Union, your way of making love, and compared it with our way, and made those slighting remarks... when I think of that, I feel so inadequate and foolish I could just die. What do you SEE in me? Am I just another guinea pig? You've made me fall in love with you, and where can it lead?

I learned many things being with you, but where can it go? This might burst like a bubble. Self-pity engulfs me! I can never catch up to you.

So here's the sixty-dollar-question. When we've scraped through all this— what then? *Can* two people from different species find happiness together? What do we really have in common: you, a 36-foot "dolphin" from another world; you, on a higher plateau of perfection; and me- what am I but a miserable tool of my baser instincts? A despoiler, more beastlike than you, who are born a true animal?...

O how these questions plague me. For it was my portion, my karma, to issue from the vampire breed, from the peerage of ancient blood. And I was *content* with my perverse nature. I, born of the wind, wanted to go on living my old, wild, vampire existence (with a thin veneer of "civilization" to keep the bureaucrats off my back). Then you came along. You, from the wastes of space. You, who gave meaning to my life: pre-rational, instinctive, heroic; everything I always longed for.

And yet.

We're *unequal.*

You compare your Rysemian religion to all of ours— with a sneer; saying "What good's a religion that leaves you stuck in your body? You've been tricked." How do you suppose that makes me feel? I have rights too, you know. A lot of the time I don't know what the hell you're talking about. I don't know if you appreciate me or not. You, who say you love me. Is this part of an experiment, or what?

It means nothing to you that I can make truly sensational spaghetti, or pickle a mean herring; you *hate* people who eat flesh, fish, or birds, because you are yourself an animal. So. We've got a few religious differences to clear out of the way, isn't that so?, before our love can endure for the lifetime of a star.

Alas for this base culture, which casts adrift the noblest souls!...

But on the other hand: "I will give unto thee the keys of the kingdom of heaven." You have promised that after a few sessions with your clone sister Omark, I will be able to live on poetry (the real thing— not today's Twinkie-verse) and forswear blood altogether. Not only will I no longer be a vampire, but I'll join you as one of the immortals! Or as my old Romanian grandmother used to say (a free translation of her guttural, fourteenth century urgency): "Defecate, or release the pot."

As you know, Omark makes me sick; but I willingly place myself in a position of mind-enlargement under this witch doctor. And why? Let me tell you of the horrors that befell me recently, by way of explanation.

After leaving the city morgue where I was called to identify my ex-husband's body, so spent was I, that I went and steeped myself in Burton's *Anatomy of Melancholy* for several days. The profound shock of Armand's being slaughtered in that grotesque way, his corpse stuffed into a piece of modern sculpture (a Henry Moore! Why not at least a Donatello? Why not a Praxiteles?) to be discovered by giggling, and then shrieking, Girl Scouts on tour! My poor Spy— my Redford— bad enough that he was changed by the evil demon called Time into a bearded, porcine, and nondescript CIA hireling.

It appeared Armand's killers were sent by the Latin American syndicate I mentioned. One thing I never bothered to say: The U.S. government approached me several years ago and I told them to go piss up a rope. "Time travel, the greatest adventure" and all that. All of them hot after these revolutionary discoveries of mine.

So, seeking information, I began unraveling Armand's life story since the day we split the blanket. He was a brave man, but his life as agency pawn— what a sucker bet it was! Compelled to act out a boring spy story, full of frivolous subplots and false trails and lots of serious, important "problem-solving" which solves no problems, but is addictive, irresponsible, and paranoiac. And is beloved by psychotics everywhere, because it is based on "things that happen out of our control."

As Mr. Emerson says: *nothing* is out of our control. (O Ralph, where are you when we need you?)... And you tell me the same thing, my spacewoman. Awake or asleep, we set up every single thing that happens to us. Including the blinding delusion that we are pawns, have no responsibility, and can't set anything up!... Oh, how shattering. It's slightly terrible. And imagine: they name *schools* after that man and his friends. Emerson School. Whitman

School. If those devout materialists only knew what their heroes were really saying! But how lucky for Today's People that they can't read.

I shudder to think of poor Armand dying out in the cold like that. No blindfold, no cigarette— and no last request. A typical human death: forsaken by fortune, a rat in a trap...

You may be a monster, Benaroya, but you've made me see what a wretched and seedy game we humans are playing. I understand you're not criticizing us for no reason; but only to point the way to evolution. You're a missionary, right? And my pressing question is this: what should I do? Be "loyal" and act human, and eventually be interred among the potsherds with the other cave-people? Or should I risk all and come along with you?

I'm such a twit. You've no idea. I invent the first temporal translator of matter— and use it very gingerly, afraid of what I might *see*. I go back to the town of my childhood and lurk on a hillside, fearing to glimpse my parents, or my favorite, long-dead brother. Or even worse, my young self. I'm chicken. Not physically, but emotionally.

But listen carefully, my dolphin; there's another alternative. Driven by guilt, or by hopes purer than passion alone, I slipped ahead about 200 years, and glimpsed the Golden Age that is forming and reforming just around the corner.

The phone's ringing, dammit. I must hurry and tell you this. Somehow, the human race managed to walk a tightrope over the Abyss; that terrible void, lying between our present know-nothing state, and the Land of Perfection and Revelation.

(Ten ringy-dingies... Why can't they leave me alone?) It will take all the energy I've got to make the move permanent; but there, waiting on the Shores of Fate, I saw the ghosts of things to come. And the future *is* endlessly beautiful. It is everything we hoped and more— isn't that smashing news? Humanity finally managed to escape what T.S. Eliot calls "the immense panorama of futility and anarchy which is contemporary history."

The power of time; of persisting in time; of basking in the gardens of Elysium, is mine, if I have the guts to take it. Yet... the scales do not lie! and if I stick around here, I cannot hope to elude punishment at the hands of these terrorists when even a trained agent like Armand could not do so.

The ringing has stopped, thank heaven. So now, it's either 200 years into the future— or I go to Rysemus with you. Could I stand it?, two lovers swimming on and on in mile-deep, heavy waters? Making love in the cones of submerged volcanoes. Using one of your huge, blubberfish bodies while my own sweet bod hangs by the heels in cold storage. I hope you don't feel insulted; I'm so tired of the social lies we Earthies are forced to keep telling each other, even though we are all telepaths, and know what's going on, while trying like mad to hide it. Because it's "rude" — can you believe it? Earthies accept criminal suppressives, but not telepaths. They won't make this mistake in 200 years, though. *The Renaissance is coming.*

So: honesty. You know what I think of your Basic Body, so outlandish, so repulsive that even a picture of it makes me feel ill. The Virginia Woolf body is sexy, but the fishbody— ugh, ugh, and again ugh! and I know you think the human form is a storky, buttocky toothy laughingstock with rubber features and a vertical smile, and all that.

But so what? I love you, my angel, and we function well together; yet I'm uneasy. I must tidy up my affairs, but I'm being watched, and I don't like being shot at. Although as you keep telling me, nobody ever dies, they just come back and back in a compulsive manner, while pretending they don't. Because people *want to believe* they die. Otherwise it's too much hassle with all the responsibility and everything. In any case, it's disturbing. I'm quite frantic at the moment, although hiccupping grandly, and nicely gorged with blood (from the insurance man), which satisfies at least part of my nature.

But oh, Virginia, I'm scared *witless* to have a corpse in my freezer!, her skin a grayish tinge, and her lips still lipstick-lurid… and half of her face blown away. Knowing that I'm a murderer… however neatly tucked in she may be, and well hidden under spinach and frozen orange juice.

Poor, flaky Patsy, with her inbred, negotiable vulgarity! and her Eastern prep-school accent from Oklahoma; she was a typical Today Person, and now she has been blown away by her own gun. And can the Inner Core help the poor twerp any more? Not at all!, not even as the supremely powerful Intersystem that it is, with a finger shoved up each of the world's intelligence orgs, moving their heads and arms, like the Punch and Judy dolls I hated as a child in Europe. I hated it when they whacked each other with clubs! The other children all howled in delight. The *normal* children. The bloodthirsty little non-vampire children — which may tell you something.

You know what?... I bet you won't even bother to run "Inner Core" through your ship's computers. An Earthie spy ring. Small potatoes. You are worried that Beel is going after our thoughts with the A-O; but isn't that just what the Core does? On a lower level, sure; but still— Patsy Cox and Johnny File both worked for the Core, they lived for it, they worshipped it. And not for serenity, or fun, or eternal life. Not even for "money" (Johnny has bushels of it). Only for "power."

It's a joke. An illusion. People are such snobs about their "power" and their bodies and it's absurd; they're all dead in 80 years anyway. But: when the pupil is ready, the master will appear, and here you are, and I don't know if I'm ready for it.

I'm thinking now of my dear friend Jean Cocteau who said, "The fantasy writer is a terrible individual easily confused with the poet." Jean knew that to get any hearing in this world you must disguise yourself as a whore, a cop, or a jukebox. You must compromise your integrity. You must be a File or a Cox; the Inner Core came into being and sucked the pair of them in, and if this sounds like high-powered hokum, take it from O'Blivion who has seen the future: the incredible *can* happen. True, a race that consistently favors the mediocre must go through hell before the light finally dawns; but dawn it will. I've seen it with my own eyes.

These Core members, mind you, are ordinary people. Neither "right" nor "left" but merely desperate. Hungry— to throw the world into a state of supercontrolled slavery, where everyone is *safe.* The only way to stop them is to evolve. Stop being a race of tiny-minded thieves and stupidity addicts. Make all information available to everyone, instantly. Develop some character. Learn to put in a good day's work. Above all, regain the lost telepathic abilities. It may sound impossible; but it finally happened— and *we started it*, you and I. We planted the seeds for this Arcady, this Golden Age, with our FMTC and our attendant crazy plots and projects engineered to jolt Homo Sap out of his moldy rut. And now —

The phone rang again. It was Johnny, with his usual inspired timing. "Meet me in the coffee shop, Sterling! Get down here *fast.*"

What now? On with the plot? Does File suspect Cox's body is in my freezer? He can't know that I wrestled the huge pistol out of the little fool's hand and it went off in her face. I must handle this. So until later, baby, I remain yours in frantic isolation,

S. O'Blivion

NINETEEN

It was a blazing Sunday in Miami. The afternoon was just beginning and already Vicki Bauer felt wilted — just sort of hanging there, like the flags and pennants that drooped around the football stadium. It all felt unreal; football should be part of cold snappy weather, icicles on eaves, couples cuddling under a wool robe and nipping from a flask and all that. But this scene was almost nightmarish — hot sun, palm trees, fake grass, the crowd in summer clothing. Vicki wasn't used to the heat and she felt suffocated.

She was wearing a powder blue suit from Saks, chosen to minimize her weight, with pearl earrings and a strand of natural pearls. A bit dressy for the game, but Vicki had an important date afterwards. Usually in a crowd she would begin to feel all shaky and withdrawn; but today she felt calm and purposeful and this was because of her terrific new job. The nice bank account helped a lot, too. Today was the big Bowl game and she was stalking Larry Cram, a running back who was very popular with FMTC customers. Vicki had arrived in Miami on the early flight; her assignment for this afternoon was — Get Cram.

The game should be starting soon. After the band left the field Vicki didn't quite know what was going on, but it was exciting, all those husky men in their tight pants running onto the Astroturf. Larry Cram's team wore red jerseys and the other team wore white. Cram was number fourteen. She'd seen a thirty-minute film on him at the office. He was cute and boyish but with tremendous shoulders, hands like a pair of giant octopi, a slim waist and powerful legs. No wonder all those women were clamoring for a Package of him.

Vicki took out a Kleenex and swabbed her face. She didn't care who was watching; she didn't know anybody here, anyway. It was hotter than sin today. The Goodyear blimp was droning by overhead and people craned to see its underside. Last week a blimp had passed near the office building and Benaroya'd gone crazy, laughing until she cried and pointing. Kind of weird to laugh at a blimp. Didn't they have blimps in her country, or was she on something— speed or something? She seemed to have more energy than three racehorses. Vicki kept thinking about Benaroya; maybe too much. But then it was only natural, because she owed her boss literally everything: money, clothes, trips, prestige, you name it.

The Braves, Larry's team, were out there running around and rapping each other on the shoulder pads with their fists, taking deep breaths. Larry was running in place with his knees high. Warming up. She knew he had trouble with those knees. He had scars all over them from operations for floating cartilage; she'd seen a closeup of his scarred knees in that film. How could he still play football after six operations? Especially since the other teams always went for his weak spot, trying to tear loose more cartilage. Vicki shuddered. Men were really brutal.

Now both teams were lined up and she heard the whistle blow. This was going to be exciting. Vicki bought a hotdog from the vendor, slathered plenty of mustard on it, and ate it gratefully; that damned diet was driving her crazy; she could never keep it up. Heat and thirst made her gulp an orange soda. Well, a working girl must eat, she told herself with masochistic sarcasm.

A man scrambled into the empty seat next to hers, almost stepping on her toes on the way. He smiled, apologized, and settled in. He was chunky and middle-aged; really quite homely; but he was alone. Maybe if she worked it right they could get to know each other during the game. She was so sick of being alone! This man's hair was thinning and his teeth were tobacco-stained, he had a sickly pallor and wore rummage-sale clothes; but any port in a storm. Vicki felt a flash of disgust with herself. Forget it. In the first place she had work to do. In the second place, she was rich, and could afford to let things develop naturally.

This new job was really a blast; she'd been all over the country in the past two weeks, getting Packages from celebrities. Ronnell and her Krishna friends were just about crapping with jealousy, putting FMTC down like mad; it was satisfying to hear the envy creep into Ronnell's voice! because Vicki was having such an absolute ball. Meeting movie and TV stars, especially, thrilled her. The only dud had been Brian Jones, the tutti-fruity of the year; when she'd attempted to collect a sample from him, he had run screaming into the bathroom and locked himself in, crying for his boyfriend. Vicki had to send a cab from the sperm bank for him the next day. They finally scored a Package but only after she practically tied the $50,000 on a stick like a carrot; and once they got to the medical lab, Brian would talk to nobody but a handsome male intern. God, what a weirdo. If the American Public ever found out that their number-one macho symbol was a screaming, prancing queen, what would they say? Probably wouldn't believe it.

The client she'd really enjoyed was that Living Legend of a Governor who, when she'd finished, presented *her* with a check for $5,000, saying he wouldn't take payment for upgrading humanity! Of course he meant it as a joke. But he was dreamy. She just swooned over him. Too bad she was still the blobby fat girl. Nothing could change that. Oh, she could take off a few pounds at a health spa but she'd never be a stunning beauty like Benaroya. Even the money flowing in didn't make up for her lack of beauty; and beauty was the only thing that counted. Wealth hardly mattered; if you weren't young and beautiful in this country you might as well commit suicide.

One of the red jerseys kicked off. A white jersey caught the ball and ran. He was immediately tackled by a swarm of reds. Vicki had to buy a 7Up from the vendor; she was dying of thirst again. The whites, she guessed, were advancing their ball. The reds huddled. Larry Cram wasn't so cute with his helmet on. You couldn't see his flowing blond curls that the women swooned over. Casually, Vicki spoke to the man next to her.

"Do you know what's going on?"

He glanced at her. "The whites tried for a field goal and missed, so the reds are advancing."

Vicki finished her drink. She was enjoying these rough collisions and pileups on the field. Football was really very sexy, in an S&M sort of way. She wondered what Larry Cram would be like, later, when it was time to get a sample from him. Would he be nice, or mildly sarcastic, or would he be really insulting?

Her most interesting client to date had been Vernon Birch, the famous writer and film producer. She'd been a little scared to meet him because he was such a big intellectual. He was *so* intelligent you couldn't stand it. The government even chose him to go along on the next moon shot, as official writer, because astronauts couldn't describe a breathtaking trip like that, and Birch's prose was supposed to be immortal and then some. Vicki'd heard that he attacked his first wife with a corkscrew and scarred her face badly, and this made Vicki a little nervous; but, geniuses were like that, and Vernon Birch had turned out to be putty in her hands. She had to smile at the phrase. Anyway, he'd enjoyed Vicki's attentions almost as much as he enjoyed the impressive FMTC check she'd handed him.

Well, that made three Nobel Prize winners, plus one French existentialist, one living legend type playwright who did cocaine and made scathing remarks; plus that German rocket man and two poets in their eighties. (Vicki sent both of them directly to the sperm bank; she didn't want any heart attacks on her conscience; and anyway, old men gave her the ickies.) And of course the many sports and entertainment personalities that she had scored.

She wished she could keep up with this game. She'd have to read some books on football. A white jersey was running. Five reds, including Larry, smashed him flat and piled on top. The tackled player jumped up fighting mad; he took a wild punch at Larry, and Larry slapped him across the face. (Cram had a rough reputation, she knew.) Officials separated the two players. Nobody was penalized. Cram had the ball on the next play, and he was running with it and the crowd was screaming.

It was so hot and sticky she couldn't imagine how they could play football. The man next to her kept mopping his face. Here they sat, strangers, sweating together. The idea made Vicki want to laugh, so to cover she asked him, "What's happening now?"

"Well, the quarterback, number 42, just took the snap from center and handed off to Larry Cram," his voice was rising to a yell to be heard over the crowd. "That's number 14; look at Cram move, he's clear, and it's a touchdown!" The whole stadium was exploding.

"Thank you, I'm trying to learn more about football. It's sure interesting," Vicki gushed, when it was quiet enough to be heard.

"It's a wonderful game," the man said enthusiastically and smiled at her.

His teeth were stained and none too clean, but the smile was a good sign. Les Rogers, one of the white jerseys, threw a pass. Vicki was slated to get a Package from Rogers tomorrow morning. She always enjoyed seeing the men work at their specialties before she approached them for a Package. It doubled the excitement! Before she was done, she would have a Package from the entire NFL and AFL, except for a couple of holdouts.

God, she owed Benaroya such a lot. What a stroke of luck it had been; the miracle Vicki had been waiting for— seeing that little ad in the paper, getting this terrific job under this fabulous boss. She admired the dynamic leader of FMTC so much it hurt. The boss absolutely didn't care what anybody thought. She'd put her feet on the desk or flip a letter opener into the wall right past your head, or guffaw loudly when something struck her funny. Part of Vicki's admiration was sheer envy, and she knew it. She'd give anything to be Benaroya!

But the boss said some very weird things, too, especially when they were all at lunch together. Like… "Your society's a stagnant pond. You must evolve into fully developed beings," and, "Every person in the U.S.A. must have a change of heart. You must understand, fully and completely, that what you call 'physical reality' is created by you, lock, stock, and barrel."

They'd all argue and squabble and she'd say, "Your blindness doesn't change the fact. *You* build reality. You made it a straitjacket. Now you must change it," and stuff like "You've got a basic right to *be* in this space-time and by golly you gotta trust that right. No more of this killing off of your own creative powers within yourself. Sure, your parents and teachers strangled those abilities within you, but today, this moment, you gotta declare independence and move on out into a glorious new life. And now shut up and eat your tacos."

But here was the oddest thing Benaroya had said. It was in private, to Vicki. "Soon you'll score your fiftieth Package, my dear. The company would like to present you with a special award, and I happen to know what you want more than anything else in the world: a new body. Now who would you like to be?"

It was another crazy gag. Vicki laughed and said, "Marilyn

Monroe," - picking an oldtime movie star whose old movies she'd enjoyed.

Benaroya said, "All right, after your fiftieth sale, you'll become Marilyn Monroe in her prime."

"I bet," Vicki had laughed. Very weird. Now the stain-toothed man was saying, "Watch it. This is it," so Vicki peered at the action.

Les Rogers threw another pass. A white jersey caught the pass but fell out of bounds, and all of a sudden the game was over. Fans were running out onto the field screaming; the stain-toothed man stood up, collected his field glasses and cheap camera, said goodbye with a pleasant nod, and got lost in the crowd.

Vicki felt a flood of the most desolate loneliness. The creep had *rejected* her! Walked right off and left her sitting there— him with his stained teeth and repulsive pallor and wattles! If she'd been good-looking, not so fat, he never would have done that. He would have asked her out for a drink at least. She was sick of being rejected. What right did this sickly little turd have to reject *her*? She, Vicki Bauer, had an engagement with Larry Cram! She was going to get a Package from Larry Cram, right now! She got up and stalked out. They could all go to hell. She had work to do.

Benaroya had explained that Vicki just needed to get the celebrity's signature and his promise that he would show up at the sperm bank as a donor. But Vicki always liked to do a thorough job; and Benaroya let her people handle things their own way as long as they produced. Vicki had phoned Larry Cram earlier and made an appointment to meet him after the game. He'd already checked FMTC out and knew he'd be given a certified check today, but that was just good business.

She was waiting outside the dressing room when he came out. Six women made a noisy grab for him but he pushed them aside. For once, other women were being brushed aside for Vicki! Too bad it was just business. She knew that a parade was being given for Larry later today and the mayor was going to award gold medallions to him and his teammates, so she had to hurry. She only had two hours to spend with the football player at the very most.

Larry Cram greeted her pleasantly, thank God; not like that

faggy Brian Jones, or that playwright who'd sneered and made nasty cracks about the size of her butt. Larry was polite and gentlemanly. He looked impressive off the field; he was about six-four and weighed well over 200 pounds and was only 23; but up close he looked tired and older. There were bruises on his face that must be hurting.

"You're the lady from FMTC," he said by way of greeting. "Well, what happens now? My place or yours?"

"Either," Vicki said, a little flustered. His car was in the staff lot, a dreamy white convertible. He held the door for her. She slid in, pulling her legs together and arranging the skirt over them. Why couldn't she have a slim rear like Benaroya's? Why couldn't she be wearing a miniskirt like those cute tanned cheerleaders? Why couldn't Larry fall madly in love with her, dammit?

He started the engine and headed out of the lot, saying, "So you're going to pay me fifty grand, for what you call a Package. That's really far out." He slid through the aftergame traffic under the palms, heading for the row of swank beach hotels.

"You're very popular," Vicki said demurely. "Dozens of housewives have put in requests for you."

"That's the wildest thing I've ever heard. It's very flattering. I don't mind doing it at all, really. Here's my hotel," and he turned his convertible over to the doorman.

He ordered drinks as soon as they got to his suite and then was busy answering calls while Vicki looked around the room. It was nice, but sort of noncommittal; no personal things, just a place to sleep. Larry gestured to her when room service knocked and she opened the door and brought over the bill for him to sign. It would be fun to do things like this for him all the time; travel with him, maybe even be married to him — whoa, girl, keep your mind on business, she told herself hastily.

When he was off the phone, she outlined the program briskly and brought out a contract for him to sign. He read it over and signed it, saying, "Now what?"

"Drop your pants, please," Vicki said.

"What?"

"Just relax, Mr. Cram. Lean back on the bed if that's more comfortable for you." She unzipped his pants. "You could do this at a lab tomorrow if you'd rather, but personally I think this is more meaningful, don't you agree?"

"Yeah! Yeah," he gasped, a little nonplussed, but not unwilling. Vicki took a small tube of lubricating jelly from her kit and creamed her hands well. Larry watched her.

"This is different, but what the hell," he said. "This is really heavy, it really is. But with my trick knees I'll take the fifty grand." He gasped again as her cold hands touched him.

"We're very glad you agreed," Vicki said primly. "You'll make a lot of women very happy." Mentally she catalogued the size of his equipment; bigger than average, but still topped by that black rock musician who was impossibly large. But she didn't want to think about such details; she wanted to do her job and do it well.

Larry Cram was spent and breathing deeply, with his eyes half shut, when Vicki finally said,

"This is a special glass container that will freeze the sample immediately. When you affix your thumbprint, it is permanently sealed; then you sign and date it below. Of course every Package must be tamper-proof and genuine."

Larry Cram opened his eyes a fraction. He set his thumb onto the glass, smiling in a satisfied way. "That's okay by me," he said. "I hope every neighborhood will have at least one little Cram playing sandlot football, you know? That would be worth even more than the cash. I love the game of football. I want to help it in every way possible, so thanks for asking me."

"I understand." Vicki nodded. "Here is your copy of the contract. It specifies that we can claim a repackage any time during the next five years for ten thousand dollars. And it guarantees there will be no other involvement on your part."

She handed him the $50,000 check signed by Benaroya.

"Thanks," he said. "This is the easiest fifty Gs I ever made. It even beats commercials."

He tucked the check into his shirt pocket. "By the way, one of my teammates, Mitch Keefer, was asking about the program. He'd like to contribute if he's eligible."

"Our Director will contact him," Vicki said.

She used the bathroom, patting cold water on her face and combing her hair; she was a little flustered and nervous, and the cold water made her feel better. When she came out, Larry Cram was already snoring.

Downstairs she headed for a phone booth to call Benaroya and announce victory. The lobby was crowded with postgame celebrators. She got Blake Reardon, the second-in-command. He was another one of these snobs who were always rejecting her.

"The boss has been gone for two days," he said. "No message. That's not like her. I'm a little worried."

"Don't be. She can take care of herself. When she comes in tell her I scored one Package from Larry Cram, all signed and sealed. Tomorrow I have two more football players and I'll be back on the dinner flight. How're things otherwise?"

"Edgy," Blake said gloomily. "I rang a doorbell and a Holy Roller broad chewed my ears off. She said the FMTC was against God's will. Tried to beat me with an umbrella. Was calling the heat when I left, so I pulled the crew out of the neighborhood. Then back at the office I get a call from an irate husband who says he's going to liquidate my assets because I sold his wife a Package of Billy Graham. Outside of that we're all getting wealthy." He hung up.

Vicki headed for her hotel room to take a shower, freshen up and rest.

She'd probably see a movie alone tonight.

All of a sudden she wanted to throw something at the wall.

Dammit, it wasn't fair! Here she was, having just made five thousand bucks plus expenses, and she was feeling as slighted, lonely, and rejected as ever. The phone was ringing inside her room. She couldn't get the key into the lock; she had it upside down— oh gawd! she hoped this was the bosscalling with comforting, inspiring words-- finally she threw the door open and was grabbing for the phone.

"Hello?" breathlessly.

There was a brief pause. Then, "Hello, my dear. Please forgive me for interrupting like this, but I've seen you in the elevator and I'd like to take you out to dinner."

For a minute Vicki couldn't utter a word. "Who's this?"

"My name is Sylvester Beel," purred the most thrilling voice she'd ever heard.

TWENTY

Eating licorice allsorts that bristled with the tasty lint from her pocket, Virginia Woolf left the office for a breath of fresh air.

FMTC had made eleven million dollars, and that was *good*. Blake Reardon and Vicki Bauer had been kidnapped by Beel, and that was *bad*.

Sterling's letter was tucked safely in Woolf's boot. She had covered it with many lipstick-print kisses. The letter didn't make a lot of sense, but it tugged at her heart. She was in love with that luscious vampire and was going to marry her and live happily ever after; but boy— all that guilt and anxiety of Sterling's was really funny! and all this "Do you love me" granola— Holy Moses. Rysemians didn't live shared lives; they were cloned, telepathic dolphins. But for the sake of the grand experiment it was important to do things the Earthie way. And besides, if a 700-year-old human couldn't evolve, who could?

Blurp: her mouth was so full of allsorts that half of them were falling out— Ha ha!— but she pushed them back into the opening and wiped her ugly face so nobody would get mad. They tasted a lot like rabbit poopoo, which she preferred, but you weren't supposed to eat it. All these damn, dopey little *rules!* you were supposed to obey while keeping that grim, morose, important look on your face. "I am a human. I am much more important than any animal. I am made in God's image." That was horseshit, but you had to keep saying it. Otherwise the truth would grab you, and you'd be in hot water. Anyway, Earth had been found to be a good-luck planet, and great things were in store for its deserving people. Sterling said so. Hot dippity. If that checked out, they wouldn't need euthanasia, which would save lots of work.

A motorist honked and shrieked at her— Ha ha!—what a tingle; no wonder the kids back home said you were fulla B.S. when you told them about it. But it was thrilling, just being out here in the sticks, in a far-flung corner of the universe where hardly anybody ever bothered to go; teetering around on two legs like some kinda crazy stork; could get killed at any second. Wowee. Woolf loved it. She loved these potentially great people crashing by, who'd be among the chosen of the galaxy, once they got over being psychotic.

"Excuse me," one of them muttered politely, bumping her. Heyyy... he'd lifted her wallet! with his sweet little paddy-paws; how skillful Earthies were.

"Don't spend it all in one place," she called after him, with a Bette Davis smile full of love and pain. But now, another bunch of cars came screaming past as the light changed: a blue one, a red one, and a yellow one that ran over her foot. And above was a layer of dark, furry clouds and where the sun reflected off their edges it was bright as a knife— Oh! she'd like to send this whole 3-D picture postcard back home, pain and all, it was so exquisitely thrilling!

And hey, the crowd crossing at 7th and Stewart had to be in the picture too. They looked like they came out of a very old religious painting, from when Sterling was a kid; only now with their innocence changed to these sheet metal expressions all smug and jaded; beautiful. All of them rushing to pointless missions, making "money," eating kelp, discarding each other and saying they didn't... it was *terrific* to be psychotic.

Holy smoke. But Sterling said they were going to change completely and become happy. They would hear the Call to simple living and high endeavor, and they would finally master life. That was keen. And it would only take 200 years. Meanwhile here Woolf stood, in the roar of commuter traffic— what a thrill for a born traveler from across the Snowy Ranges.

She leapfrogged a hydrant, then sauntered in and out of a few boutiques, winking at startled salesladies and now and then pinching a customer's rear end. She enjoyed the stifled little shrieks, the indignant glances and so forth. But under the cool exterior she was getting madder and madder the more she thought about it.

"Damn their rotten eyes!..."

The Sajorians were picking off her best people. Earlier today they had snatched Blake Reardon. He left the crew parked in the limo in front of a 7-11. He went in to get six-packs of Gatorade for the day's winners. He never came out.

Terrible.

And just now, they'd transported Vicki Bauer from her hotel in Miami.

Poor employees! Never would they see their little homes again. Woolf wondered where they were being kept, and how they felt about it all. Maybe they wouldn't mind too much. She grinned to herself. That's how Earthies thought. If something unspeakable happened to one of them, the others would shrug and say "It's for the best," or "Nothing can hurt him any more," or "She deserved it." Which was good psychology; if they faced the truth they would go bananas on the spot... ha ha.

But it was terrible. Blake's wife Susie rushed in, hysterical. "Where's my husband? What have you done with him?" Susie sobbed over and over.

After explaining the Sajorian tactics until she was hoarse, Benaroya got bored with all the histrionics and roared, "You must evolve into a free, creative race of fully telepathic beings! Otherwise we don't want your kind in the Universe. Look at the trouble you idiots cause, getting kidnapped because you're deaf-dumb-and-blind!"

But it didn't do one particle of good. Susie wailed on and on until she was blue in the face and Woolf had to call a doctor (Susie believed in their black magic) who gave her a sedative so she'd scream *inwardly* and not bother others. It was tough luck about Blake, for sure, and she'd do her darnedest to get him back, but where did you start?

And poor Vicki. Only yesterday Woolf had taken that champion sperm-collector through FMTC's bank and showed her how each little thing worked: "We can store the merchandise in these tiny bottles, in this very spot, for a million years, if we feel like it. We freeze it in a glycerol solution."

"Far out," Vicki smiled shyly at the boss.

"These methods were discovered in animal husbandry. Semen from prize bulls is shipped this way. Look over here," pointing to a set of test tubes in a tiny freezer. They were labeled *Tiger*,

Elephant, Bison, Polar Bear, Panda, Poet.

"Dreadful to realize these breeds will soon be extinct. Bureaucratic Man tolerates no breed other than the two-legged, two-faced image of himself. But here are frozen zygotes which could repopulate the world with these fabulous creatures."

"Neat," Vicki sighed without much enthusiasm. She didn't care a rap about the future, only about her own dopey problems. They stood together in the old bowling alley, now refurbished as lab and sperm bank. It was pleasantly restful, with soft pile carpets and indirect lighting. In the background, technicians were quietly centrifuging, sorting, and packaging.

Woolf continued, "Yes; we're flooded with income and fan mail and bomb threats and we've got big expansion plans. You'll have a fantastic future with the Company if you remain loyal, my dear. For one thing, we're opening a cryonics lab, for the freezing of newly dead bodies, to be revived as soon as human doctors can cure whatever caused the death. If ever. Bodies cure themselves, you know. Or else they don't. Ha ha. And as everybody knows but won't tell, every death is a suicide."

"Uh-huh."

"We've tested the market; a spinoff of this type would be commercially feasible. Then there's parthenogenesis. We give an egg cell a tiny shock as it comes down the tube, causing it to develop into a baby without a father, for rich women who don't want to mix their genes with those of some schlemiel. And that's just the beginning! Wait until you hear what we've got planned for the entertainment business!"

Vicki gave a damp little smile. She was bored by all the facts but pleased by the flattering attention from her boss.

Woolf did her best to teach the poor twerp, explaining all kindsa interesting facts to her. "A prime test for madness and paranoia is called 'insurance.' If a species has 'insurance,' it is patently doomed. Only a toylike, salivating, pent-up bunch of gruntlings could conceive of such a sociopathic type of gambling.

"Another test is called 'forms to fill out.' Any person or organism that asks you to fill out any kind of a 'form' whatsoever is an entrapment specialist of the sneakiest kind and should be avoided or if possible shot."

"Uh," Vicki yawned, in that apathetic way Earthies had—thinking about lunch and hoping Woolf couldn't read her mind.

If the silly twerp only knew that a Marilyn Monroe-at-her-best body was being readied for her to walk away in!, complete with wardrobe, yacht, typhoid shots, and an all-expense tour of the Greek Isles! And all this as a reward for her excellent FMTC teamwork. And now the poor, foolish little bovine had been snatched away by Beel, never to appear again on her native planet. How very, very tragic.

Aside from all that Woolf felt terrific, cracking her shoulder bones, gulping the piquant smog and experiencing her body as the finely tuned precision machine (slick to operate, interesting to push toward its limits, if any) that it was; with a fantastic, multidimensional computer lodged in the skull. Possessing unnamed talents. And to think humans were issued these bods without an owner's manual and didn't know how to use them. But in this storybook world of theirs, they should certainly feel this great all the time. No tantrums, no depressions; no dumb, mind-forged manacles of any kind.

What the heck: the dormant abilities they possessed were unimaginable. And this business of keeping their chins on the ground while going to a made-up "job" for eight hours a day, wasn't that insane? Why, they should be having *fun*. That's what life was all about! Holy mackerel! Instead of sitting around, awarding each other Nobel Prizes for pretending that matter wasn't an emanation of mind. No sir. Becuz all you had to do, was jump in without fear, and invent any reality you wanted, and stop pretending somebody else did it.

"I'm looking over a four-leaf clover," she hummed.

Singing loudly off-key, Woolf tapped up the street, twiddling her fingers at people and bobbing her head. They were embarrassed by all the singing and twiddling— how adorable! She wanted to run up and chuck each one under the chin, but didn't, because they would fend her off with blows and later become ill with indignation or embarrassment. So she took a path that forked off into the park.

Suddenly there were some men following her. How very sweet of them. There were a lot of them, putt-putting along the dry and woodsy path on lounge-chair motorbikes and right away Woolf took a liking to them.

"Hello sweethearts," she yodeled. "Are you aware, that your potential is greater than anyone ever realized, and that I admire you-all so much it hurts?"

Nuts. That made them back off a bit... Doggone it! She should keep her big trap shut. But no use getting lathered. Eventually she'd learn to conform, and then human society would open its portals to her. Yep; just as soon as she learned not to keep sticking her foot in her mouth.

Another of her big problems was that FMTC was making money like it was going out of style, yet was about to be shut down by Regulations. Humans could not tolerate success. Making money was considered evil unless you were long-established. It was part of the Trap that kept them insane-but-tame. But it didn't matter a particle, because the wheels had been set in motion; FMTC had made folks glimpse the fact that they could control their fates, and in another 200 years they'd be able to wash the bureaucracy right off their cute little paws. Sterling said so. Boy. It was going to be neat: a planet of lush green trees with ripe, tangy fruits, and happy, sane people to enjoy it all.

The dear lads following her wore jackets with coiled, fanged, constipated-looking serpents upon them. How funny. The lads oozed hostility, poor little mites, not knowing she could kill the pack of them in about two seconds. She walked downwind, enjoying the ever-popular reek of the lower orders... and trying to remember the protocol here.

Let's see: they could cut your head off and that was all right, but if you called them "illiterate boors" they could sue you for being an elitist. If you swore while doing it they could sue you twice. That was becuz the majority were I. B.s and they ruled. Well, that sounded fair enough to Virginia Woolf! The lads wanted her to be scared; they disliked it when she sang and twiddled, so she shut up and projected fear. (Be polite, for gracious sake. When on Earth, do as the Earthies do. *Her* fear made *their* chronic fear a lot less painful to them.)

"What do you want!" she croaked as if on the verge of tears.

Terrific. They loved it. She'd like to pick each one up in turn and stroke it, and peer into its pungent ears, nostrils, and rectal orifice, and sniff its bristly whiskers. Each had greasy hair and dark sweat stains in its cute little armpits.... Awww! she knew others considered them scruffy and loathsome but *she* thought they were darling. Right now, though, she had a lot on her mind... Boy it was rotten that the faithful lieutenant Blake Reardon had been kidnapped! He'd admired her so; always shuffling his feet, standing close to her and whispering, "You're spectacular."

"What, commonplace old me? Why I'm just a plain, down-home girl," she always demurred, adding a witless giggle because it made him so happy.

Well, maybe the Sajorians would release both Blake and Vicki if she threatened to draw and quarter Scaulzo and burn his intestines. On the other hand... why should they? Hell, Scaulzo was frozen into his body; he'd probably never do any damage again. Actually Scaulzo was the most fascinating problem of all. The devil in the flesh, who resisted all attempts to make him into a Better Person. Or even a Neutral Person. Odd. What was Satan's secret? Why did he never want to be counted among the good guys? She'd take another crack at him when time allowed, and see if Omark's release mechanism could be used on the Prince of Darkness... She was hoping it wouldn't be like releasing the evil genie from the bottle; although Omark said it didn't work that way.

Oh, what delightful grins the gang all wore. They sure were having a good time.

"What do you want!" she cried in terror, keeping them satisfied.

They lounged in their seats, putt-putting at a slow walk, wearing salacious smirks. Adorable little dolls! It was funny to read their minds. They were in love with each other but were not allowed to admit it, so wished to do violence to her person by way of revenge, and so forth, and so forth. Ha ha! They didn't know she could see right through a millstone. The things that humans struggled to hide were right there in plain sight. No wonder they feared the idea of telepathy. And yet... This scene better not get violent. She'd love a good bare-knuckle fight about now but remembered the sad clods she'd been forced to de-genital back in S.A. when they jumped her, and she certainly didn't wanna do *that* again. All that cringing and screeching hurt her ears. They sure got over being tough in a hurry. Poor little girlies. Or whatever they called them.

Heyyy, somebody'd left a motorcycle up the path. It was all shiny flake-purple with limelight shafts bouncing off, and it leaned invitingly against a tree. Hot damn! She'd always wanted to experiment with one of these alien geegaws. They were harder to manipulate than a car; you had to keep your balance, which was hard enough just walking on the two skinny pins but what the heck! She pressed the kick starter but nothing happened. H'm. What was the starting procedure for this internal combustion toy?

The motor was warm, which meant it didn't need to be choked. She opened the throttle, turned the ignition switch to ON and kicked it. The engine roared to life, but she *must* learn to lie better, doggone it. Earth culture was based on the ability to lie smoothly. That was the whole point to being a nontelepathic race, after all. That, and being self-righteous, and getting insulted easily, and shunning responsibility while saying you didn't. Wow. Choke, throttle, clutch; the machine had all its cute little violent parts labeled and she jumped on it to enjoy the vibrations, cracking the throttle a bit more, not wanting to kill the life in the beast; then slowly she extended the clutch.

The rear wheel spun. Woolf lurched forward, opening the throttle wide by mistake and jerking the front wheel to the right. The lads watching thought she was trying to escape by this ploy and were well pleased because they could easily head her off; but, her left hand had been jerked loose; the motorcycle took a leap to the right, and Woolf was flipped over backwards. She flew left and landed crunchingly, bouncing once or twice— haw, haw, ouch!, more fun than she'd had all week.

The darlings watched; each craven, nodule face split in a grin of respectful attention. Woolf hopped up and loped after the still-running motorcycle. She picked it up, accidentally twisting the throttle without pulling in the clutch, and at the same time sobbing,

"Leave me alone!" in bitter panic.

The stupid, alien bike shot ahead several feet, yanking Woolf with it. She burned her hand on the exhaust pipe and let out a sharp yelp. This time she remembered to pull in the clutch, then picked up the motorcycle to examine it: both turn signals smashed, small dent in tank, the end of the throttle grip torn open, gasoline leaking in puddles onto the ground— fascinating!

The bike was still running though, and all mechanical parts seemed to be functioning nicely. She swung her leg over again, lifting up on the shift lever to find neutral. Boy, her shins throbbed! and all because of this super-dumb body design. The bone shouldn't be in the front of the leg. The *meat* should be in the front of the leg. Any dope could see that. Her own basic body made a lot more sense: cartilage instead of bone, and plenty of padding under the squidlike skin. She let out the clutch. The motorcycle jumped ahead six inches and stopped abruptly. It had been in second gear.

"I'll tell," she wept, sneaking a peek at the audience.

The bike started easily this time. It didn't need to be choked. She put it into first and slowly let out the clutch. Yaa-hooo! at last she'd done it correctly and was wobbling down the road, the whole gang following close behind; boy, was this ever terrific! pulling in the clutch; up with the shift lever; not forgetting to let out a loud, wracking sob as she did so.

What a supreme thrill! as the machine surged ahead, and the lads receded in her rearview mirror. Woolf repeated the shifting procedure for third and fourth gears, her eyes on the speedometer... She was shooting ahead! Yeahhh, zowie, the gravel road was suddenly flying backwards underneath her, swiftly followed by a short wooden dock jutting into the polluted fringe of bay.

"Come on, ya sapsuckers," Woolf shrieked in delight.

Oh-oh.

She jammed on the footbrake and pulled in the handbrake with a sprockety Thwonk. At the same time, the motorcycle hit a crack in the boards; it stopped abruptly but Woolf did not. She sailed past a sign that said DANGER, OPEN SEWAGE, finishing reading it just before landing face-down.

As she clambered to her feet, boots sinking into the muddy bottom, a small rescue party had begun to gather; but the main audience was wheeling off in disgust. Woolf stood coughing in hip-deep water.

"C'mon back, ya cowards!" she yelped, spitting chunks of dung; but they didn't bother to answer.

"All right for you!" she screamed sadly.

Ah, nuts. The hell with 'em. Anyway, her comm ring was beeping; she had promises to keep.

TWENTY-ONE

Punctually at dawn on a lonely road outside Winnetka, the Council Chief Heidi's Grandfather met with Omark, who wore his Jennison body dressed in its buckskin and cowboy boots, its engraved revolvers, bowie knife, and silk underwear.

The agents had two problems. First was the vampire O'Blivion, about whom Heidi's Grandfather said, "Bring that one to Rysemus? Never. She can't adapt. No flexibility. Has spent too much time in the Earth hope-and-despair maze. Is an addict, a P.U. junkie, like all of them."

And Omark commented, "True, subject is overprotective of her flesh, but she has something of genius in her. Can manipulate time a little. Doesn't realize it's a simple trick, however."

"And she's packed with morbid fears," H.G. agreed. "After many centuries of life she's still only marginally superior to the common run. But Benaroya can do further testing there."

Of more pressing importance was the Sajorian offensive. Beel continued to seize many of the humans that Benaroya was using in her experiments. ("Woolf's bucking for Most Valuable Anthropologist Award!" Patton had squawked; the two competed furiously, in imitation of Earthies.) The talk now turned to Scaulzo. After a full year of testing the self-styled Prince of Darkness on a green planet created solely for that purpose, the Rysemians were no closer to any clues as to what made the devil a devil.

H.G. tapped gravel with his alpenstock. "All we got for certain is that his commercials are sweeping the Awards, even while the fiend himself is frozen into a tubercular body, under constant surveillance, laughing at us."

"Give the old boy a freeze release. Put him on the cosmic gravy train, in contact with It, directly. One way to make the devil 'good.'"

"Think it would?"

"Nothing to lose by trying. Could say it's in exchange for our hostages, so they won't suspect any pure motives."

"H'm."

Omark unwrapped the Quarter Pounders with fries the Grandfather had brought from his rickety helicopter, which waited on a nearby greensward, blades quivering in morning breeze, several sheep peeping from its windows. Jennison himself was driving the red Corvette parked behind the curve sign, an old woman sleeping peacefully in its bucket seat.

They chewed quietly, meditating on the sad species that drew them together in these tramontane forms. On the far horizon, a man walked his dog. Across the blacktop, a group of college youth at a bus stop were eyeing the Rysemians and exchanging wit. These youth wore pantaloons tight in rump and crotch, wedged into the vertical smile, but flapping at the ankles, some with pairs of socks stuffed into shorts to simulate a bulge. Many wore tight shirts upon which were printed clever sayings. It was a fad this month. It had been a fad a year ago; then it was considered terribly dated; and now, it was a fad again. Many of the youth wore newly sprung, drooping mustaches, which they constantly smoothed with their fingertips while intoning:

"Way-to-go. Radical. Radical! Do you copy? Have a good one, loser. I read you. All right. All ri-ight. All *ri-i-i-ight*," and so forth.

It was a sad fact of life that many a fleabitten zookeeper would pay top dollar for vulnerable specimens like this. Omark had seen too many of their yellowed skeletons wired to the walls of spacer bars; the Sajorian slave-raiders found a use for everything. But this season, far too many Earthies were being shuttled out, largely as a slap in the face to the Rysemian command (although humans had been a natural cargo for half a million years, bringing premium prices on Outlands black markets).

At length the Grandfather wiped his fingers on his blue smock and shook hands with Omark, who walked back across the road to his car. He heard the chopper cough and rattle, revving up, as two joggers came laboring around the bend.

The pair wore white shorts and were hairy of leg and bushy of mustache; Omark noted their oozy, uglinose grimaces. Then a woman on a bike who was pedaling by, turned and smiled at the tall, handsome anthropologist in his gunfighter suit. Last week he'd tried on a goat body for a few minutes, and a woman much like this one had backed away in disgust.

In Omark's opinion, Benaroya was a mixed-up cadet to believe there was hope for this species. Too self-fixated. Each one seemed to have an infinite capacity for bullying. "What *I* am is *right*, and if you're different, you're on an infantile level, so I have a right and a duty to bully you until you act like *me*." Isn't that what they were all saying?- no doubt including this duo of corporation lawyers having a run before breakfast. Omark remained in bond with H.G., who was still very much preoccupied with the Sajorian crisis as the chopper lifted off, turning sharply northward.

A bus now picked up the waiting students. This was going to be one long, risky day. He'd do Virginia Woolf a favor, maybe try to get a line on her missing sales crew she was so upset about, maybe try to figure how to stop these unfortunate daily raids... of which "the media" hadn't taken notice as yet, as only a few thousand were missing and that happened all the time. The worst of it was trying to penetrate the slippery Sajorian mentality. Antitelepathic shields, loaded with charge, slapping at you from every side... But, so it went.

When the joggers were between Jennison and his car, about 20 feet away, sweating and straining for air, their legs pumping tiredly, he glanced up; then seeing his mistake he cursed and turned to run but it was too late. Slugs caught him in the upper body, lungs, heart. First came the dull thud of the freezegun; after that came the pouring hot lead. Jennison spun to one side, a vermilion slash crisscrossing his chest as he staggered and collapsed.

In the Corvette the old woman woke up with Jennison's curse on her lips. Devil take it! now he'd have to go to South America as Mary Worth, the backup body, as there was no time for another switch. Mary slid the car into gear and purred off, while the two "joggers" were flopping Jennison's corpse over onto its back and grinning with satisfaction into its death-hooded eyes.

That was amusing. Ha ha! The Sajorians had to work hard for their bread, despite all their technical brilliance. They were obsessed in the same way Earthies were. And agreeably, this Worth bod was in fine trim: lean and sinewy, never pampered, but hardy and with lightning reflexes, especially after the nose had been flattened and several teeth knocked out in training (courtesy of General Patton).

These assets would be put to good use. At the moment Omark was carrying the ball: a lead concerning a mysterious prison camp 200 miles inland from the coast of Argentina. But if she hoped to be in Buenos Aires before nightfall, she'd better shake her bootie.

Mary Worth brushed her teeth (for the last time? very likely) at O'Hare shortly before takeoff and then studied herself critically in the ladies room mirror. Saber scars on both cheeks, powder burns on the forefingers; general shape, tiptop. "In the pink," Patton had judged her. If truth be known, Omark was bored with defending Jennison's manhood all the time. Maleness was an anchor. Always the chip on the shoulder, morose, serious, looking for insults. "Machismo": an incredible bore. Never allowed to cry or be spontaneous; couldn't kiss a man if he felt like it, or suck his thumb and play baby, or express a sense of humor above the dumb-brute level. Forced to approve the killing of ducks, fish, and deer, to show how "tough" he was (despite the fact that any insane five-year-old girl could slaughter animals after an hour's training). Forced to dramatize the same crafty psychosis night and day, to "prove he was a man," by the tenets of this low-toned culture of theirs.

Bah. And what's more, the Jennison bod had a regrettable tendency to pinch its genitals while mounting horses and suchlike. Too floppy. Whereas the Worth bod was sensibly compact; no excess bulk, no dangling parts, and it required far less food, space, oxygen, clothing, care, and flattery. It looked good in the mirror too, in its torn blouse and gaucho pants, its old Nike runners, dirty cowboy scarf, and shaved head.

Omark felt pleasantly at home in this getup. On Mary's head she placed a checkered golf cap, in honor of the thriving, sporty metropolis that was Buenos Aires.

She went directly to the Rio de la Plata to take a stroll on grass-and-concrete waterfront and drink in the character of this wealthy, bustling spaceport, the air of which stank thrillingly of creosote.

Peculiar how Earthies *never* found out they were constantly being visited by other species. Mary stood admiring their dredges, cranes, loading belts, and shiny grain elevators. She waved at some stevedores who were shooting craps on a passing tug, but they ignored the funny, embarrassing, old lady. It wouldn't be macho to wave back. Maybe she could jump the distance, board them, humbly ask for a little game and then clean the dummies out— but no; gambling was for after the job was done. Right now she needed to steep herself in the bracing insanity of this Paris of South America, erupting with turnpikes, skyscrapers, meat-wagons, gluttony, and poisoned air.

In her lab-dirtied Nikes, Mary Worth wandered to the suave downtown area, wishing to be absorbed as quickly as possible into the Arena of Life. She sauntered up the Avenida 9 de Julio. She saw the resplendent Palacio Hotel and crossed thick carpets under gleaming chandeliers to a sumptuous front desk.

"A suite, if you please," she told the attendant, raising her cap to rub her scalp where it itched from shaving.

"Out."

"...Come again?"

The clerk smiled bitterly, folding his manicured hands.

"Get your ass out of here this moment, or you'll sleep in jail."

Omark was surprised, but decided not to press the issue. No doubt the little Mary Worth in her checked hat, with gray fuzz on her scarred old cheeks, didn't look what they called "impressive." Meanwhile she should not forget that humans, in general, are of such low intelligence that they can only judge superficially. If she'd stuck to the Jennison body, this boob would now fall all over her. He would become a "Si-Señor" machine, simpering, fawning, and offering his vertical smile to the macho Jennison, but what good would that do? Obscurity is much to be preferred to the adoration of drooling idiots.

So Mary hiked with long easy strides to Nueva Chicago, the stockyards where cattle were trucked in from the pampas. Here, men slaughtered live beings by the millions, calling them "animals" to prove it was no crime; assuming they'd never be punished, while imbuing their environment with an atmosphere of bloodshed and corruption. And they wondered why their lives were short and barely tolerable! What brain-boggling idiocy.

Adjoining this terrible place was a Villa Miseria, a misery town with its jumble of reeking shacks. Mary loved industrial landscapes; and here, sources of a most revolting delight lay everywhere. A scarred and sooty vista, with heaps of interesting trash to poke through. Plenty of grime, puke, and urine splashed on old newspapers. How fulsome, the reek of ammonia and burnt chicken feathers; how inspiring, the far smokestack, and the gorgeously crooked houses washed in brown light.

This was good stuff, all right. Much better than some snob-ridden hotel with polished plumbing and scalding water, where you learned nothing. Mary found an empty packing crate and moved herself in. She approved of the view from her front door: acres of weeds bisected by railroad tracks, sparkling with bottles and foil half-sunk in cloroxed mud, jammed with sordid little hovels, everything overlooked by condominiums atop the soaring monoliths of a proud city. Who could ask for a view more typical of the human mentality?

Her neighbors were also wonderful. There were several poets and a few sick junkies who vomited constantly, but most of them were ex-gauchos, ex-butchers, or ex-stevedores, a wretched gang of destitutes squeezed out by young competition or beaten by inflation, picking up a living like the pigeons of the air.

Enlightening, to share their grief at being unable to solve the age-old "mystery" of why their lives were a decaying mushroom. Mary savored dipping into these spookily unclean, alien minds. She could enjoy total contact, undetected, because they insisted that telepathy did not exist. She spent hours gossiping outside her windy shack, seated on an oilcan, or reading comic books (*La Pequena Lulu* and *Superhombre* were among her favorites) to be found by the carload at the dump.

As always, she introduced herself as "from a far planet," and as always they gave her a covert shift of eye or curl of the malleable blubber around the mouth.

Evenings, she rested with her friends on warm cinders and savored tidbits from a garbage can as they spoke of politics, *beisbol,* and rising prices. The ragged gang sat watching the orbed redness of "THE" sun (as they so respectfully called it) "sink in the west" (as they always spoke of it). During these times, Mary Worth tried to insinuate that they were divine spirits who created their own reality. She offered to show them how to make a lot of money; but whenever she got onto these subjects, they would react negatively, until she stopped it and flattered them by agreeing with them.

At first she had foolishly ventured remarks such as,
"There is no 'harsh reality' except as you create it."
"Shut up, you crazy old whore," they had explained.
"No human should be miserable. I'll teach you how to get what you need by postulating it and visualizing it."
"We'll bust your ass first," they pointed out.
"You begin by taking full responsibility for your actions — and by that I don't mean 'blame,'" she said warmly.
"Stick a shoe in her mouth," someone advised; and when this was carried out, Mary knocked off the philosophy.

How could anyone wake these deluded monsters out of their self-imposed nightmare?... But missionary work would have to come later. Right now, a bed of banana peels and straw was luxury to the tired Mary Worth, who was remembering her very first Jennison body, copied from the 19th-century frontier hustler, which had been gunned down months ago by Scaulzo and was still on ice in the Naples morgue. It would be a good joke to reassume that body and sneak out through the front office, scaring the pants off secretaries and clerks; walking all stiff and gaunt, with several feet of intestines dangling, and blank spaces here and there where eager coroners had dissected out other organs.

She slapped a flea, rolling over in the straw. She'd kept nothing from that life; nothing. Even her revolvers had been stolen by the Italian police. Meanwhile another pair of authentic 1860 Colts had been issued her from the *Vonderra's* smithy. These guns, identical to the standard model right out of the old Colt factory, were stiff and new and not prepared for a professional gunfighter. Had to get cracking on that job.

The next evening Mary gulped her supper of two boiled potatoes shoplifted from a local market, then sat in her shack after dark and worked on the weapons by candlelight, modifying them to her own taste. The trigger pull was heavy. They were hard to cock, needing a hellish amount of pressure on the hammer spur. Mary stripped both guns and used a whetstone on the edges of the half-cock and full-cock notches on the hammer, grinding them until they let off slickly when she pressed the trigger. Then she polished and rehardened them.

The mainspring badly needed replacement. In a gunfight, a hammer had to be cocked faster than the wings of death. Mary removed the factory mainspring and replaced it with a well-tempered little whip, so that the piece could be cocked with no effort but would come down on the cap with enough force to explode it. Wearing her golf hat backwards, she filed, polished, tempered until the action was smooth and reliable.

Daytimes she spent visiting neighbors or sorting bits of garbage while learning the ropes of this fine, stinking "laid-back lifestyle" as they called it.

She began hanging out in a tough bar of the district, where the flow of information was better than average. The plan was that she keep both ears open and wait for the right contact. Luck finally showed itself in the form of a young gaucho called Pepe, who blew in bragging about his job on a ranch known as the Morales Estancia, 200 miles due west on the pampas.

"Give us a kiss, old woman," Pepe roared, drawing Mary Worth roughly onto his lap.

Should she pucker up her mouth, or stick a pistol in his nostril?... Worth sat and pondered as Pepe took a long pull from his hip flask.

TWENTY-TWO

Daybreak. Indian summer of the year 1289.

As usual I went into a fit of numb lassitude, lurking here in the orchard of my childhood home; dreading that a friend or relative might see me (but they didn't— at least not that I ever heard of), and at the same time longing to "go back," "make things right" and be the person my parents had wanted me to be... and all that.

Foolish? Of course. But that's my middle name. Sterling Foolish O'Blivion, who was impulsively picking a red-green apple and taking a bite. Such an apple: shiny-tangy, running with juice, and snappy with the frost of night on it.

But just eating that apple might cause radical changes. It was the old paradox. "Suppose you go back in time and shoot your grandmother; then you'd never have been born," etc. Woolf always got impatient with such caviling. "You *can* change the past," she'd insist. "Just jettison that old victim mentality and set it up right." *But.*

My fears were emotional, not mathematical. Of course you can be popped from your space-time like a migrating pea. But the idea of generations that *succeed* each other: to me this is a lonely and frightening plan... And I was scared of seeing myself as a child, or seeing others I'd known; so each time, I can only stay a moment in Old Transylvania and then it's back to my starting place in the Drake Hotel.

I'd been away five minutes at most. Before that, Johnny had called, asking me to meet him in the usual place; I'd needed a moment to think; now, I had to get down there as fast as possible.

But once at our usual table I wondered why I bothered hurrying. Johnny expressed condolences at Armand's death; he pretended to be my friend; then right away he started pumping me.

"They took a shot at me" was all I gave him.

When he started the "Who? How? Where?" routine, I dearly longed to bring him upstairs and show him the contents of my freezer— but didn't. It's strange that people can't see the future. Little did Patsy know, when she sneaked in to burglarize my apartment, that she'd never leave it alive.

How did the lovely spy get in, past all that security? I was hovering at the suite door ready to slip my key into the lock. But something felt wrong. Maybe traces of her perfume were lingering in the elevator. A subliminal signal; I couldn't place it. The door *looked* wrong. So I slipped in very quietly and stood in the dark, leaning against the wall, and sure enough: the merest slit of light, under the study door. Where I keep the two chips and the dandelion puff. My ttm.

Then— a noise. Papers being shuffled. I crept down the hall and stood listening. What to do? Go out and call the police? The intruder would fly by the time they got here.

For some reason I thought it was Johnny in there, going through the very papers I didn't want him to see. (It didn't cross my mind that he could *use* the ttm and escape to past, future, or whatever. Even if he found the correct data, he couldn't apply it. Or at least not quickly.)

I waited.

While I stood wondering, heart in mouth, Patsy Cox opened the door. She let out a yelp of surprise when I moved in on her, knocking the cigarette out of her mouth— with the intention of grabbing the briefcase in which I knew were my papers.

"Sterling!" she yelped— the last word she ever uttered.

Somehow I never thought Patsy would be carrying a gun, the poor stupid would-be glamorous disco-teacher-spy.

When you get to the bottom line, the mistakes we make are always incredible bumbles. Maybe Patsy craved attention; she hungered for love, possibly, or at least *contact*— if so, she really got it. We wrestled. There was a lot of frenzied *contact*.

Then the gun went off. The whole side of her face was blown away. I didn't know what to do with the body, said a few hysterical prayers over it, wrestled it into the freezer all gray-faced and doubled over, then got her blood out of the carpet with two boxes of Arm & Hammer. But her perfume is still here; and spray deodorants do not take it away.

What papers of mine were in her briefcase? Literally everything: all my time stuff, including workups and projections, a lot of which would make absolutely no sense to the Inner Core. What would these twerps make of the fact that the Renaissance will definitely take place in less than two hundred years; that all the old, cold-eyed humanity with its lies and strangleholds will be as dead as the Stone Age, and that the new times will be just as glorious as the 1980s were ridiculous?

No use worrying about it. Patsy and her tribe finally passed on; by the year 2190, the "rubber-faced bipeds with their slithery economics" (as Woolf termed us) no longer existed as such... and *Homo sapiens* had at last begun to tap the awesome power of self-recognition.

I was going to tell Johnny a little of this but something warned me to keep my mouth shut. Instead, I let him read Armand's letter. He refolded it.

"This is true, Sterling. I was with the Core but I quit them. I swear it."

"Okay, let me guess: you're here to warn me... that somebody's upstairs ransacking my rooms at this very moment. Is that right?"

He was more subdued than usual, shoulders hunched, drawn into himself. "I don't blame you if I've lost credibility with you, but for God's sake please take this ticket and use it."

I opened the folder. Inside was a Pan Am pass to Acapulco.

"You've got to be kidding."

"Take it. Use it. Before it's too late."

I ordered an avocado from the waitress. I cut it in half, removed the pit, sprinkled the hollow with salt and calmly began squeezing lemon juice into it. And thought of the 1289 apple I'd eaten a few minutes ago.

Woolf had taught me one thing: to change a condition, you had to *will* it. You had to postulate it, command it, make it happen... No, I wasn't up to that. I said:

"By the way, I killed your friend Patsy and stuffed her body into my freezer. Flies are circling it right now."

"Sterling, you don't have to prove anything to me; I already respect you and love you."

"Terrific!" I chose a silver spoon engraved with the hotel's cursive D, adding, "Go suck an egg. If you want cooperation from me you'd better give me the whole damned story from the beginning."

"All right. In capsule form, because we have no time: I joined this outfit six years ago. I thought they stood for a lot of things I believed in. I found out different."

There was a note of sincerity in his voice that relaxed my guard somewhat. I spooned avocado, saying, "Go on."

"Well, skipping over the disillusionment, and ignoring the fact that (like a lot of things) it's much easier to get in than get out—"

He stiffened, and gave me a strange gentle look, at which something stirred in my heart. Then he slumped forward, dead.

The cops questioned me but I wasn't detained. Obviously I couldn't have put the silenced bullet into my associate's back. But now that Johnny was dead, I felt a flicker of love for this man whose army buddies were all in PR and whose fraternity brothers were in publishing, and so forth, and so forth, and what good were his cherished "contacts" now; and... briefly, I wondered what the real John File (if there was such a person) had been like, under the dreary mask everyone is forced to wear in this dreary society.

But I had no time for grief. Or nostalgia. I had to rush along to the next stage of the terrible game.

TWENTY-THREE

From that first meeting it was Pepe's mania to tease Mary Worth without mercy, calling her a dried-up old streetwalker, fishwife, whorehouse madam, toothless monkey, or (worst insult of the late twentieth century) "woman"; or decking and standing upon her prone form; then polishing her shaven head with beer, weeds, and saddle grease; and laughing at the way the Field Commander lisped through her missing front teeth.

"Where did you get those guns, old monkey? Did you roll a drunk?"

"*Si señor! Nada mas,*" Mary would cackle with the manic, nodding leer that made such a hit everywhere she went.

"Where did you steal the nice gun belt? And those holsters all lined with steel for fast drawing, did you lift them off a croaked gaucho?"

"*Si, un refresco sin igual!*" she'd screech.

It took nearly a week for Mary Worth to break through Pepe's incessant bragging. He claimed to be a riding, roping, drinking son-of-a-bitch, nightly in bed with four ladies simultaneously (Mary never saw it happen; possibly this was his week off) and yet he liked this leathery old witch, who made such an excellent soccer ball.

Slowly it dawned on Pepe that his newfound pal could have both six-guns firing before you even saw her hands begin to twitch. At last the Field Commander was learning "bragging": the quintessential, macho-male skill. Pepe would throw cans and rocks into the air and the old monkey would blast them to bits at any specified point in their rise or fall, or anywhere in their trajectory. Pepe admired this talent so much that Omark agreed to teach him a little of the gunfighter's art.

"Target skill is not enough, my friend. The main thing is presence of mind. You must be perfectly cold-blooded and kill the other man before he kills you."

"What, you like to kill people?"

"*Un refresco sin igual*," Mary cackled in her manic, fishmonger roar.

Pepe didn't know if the old reprobate was putting him on or not but he wasn't about to test it. Actually they were a great pair: a gangly, swaggering cowpoke and a bald, sunburnt, armed senile delinquent.

"How many gunfights you been in?"

"Thousands," Mary bragged. She always hung around her pal Pepe and bought him drinks, and fixed his old Ford for nothing.

He'd answer, "You fulla bull!" and throw Mary into the air, or the mud, and rub her head with it severely. Pepe enjoyed roughhousing Mrs. Worth; they drank together nightly; she was one cool operator. She was even-tempered, smart, no ego challenge, no threat whatsoever, being only an old type who'd probably done time for shooting her old man or something like that. But all in all, she was a swell loafing and drinking buddy.

One day she asked him, "Can you get me a job?"

"Where I work, you mean? Sure, you can tag along if you want to." Pepe cleaned his nails with a fishknife. "They always need a cook or a mechanic out at the Morales place."

The bar they frequented was adobe painted primary yellow and blue. The proprietor served smoking-hot pot roast every evening at four. This evening they were waiting for the feed, sniffing succulence of beef and vegetables, and drinking from brown bottles of cerveza.

Mrs. Worth asked, "Just who is this Morales guy?"

"Owner of the estancia, of course. There's a father and son Morales and some cousins. Funny thing," downing a slug of beer, wiping his nose on his sleeve, "I called collect for an advance and some stranger wouldn't take my call. Said the Morales family is on vacation."

"What's funny about that?"

"All of them away at the same time? Never happen. Unless maybe an important relative died. Anyway it's not my damn business as long as they pay me." Pepe attacked his pot roast.

Unlike Benaroya, Omark had trained himself to eat meat like a cheerful cannibal, and the food in Argentina was excellent; the meat really tasted like meat and not like assorted chemicals marinated into soft leather, the way it did in the States. Mary ate with gusto, all the while asking questions in her sleepy, offhand way. She knew the Morales ranch had to be a Sajorian headquarters. Beel himself would be out scouting for new abduction victims, but the ranch was a likely place to store them. Benaroya and her vampire friend O'Blivion were hoping against hope that their FMTC staffers had been taken there, at least temporarily.

"Juan Morales left in one hell of a hurry." Pepe mopped up the gravy with his bread. "He didn't even have time to round up the cattle. Must be a thousand head out there, wandering around loose."

"Think something's going on?"

"Monkey, if they pay us, nothing's going on. If they don't pay us—" He drew his knife across his throat and stuck out his tongue.

"*Un refresco sin igual.*" Mary Worth was forced to agree.

They left next morning in the gray chill before dawn, turning the heater in the old Ford on full-blast and gulping scalding coffee out of a thermos. Pepe drove silently through cattle country. Mary dozed, letting the truth of the hushed and windblown pampas land seep into her bones. She threw an occasional probe into adjoining time slots but found nothing, nothing but brick walls on the other end.

Around nine in the morning they pulled into the driveway of the Morales ranch house. Chickens squawked and flapped out of the way; a pack of dogs bounded out yapping hellishly. Pepe kicked them aside and walked to the door.

Mary sat in the truck rolling a cigarette, looking the spread over through sleepy eyes. She thought about Woolf's sales team, and wondered about Sterling O'Blivion— so confused by the A-O she'd been jolted out of the last of her complacency. A man in business clothes stood on the porch talking to Pepe. Mary hopped out of the truck, grinning. She struck a wooden match on her thumbnail and strolled over, lighting her Bull Durham.

The rancher, who had a face like a hatchet buried in permafrost, snapped questions at her. "Ever steal anything?"

"What, me? No, *señor*, no-no."

"Your son says you boost from shops."

"Does the fool want a whipping? Mother of God, I'm bonded! I was a Sunday School teacher before the government taught me mechanics," crossing herself repeatedly.

"Can you repair a generator? Can you fix that Bluebird bus over there?"

"My beautiful mother can fix anything," Pepe bragged.

Mary probed the rancher, who claimed his name was Sanchez. The rancher expected no trouble from this talkative young cowboy and his battle-scarred old lady. Mary held her breath for an instant. One of Beel's bullies!

The installation must have been operating here for months. Probing, Mary kept her own shield battened down tight. Sanchez suspected nothing; why should he? They were only two drifters wanting temporary work. Sanchez rested his eyes for a moment on the pair of antique revolvers Mrs. Worth kept holstered within easy reach of her hands. Not unusual for an old-time ranchwoman.

"All right, let's see if you can make that bus run smooth. It chugs and shimmies and smells like it's going to blow up." Sanchez went back to the darkened interior where a TV muttered away to itself.

Pepe headed for the bunkhouse with his gear. Mary Worth sauntered to the bus and looked it over, stroking it softly. She got in and started the engine. She enjoyed tinkering with these inefficient little toys, these internal combustion fuel-gulpers with the steel bodies and the oversized wheels, which Earthies held so dear to their retarded little hearts.

One listen told her that rough roads had jolted everything loose. The bus was ailing; it needed a motherly hand. Mary yanked the carburetor and blew through the gas entrance hole. The float needle wasn't holding. She removed the four screws that held the float chamber and lifted the cover off, handling the gasket with tenderness. She saw that vibration had loosened the needle valve assembly and it was about to fall into the float chamber. She tightened it up, put the carb back together, and did a quick tune-up, tinkering and stroking until the engine purred.

Very good. Leaving her body bent over the idling engine, she explored the acreage, or at least sections of it that were not tightly shielded. Right about then, the rancher came back and began watching her narrowly. Mary invited him to try the bus.

When it bowled smoothly along the drive, Sanchez said, "Not bad. Now we have a generator in the storehouse that needs repair."

He gave Mary a box of tools and some directions and left her alone. This was perfect. Mary fixed the generator, which had been gas-primed a few times too often. Then she wandered idly around, looking things over. She'd brought a small folding telescope which opened out to a four-incher; this she set up on a rise, well screened by bushes, where she could check the area thoroughly.

About a mile down was a stockade connected to a barnlike building. Mrs. Worth studied this layout carefully. There were steel bars on all the windows.

What kind of beast requires barred windows?

Sanchez would think she was hard at work on the generator. In case the rancher came looking for her, she'd have plenty of time to stow the telescope and amble out of the bushes buttoning her pantaloons.

So she waited.

One hour.

Two hours.

Nobody came looking for Mary Worth. She sat on the rise until every shadow had dwindled to a black puddle and the sun stood at high noon. Finally she saw what she was looking for.

A guard approached the stockade. He unlocked the narrow door and yelled something, and people began to file out. Men, women, even a few small children; Worth counted forty head of them. All jammed inside that tiny stockade? It must be a hellhole in there. Typical trick of Beel, who seemed to extract perverse pleasure from crowding his victims into small spaces. The prisoners milled around the yard, exercising. Mary had memorized photos of the engineer Reardon and the sperm-collector Bauer, among others, but she recognized none of these FMTC people among the prisoners. She picked up that these were Chinese intellectuals dressed in the clothing of farm workers.

How many compounds like this did Beel operate? How many terrified Earthies were penned up, awaiting shipment to unthinkable destinations?

A Bright Lights culture would never stoop to display any animal, not even a living human being; but there were plenty of creeps out there who'd snap these prototypes up as slaves, exotic pets, novelty or joke gift items, lab animals, or simply to be butchered for the burgeoning fast-food joints, the McDonald's Golden Arches of the Spaceways that were springing up all over since "long pig" had been found to be a delectable, cheap source of protein.

It was really too bad. And think of the bereaved relatives posting "Missing Person" notices in public places, perhaps for years afterward, to no avail.

Mary went thoughtfully back to the ranchhouse, attracting no attention. She lined up for chow with Pepe and the other hands. They wolfed down beef stew and coffee and then leaned back, rolling cigarettes. Pepe brought out his guitar and began strumming chords, squinting against the smoke. He said, "Sanchez likes you. He told the foreman you can fix anything."

"What's the setup here? Did Morales hire Sanchez and his men and then take off?"

Pepe grunted. "If you're worried about getting paid, no problem; they pay every Thursday like clockwork."

That afternoon Mary Worth fixed a grain thresher and a couple of pumps. She had chow with the hands, crawled into her bunk and waited patiently until the whole staff was asleep. Then she moved outside noiselessly. She got into the Bluebird bus, eased off the brake and let it roll until she was far enough from the buildings to start the motor; raced it for half a mile, turned the key off, and coasted the rest of the way to the stockade.

The moon was rising over a grove of scrub aspen near her vantage point. She took out her telescope to watch the stockade by moonlight. There was one guard, sitting on his haunches under the bushes, chain-smoking, and taking healthy nips from a bottle. Mary probed.

Yes, he was Sajorian, bred to give no quarter; a being who had absolutely no sense of guilt no matter what crimes he committed. Lucky? Perhaps. This bully wore two guns. One was an ordinary police special. The other was an H-2 unit.

Mary shut her eyes. To be stuck permanently in this body until it died — how would that feel? Horribly frustrating. Like Benaroya that time, kicking and spitting, or like the Quatzler that Omark rescued from such a disgusting condition; or like any Earthie, poor imprisoned souls. In any case, she'd be a swiftly moving target and not get frozen.

All was quiet in the stockade. The prisoners must be asleep. Mary moved quietly, snapping no twigs, keeping an eye on the guard, who dozed under the bushes.

It was a dark night laced with patches of moonlight. Rooftops were sugared by the crescent satellite. If the guard woke up he'd sure as hell spot Mary tiptoeing between moonbeams. She longed for a freezegun. But she'd have been blasted right away if she'd tried to smuggle one in. A bird stirred and chirped a few notes somewhere close, as Mary crept onto the ground above the dozing guard. From here she could jump him. If she moved quickly and got the correct momentum it would be simple.

She jumped.

She hit the guard with body stiffened like a ramrod, jamming both her thumbs into the cervical nerve junction. Owf!, an ounce more strength and she'd have it made. As it was, the wiry Worth carcass, perfect for stalking but lacking in sheer meat-bulk, didn't have quite the strength; so the guard brushed her off with a jackhammer fist.

This guard was a bruiser. Six-four at least, shoulders like a bull, with elephantine feet in swiftly moving, steel-capped boots. He kicked Mary Worth a couple of explosive, numbing kicks. He had both guns out. The .38 in his right hand. And in his left hand… the weapon of nightmare.

"Get up," he snarled.

"Excuse it, *Señor*! I badly needed a swallow of booze," with an eye-rolling leer.

The guard looked her over. "You must be the grease monkey."

"*Nada mas*, pretty person."

"Why didn't you just ask nice? You drunk or crazy?"

"A little of each," Mary smirked, writhing because her ribs were somewhat crushed. "Hey, you got the nice guns, *Señor*, but can you shoot them?" with a friendly giggle.

"You drunken old bigmouth, you want your ticket punched?"

Pleasant nods and giggles.

"What you want is ten lighted splinters under the toenails," affirmed the guard.

"Oh, you funny," she laughed. And spat a little blood, probing this guard who was definitely bored; nothing to do out in these boondocks week after week except torture the prisoners, which had become boring. No challenge, because even if somebody lucked out and killed him he'd bounce back to his ship and pick up another body and stay in the game. On the other hand, if he destroyed this foolish old woman, that would be permanent and something of a diversion, so Mary needled him with a smile,

"You like gunfights? You want fair gunfight?"

"With you? Don't make me laugh."

"You chicken."

"Get out of here. Sanchez can't use a dead grease monkey."

"Fair gunfight."

"Go hang yourself and save me trouble." The guard holstered his guns.

Mary said, "You draw first."

"Go home."

"Draw."

The guard laughed.

Mary scrambled to her feet. "Come on, gaucho, chicken."

"I thought you wanted booze."

"I'll steal it off your corpse."

That irritated the Sajorian. He stood glowering, wondering whether he should kill her or not. Suddenly his hands went for his guns.

The Field Commander knew it was a myth, generally speaking, that a gunfighter can give his opponent first draw and live to tell about it. A human with very fast reflexes needs one-fifth of a second to respond to any signal. Human bodies are at best pathetically slow. If both men can draw, fire, and hit in less than half a second, the man who draws first will always win.

But Mary Worth had hours of practice under her belt. She had cutaway holsters lined with frictionless steel. She had Rysemian guts and brains, along with the killer instinct that came from knowing that she was facing a freezegun and that to lose this match was to lose everything. Her guns were blazing before the guard reached his holsters. The big man crumpled; Worth grabbed the priceless H-2 unit, let him have a taste of it, and rammed it into her own belt.

Then she took the Sajorian's keys and flashlight. Too bad there had been shots; she'd wanted to overpower the bully in silence, but didn't quite have the beef. Now she'd have to shake her bootie.

In the stockade Beel's prisoners were huddled around a stewpot, which steamed over a few hot coals. Worth probed, flashing her torch. These were "Communists." Fascinating. They believed they came from the most advanced form of Earthie society. Indeed, it was rather beautiful how they'd subdued their inborn greed and were sharing everything equally. A hacked corpse had been strung from the rafters: the smoked body of a Chinese male; missing an arm, leg, and part of a ribcage. The right arm, doubled at the elbow, was stewing in the pot.

Very practical at that. The anthropologist recalled this culture's working philosophy: we are not spiritual beings, but meat animals, highly intelligent problem-solvers with lots of chronic shortages. Nothing can be created; so, in the name of Lenin, we will share all things equally.

And they had hewn closely to that religion. Each person was gnawing upon one-half of a finger or toe, split lengthwise. Human reason and logic had won the day.

The prisoners looked like starved corpses themselves, blinking and gaping in the flashlight beam.

"Get a move on!" Mary yelled, shining the torch on her own face so they could see she wasn't one of the guards. The victims had been snatched from a farm commune on the Chinese mainland, except for the half-dozen who were of the Morales clan. She fired rapid commands at them. "In the bus! *Andale.* Chopchop, shake your booties. Who wants to drive?"

It took a long time to herd this dazed crowd into the Bluebird. Morales, owner of the bus, took the wheel and headed up the road. Mary was holding her guts, which bled copiously, internally. She scrambled to the top of the vehicle and twined her weary body in a luggage rack, so it wouldn't fall off as they jolted over the ruts.

Bad luck! Sealed beams were approaching. Still a quarter mile off but closing the distance fast.

"Floor it, Morales," Mary shrieked. When the other car was in range she opened fire and blazed until she exploded a tire, spinning the pursuers into a ditch. Then more headlights sliced the night behind them.

Mary Worth touched her comm ring. Both legs braced in the luggage rack were all that kept her from flying off the bus.

Virginia Woolf's head swam into view. "Where are you? Did you locate my people?"

"No, I—"

"Do you know how dopey you look? Is this another of your frivolous, comic strip games?"

The sublime creature: never had she seemed so beautiful. Or so maddening. Virginia Woolf had been too cocky since her freeze release, figuring that nothing bad could ever happen to her again... invariably a foolish posture, because life's tough, and always tricky. But with great presence of mind Mary Worth screamed,

"Do you want a detailed account of how I'm croaking? Listen, I'm bringing this carcass in. Have things ready so I can make the transfer in one hell of a hurry."

The bus was violently shaken, probably by a grenade bursting nearby; Virginia Woolf thought it was funny. Mary Worth, with a look of command, yelped at the impertinent cadet,

"I've got a mouthful of midges plus a load of high Communist Party elite— bankers, neurosurgeons, they all share farmwork in the People's Republic— so step on it and call the local cops and get them shipped home. They think it's an international incident. Might be touchy for the Argentine government but it's not our problem," and clicked off.

The other car was closing in fast. Mary Worth reloaded from her cartridge belt using teeth, elbows, anything, as the night whistled past. They crossed a creek on a swaying bridge, then past fences, Mary hanging on tenaciously when scraped by the limbs of a chambala tree.

Jets of lead sprayed close, too close; a slug nicked her ankle, and just after that she felt the thudding charge of a freezegun blow past one cheek. Time to scram, baby! Her next bullet shattered the pursuing car's windshield and it went skidding end over end into barbed wire. Inside the bus, the party officials set up a muted yell of victory.

Mary Worth blew smoke off her muzzle, spat a pint of blood, and passed out, in the act of beaming back to her ship the *Vonderra*.

Poor old Mary Worth. She was deader than yesterday's rock star.

They hung her skinny old corpse in the Nothingness Room to

be dealt with later. Ah well: Omark was just as happy. He enjoyed being the irritable, sardonic Jennison again, slapping people around with amused contempt. It seemed that whichever of these nasty, brutish lives you were living, that's the one you preferred above all others. As Jennison, he had the swelling buttocks that Earthies worshipped; and he was very large, which meant he could consume an outsized amount of goods and services. Also, the pleasure of awakening each morning as a macho killer was rather keen.

Booted, spurred, and leather-clad, Jennison stretched out in his quarters (he'd be much happier back on Rysemus doing a paper speculating on which barbarian identity was the absurdest, but this was O.K for now) and began stripping the freezegun he'd lifted off the Sajorian guard. Its shell was a dummy, as usual, and the mechanism was simple: a laser-based implant needle which could plow the suggestion "You are your body, and are mired in flesh forever" into any being wearing any type of carbon-oxygen carcass whatsoever.

Horrible? The very definition of Hell. It took a Sajorian to invent such an instrument.

As for Woolf, she'd been devastated to learn that Blake Reardon and Vicki Bauer were not among the rescued prisoners. Those two, they'd probably been shipped out, and were light-years away from home by now... poor devils.

To finish an earlier cycle, Jennison went to Buenos Aires and took a taxi to the same Hotel Palacio that had thrown him out when he was a scarred, bald old Mary Worth in tennis shoes.

Fortunately the same gilded clerk sat at the same desk.

Jennison swaggered across the soft pelt of carpet. He spat neatly into where the cuspidor should have been.

"I'd like a suite."

The clerk blinked, smiling warmly.

"Certainly, señor. Two rooms or three? One bath, or two?"

Jennison leaned over and lifted the clerk by his necktie. Eyeball to eyeball he snarled, "You deserve being a human being," then dropped the surprised clerk with a thud and walked out.

Horrible thing to say, maybe; but he felt better having said it.

TWENTY-FOUR

Every so often, Sterling would run into someone she'd known in the past. It could be an old friend or lover, or an employer, neighbor, or landlord; once it was the handsome butcher who used to set aside choice cuts for her; once, her former flute teacher; and so on. Sterling usually didn't recognize the faded old party.

But invariably the friend recognized *her*. The vampire's heart would flip-flop and almost stop cold when she met that penetrating stare and heard those words: "Good lord. Aren't you—? But of course not. That must have been sixty years ago. It's amazing; you look just like her," and so forth.

Each time it happened, Sterling was so strung out she'd pull up stakes and move on. In this way she moved from Paris to San Francisco, from San Francisco to Sri Lanka, to Hong Kong, New York, Zurich, Chicago— always afraid the old friend would get to wondering, and putting two and two together, to the vampire's disadvantage.

Sterling had eluded the Pointing Finger for so long that she was totally unprepared when finally it swung in her direction. The great Max Arkoff himself blew the whistle on her. He rang her doorbell one evening, accompanied by two burly men in business suits. When Sterling peeped through the peephole and saw the boss of the whole Arkoff Studio disco chain, she was so thrilled she nearly fainted.

"Come in, come in," she fluttered. Not only was Max her Boss, but he was a giant of the silver screen, idolized, unattainable; beloved by millions.

"Come in," she bustled, flushed with delight, like a schoolgirl whose wildest wish just came true. As the trio loomed in her doorway, the vampire began rummaging for that special bottle of champagne she'd brought from the old country.

There he stood— Max Arkoff! It was unbelievable. How she'd doted on that genius of a dancer when he was a rising young star, so debonair in those old movies, and with such beauty of movement that everyone in Europe and America had a crush on Max. Nobody ever danced like Max; not even the famous dancers of history; not even Nijinsky. And as for *class*, and *style*— Arkoff set the pace for three whole generations.

"Don't just stand there. Come in and make yourselves at home," she chittered.

But all Max did was rake her with ice-cold eyes and say in a voice that vibrated with scorn: "You're terminated."

Bang.

Just like that.

Sterling felt it as a physical blow. She reeled, and then pulled herself together enough to ask, "Why?"

"Get your junk out of the studio by noon tomorrow. You're not fit to be on my staff."

The weird part was, Max didn't even look like himself. He looked like some evil cartoon of his film-idol self. A white, self-important slug, in an expensive hairpiece. Sterling was shocked to her toes— more by the way Max *looked* than anything else. He seemed the exact opposite of the person he played in the movies. His face had been stripped of joy. It was shriveled, cold, and disfigured by self-righteousness.

As for the two bodyguards, they acted as if Sterling was some kind of cheap slut, or worse, that they could get off on by insulting. They had a smirky, lascivious air that threw Sterling into confusion. What was going on here? Never had she known men to treat a vampire like this. Not respect a vampire? It was unheard of! They might hate, despite, fear, or kill you, at the drop of a hat; but *patronize* you? Don't be crazy.

How could this happen? Max's hostility tore her soul; he wouldn't answer her questions, just turned on his heel and marched off, the henchmen following, and Sterling was left standing in the doorway, her world crashing around her ears.

"Why? Why?" she wailed the next morning, getting her things out of her former desk, and her pictures down from the office walls, and so forth, while syndrum flourishes rolled across the dance floor.

And everything had seemed to be going so *well*. It made no sense for Arkoff to fire his best manager at a time like this— just when she was home free! Crepe had been tacked on the doors and they'd all mourned Johnny File for a solid week. Patsy had been replaced by another charming young lady teacher. Sterling had paid $5,000 in Krugerrands to a button man of her acquaintance to haul away the freezer (with Patsy's remains inside, all identification marks removed) when she was out shopping one morning and didn't have to watch; then she got a brand new Sears Roebuck freezer. Things were gradually getting back to normal. Why had Max fired her?

"Condemned without trial," she raged. "Not a word of explanation. *Why?*"

Patsy's replacement, a starlet called Bubbles, with Italian marble eyes, didn't mind answering that question. "Because he thinks you're a dyke."

"Wha—?" Sterling had never considered such a preposterous idea.

"You were holding hands with that woman Virginia Woolf. You were kissing right out in front of God and everybody, and that's a definite no-no."

"But I thought the sexual revolution was over! I thought prejudice was a thing of the past."

"For men, yes, if they're discreet; but for dykes, never."

"And why the hell not?"

"Because it's supposed to be boy-girl, boy-girl."

"Who says so?"

"Everybody! The majority! Where've you been all your life? Gee, Ster, you're lucky I'm around to explain things to you. People look down on dykes. Dykes are at the bottom of the heap. Dykes are garbage. Except, of course, when they're useful; to titillate some impotent male who gets off on the idea— understand?"

There was absolutely no respect in Bubbles' whispery drawl.

Such a thing had never happened to Sterling before. What hurt her most was the idea that if she wasn't willing to conform on this idiotic level, "they" could gang up and rob her.

"Yeah, I understand," she flared, barely holding back the tears. "It's a whore's world. In which faggots are welcomed because they serve *men.*"

"You got it," Bubbles smiled. "You're a lesbian? Into the meat grinder. It's as simple as that. And the real irony is— Arkoff's a faggot."

The new teacher gloated openly, true, but was not lacking in sympathy. But however Sterling looked at it, she herself was *out*; out flat on her tail. And she'd thought at least she had job security!

Bubbles buffed her nails. "Why not trot over to Fred Astaire or Arthur Murray? They'd hire you in a sec, Ster. Unless Max blackballed you."

"Screw 'em!"

"And if he did, you can go to the Human Rights Commission."

"Screw 'em all! This whole society can go straight to the devil. I'd rather do something *meaningful,* as all you turkeys keep repeating— with your hands stuck in each other's jeans," and the vampire flounced off, carrying her silver bud vase, her autographed pictures of dancing stars, her three disco awards, and her desk bottle of Jack Daniels.

The confusing part was: Sterling was deeply, sincerely in love for the first time in her life. But she couldn't even extol her loved one's eyes, lips, hair, and so on; because it was not a body she loved, but a person.

True, her loved one (the nonpareil Virginia Woolf) had petal-pink lips and porcelain skin; and an air of detached amusement, at once pure and tough; and that person swept aside all paltry considerations and went on with a driving purpose—

"Max Arkof fired me," Sterling wept.

"That's the best thing that ever happened," Woolf said gaily.

But the vampire had been plunged into despair and darkness. She was a tragic figure; and the more upset she got, the more the Agony Organ slashed away at her mind.

What was "real"? What was "irreal"? By now the $E = mc^2$ of the dream world had the vampire in its coils and the harder she fought, the deeper she sank. In her diary she scribbled, "Woolf came by today, and suddenly the powerful attraction overwhelmed us. Her arms pulled me close... After the long wait, my desire for her was if anything too intense."

And she wrote: "The Rysemians are all that keep me going;

but it's slipping away from me, though Woolf again explains how my own fear augments the A-O and she tells me, 'Don't send out evil thought waves. That's what powers the thing.' Yet each time the seizure is over I start to worry about my hellish, impending fate...

Their kiss had been interrupted by General George Patton who beamed in to brief the two women for tonight's action. If anything, the captain of the *Vonderra* was even more threatening to the vampire than Jennison had been. He showed up in full dress uniform: square-jawed, radiating confidence, just like his pictures; but when O'Blivion looked him straight in the eye, he was evasive.

"Hit 'em with everything you got," Patton barked, setting up the charts. "You, O'Blivion, must live up to your mythology and get rid of all hypocritical guilt feelings, do you copy?"

Woolf explained that Sterling had suffered a series of blows, had been rocked by multiple deaths, and fired in humiliation; but Patton rippled his jaw muscles and snapped,

"Bottled up fear and fury, egged on by whatever A-O emanations you pick up (and I'm here to tell you, they play over your species constantly)— you're a ticking bomb. Either you go off tonight, or you pass this mind-expander at some safe spot and get lost."

Woolf made drinks for all of them, which settled Sterling's nerves a bit. On top of everything else, the Sperm-of-the-Month Club was under injunction to cease operations. Sterling and Woolf had pleaded guilty to six counts of income tax evasion; the FMTC books were in a mess, and the IRS had confiscated every sperm sample, which by now were thawed and ruined. It had done no good to argue "We did it for research, not bucks—" What did the IRS care about *research*?

And Sterling, already lonely, indecisive, scared half to death, was even more shattered that Benaroya just laughed and said, "On to new games!" bouncing around singing Christmas carols and declaring,

"Now for a good, cleansing romp of butchery patterned after Viet Nam, so we can set fire to huts with kids in them, and hack heads off and all that; you're gonna love it. If we get separated, remember: it's only a game, like everything else."

It was a raw December night just before the holidays. Sterling was trying on a wetsuit in front of the bathroom mirror, cursing and shaking baby powder into the tight black neoprene that would fit like a second skin, if she could ever get the damned thing on. And with all the vivid, disturbing illusions, she didn't know if she'd heard correctly. Did Woolf really plan to kill *children*?

"Yep; but they're only mermaids. Intaglios, you know."

"I can't do it."

"Of course you can, baby," Woolf encouraged. "A lot depends on this roll of the dice. We're gonna smoke out Beel in the flesh!" And she handed Sterling a scuba tank, asking, "Do you know how to use one of these?"

"I've seen them in the movies."

"Well, we'll be in close telepathic contact down there, so don't let what happens freak you out."

The Sajorian emplacement had been pinpointed at the bottom of Lake Michigan. Sterling thought that was impossible, but Patton had set up an office right there in her apartment complete with filing cases, a library desk and an overhead projector around which he strutted, indicating target areas on radar, using his riding crop to outline castles, with six-foot sturgeon swimming through them like goldfish in a bowl.

Sterling watched the general between narrowed lids as he flicked his crop against his beautiful breeches.

"'Americans love the sting of battle. The thought of losing is hateful to an American,'" quoth he. "So, Vampire: are you prepared for the great leap into the Unknown?"

"Why me?"

"Because you're a changeling, what else? Nobody else even comes close. My God but you people astound me with your self-imposed limitations," Patton said in a snotty voice. "Don't you ever get sick of the cycle of war movies, anti-war movies, anti-anti-war movies and the same old boring game played over ten million times with slight variations?"

Sterling asked what the alternative was.

The general said, "Ask yourself these simple questions. Where do people come from? What are they doing here? Why are there more people here now than a hundred years ago? The answers may surprise you."

Sterling said she didn't care.

The general said, "Do you *want* to be freed from an Earthbound state or not?"

"Of course she does," Woolf shouted, hugging Sterling tightly.

The general said: "You draw it to yourself! It's all mirrors arranged around a cut in the continuum. You saw the whole routine in a previous existence. You've done this an infinite number of times and always in the past you didn't make it. Always you chose to return to the meat animals. How about tonight?"

"She's learned her lesson," Woolf squeaked.

"Go suck eggs! Get off my case," the vampire told them.

Patton reached for the champagne (the same bottle that had been uncorked for Max Arkoff), and he kept after Sterling as he poured. "We're giving this top priority for reasons that you'll know soon enough. First, you must accept the demon-beast in yourself. I'm here to monitor your soul's progress; so lock your mind into the 'open' position and lay off the guilt trips, is that clear?"

"And if I refuse?"

"Then your name will be stricken from the book!" he trumpeted.

Woolf made an impolite noise.

Sterling hedged, "Let's discuss this rationally."

"By that you mean according to the tenets of the superstition of Megatechnics," Patton told her. "But the psychic law is: physical matter is only stuff. Get that through your 'head' (which of course is not where you store information) once and for all."

He poured for the women, then lifted his glass. "Speed the conquest! Here's to life eternal!"

"Down the hatch," Woolf roared.

Sterling took a couple of sips and said, "That authoritarian approach never works with me. I want factual evidence."

"And you deserve to get it," said the general. He took a sheaf of maps, unrolled their rubber band onto his wrist and spread them out on the top of the new Sears Roebuck freezer. Sterling examined the maps closely.

"There's no way a tracking station can tell what's going on down there in the bottomless dark," Patton said with satisfaction. "It works like a radar-jamming antenna and it looks perfectly normal— like you, my dear," with his gravelly chuckle that set O'Blivion's teeth on edge.

"You know all the dangers," he went on, "The Sajorians are zeroing in on you. Many of your friends have already been abducted. Admittedly, that's partly our fault for attracting attention to them; but you must understand how quickly their families and friends forget them. Nobody wants to think of *unsatisfying* things. Of course they want nice little stories that flatter them, by showing them solving neat problems that won't confuse their cluttered little minds. They want to be entertained. By something titillating; or of a mechanical, medical, or phony-spiritual nature, just so long as it's false. The one thing they cannot tolerate is the truth."

"So what's that got to do with me?"

"Make a decision. Either you confront reality— which is not the one-track railroad you people thought it was— or get off the lines."

The vampire felt that this was ambiguous, but put it out of her mind and tried to concentrate on the various maps. The installation was about a mile offshore at Oak Street, and three hundred feet down. Woolf and O'Blivion had been assigned to check it out. The village was protected by a simple sonar sheet. With any luck, they would put a small scrambler inside, so that within a day the whole village would just be part of the lake again.

"It'll be fun," Woolf exulted. "I have my destructive impulses too. Their staff is a bunch of chimera mermaids. We'll kill the lot of them. But just for fun. To kill is not always a crime, but to kill in punishment is always a crime."

She'd brought the half-inch wetsuit for Sterling, together with fins, flashlight, regulator, a stungun, and an H-2 unit. Sterling was reluctant about taking the stuff, but Woolf said,

"Freeze 'em into their bodies. Then when you kill 'em, it really counts."

"And don't miss," the general added. "If they capture you, admit nothing."

Sterling sat on the couch and finished off the champagne, saying,

"No way. Sorry. I can't take this on until I understand it better."

Patton drew a graph. "Soul vertical. Flesh horizontal. Dream state impinging on windows of 'the present'" (tick-tick with the chalk). "Energy bounce in and out of space-time continuum. Don't you get it yet? Is it too simple for your gadget-loaded mind?"

"He means you don't have a choice," Woolf said sadly.

"That's right," nodded the general. "The P.U. originates in the mind. It grows out of the spiritual world. This sounds like an old-fashioned notion because organized religions have cheated you, but the fact is, they can't enslave or make money off a god; it's up to you."

The fear-softened vampire had more questions; but Patton wouldn't answer them.

"It's high sec classification" was all he'd say. Except just before beaming out,

"Memento mori, kid," he grinned.

TWENTY-FIVE

Oak Street was empty at that hour except for a few drunks who didn't give the two women in wetsuits a passing glance.

"Now for the deciding experiment! Hot dippy," Woolf rejoiced. But the vampire wasn't rejoicing. She fretted about having to leave the familiar, snug hotel for good, now that she'd been given the sack. Diving weights strapped around her waist made walking seem a clumsy struggle, but the beach was close, the wind was at their backs; the lake looked black and sinister. But when O'Blivion glanced back, the skyline was garish but equally dangerous-looking.

"It's a night for wild dawgs," Woolf chirped as she slipped on the fins and adjusted the mask over her face. Then she strode backward right into the icy shallows. O'Blivion was in no hurry to follow. Extreme cold had made the city lights go all wraithy, as if they were about to dematerialize. Maybe she'd never see that familiar shoreline again. The idea made her melancholy.

Woolf told her to save the waterworks.

"Our sales team is out there! so move it. Go ahead, flop belly-down in the water, what have you got to lose?"

Sterling telegraphed an "Everything" which was waved aside. They were bound in that dreadful but miraculous mental contact which the vampire could not throw off. Woolf tried to show her what great fun this was. Grief was out of place; you could feel the bottom stones through your neoprene booties, by stepping right into a genuine Great Lake that you'd examined from 200 miles up and studied the maps of, on a strange planet, which was about the most exciting adventure a person could have. So why feel drenched and chilled, when you'll be hot in a minute as your carcass heats a film of water between it and the suit?, in this all-important team rescue.

"They hafta be flushed like rats! so stick the mouthpiece between your jaws and switch on the flashlight in your belt. And don't grab onto that body so hard. There's plenty more where that came from. Get over those age-old Earthie delusions of shortage, for corn sake."

But Sterling had begun to whine, "I was so rich and so happy and you people ruined me—" which made Woolf mad.

"Table that crap. We'll discuss it later. Now the plan is, we float over and we reconnoiter. Don't kill anybody until I give the word. Use the H-2 first and your blaster second," Woolf telegraphed, glancing at her watch. "Got it? That's very important. Freeze them into their body and *then* kill them, so it's permanent."

Could it possibly be happening? How could the gentle, compassionate Rysemian plan such things? At this moment the vampire almost hated her.

"Don't be so afraid of death; it's no big thing," Woolf said as they paddled out on the rise and fall of waves. "As to your hatred, it's a matter of indifference to me" — which O'Blivion knew was a lie, but she kept her peace until the forest of waving grass began to close behind them, and Woolf cabled,

"When I signal *down*, you throw your fins up and point your skull down and swim hard for the bottom.

"And remember, don't give off any here-I-come mental warnings or you'll be in such trouble even I can't help you."

O'Blivion fought a whirl of stomach butterflies; she wondered if she was going to die and wanted to ask how *not* to give off warnings, but followed without comment. Woolf was poking her light into a clump of weed. When a school of silvery lake perch shot out, she laughed and said, "Heyyy, just do it slow like a fish. Be lazy and look at all the pretty trout and the plants and keep kicking... with your hands not too far from your guns."

Sterling was beginning to loathe the tight mental contact with this alien. The species barrier: worse than she ever could have imagined, it was oppressive, jarring, and damaging to the self-esteem. All that energy and exhilaration of Woolf's— it made her feel tired. And irritable. A curious feeling; because if she *was* a weak link and couldn't stand up to stress, the fact could no longer be hidden.

As for Woolf, she kept her own thoughts muffled way down so Sterling wouldn't be hit with the awesome, stunning reality of a Rysemian memory bank. Even so, this tiny glimpse was overwhelming. As Sterling fought the mirages, her companion gave the signal and down they went, fins in the air for driving power, going hard for the bottom.

Even the stream of air bubbles was hateful to the vampire, who wanted to be safe in her office at the Arkoff Studio doing familiar human rip-offs, or sleeping on her red velvet couch, or being anywhere but here. Once they were down, Woolf paused and fingered shells as if looking for something. Sterling jumped as a phosphorescent, wiggly creature brushed her mask; then they began inching along with lazy caution.

"It's fairyland," Woolf exulted, flashing her light over clean, hard sand ripples that slid beneath them and vanished in the pitch-blackness all around. Sterling acted cool. But she knew she was dumb to go along with Patton's pass-or-flunk test like this; who was he to test her?, as they plunged through floating vegetation that pulled at their fins for a claustrophobic minute or two, until they burst out of the narrow gloomy passage accompanied by a four-foot pike who followed the lights and goggled at the swimming bipeds. And all the time, the mental contact was bothering Sterling more than anything else. She kept getting glimpses of that other world and what lay beyond it... an Infinity; not bearable- then something with a wrinkled beak shot past her hand, too close for comfort.

"I've got to go back!"

"Suit yourself."

The Rysemian was twenty feet ahead by now. All Sterling could see of her was a tiny light surrounded by total blackness. The vampire was afraid of being left behind, so she began to kick faster; but the near-freezing depths had taken the edge off her hysteria and she felt that things would probably go well after all, now that Woolf had begun to slow down while telegraphing,

"Your small, cluttered mind is an anchor."

"So suck eggs."

"Don't get sore. So many avenues of misunderstanding—"

There was a sensation of treacherous currents and in another few minutes the vampire needed some assurance as they swept along in darkness. And almost without realizing it, she reached for her cufflinks; the ones Woolf had given her. But they slipped out of her awkward, gloved hands and went spinning and flashing down, down, into a crevice.

O'Blivion thought she saw them gleam way down in a cleft of rock. But Woolf told her to get the hell away from there.

"Ixnay. Move forward. You don't need chunks of gold to get outta your body, you just *do* it, but not yet."

The panic had been simmering. When Woolf said, "Go ahead and dump that hopeless culture of yours, it's a sock full of holes that hasn't been washed in ten thousand years; come on, trust me —" Suddenly it rose up in the vampire's memory: she'd either pictured or *lived* this exact sequence of events, long ago. Two of them floundering in the dark at the bottom of a winter lake, traveling out past the limits of knowledge, dragged along by a force part ecstatic, part morbid, and going God knows where: to a psychic minefield, maybe.

Woolf shot back: "Just a small monkey wrench to be dropped into the machinery."

Sterling followed resignedly. Woolf, who scrutinized her every move, said slowness was okay but to proceed with caution, and pointed ahead. They were about to pass over a sunken tanker — an imposing expanse of rusted hulk, squaring itself against the blackness. It had partly settled into the sand. Woolf ran her light over a length of crumpled deck and sections of bulkhead. The tanker was overgrown with scales and shells. The beam flickered across a pilot house, then returned and held steady. Inside, a skeleton made a frozen gesture of salute with each swell. Woolf gave it a jaunty wave in return.

There was a second skeleton further on. This one was caught in some anchor chain tangled on the gunnels; it nodded and bowed, and swayed with the billows, and Sterling had a flash of anger when the Rysemian nodded back at it. She was so sorry for these drowned seamen, trapped down here in their rusty monument.

To make up for the slip, Woolf offered a taste of what it felt like to be swimming on Rysemus in the luxuriously oily water, without fear or grief.

"We're going there one of these days, together. So *evolve*. Cleanse your mind. You won't be the first human to wear an alien body on a foreign planet but you'll be the first to write home about it."

Sterling didn't want to argue. She felt too remote to care about any of this. Her fins churned the water very slowly now, but she braced for retreat when a medley of sounds came at them. Scrapings and plops: then a hiss-buzz, tweep, gurgles and ripples, whistle-grunt; followed by metallic gratings.

A monster swam up. Some instinct made Sterling remain absolutely quiet as it glided past, a metal creature of nuts and bolts, silky fins, pair of glowing eyes the size of bike wheels; at sight of it, Woolf pulled back into darkness. Sterling had a moment's panic. Her partner was lost. She began an "SOS — Mayday! Can you read me?" but then the panic subsided when Woolf reappeared again as if nothing had happened.

Soon they would pass under the repulsor barrier that the general had indicated in his briefing. Woolf signaled the vampire not to touch it. A convoluted, bubbling skein just over their heads. "Keep clear. Extreme danger—"

Beyond that, they glimpsed a sprawling maze that had to be the emplacement. It didn't look at all sinister. It was a pretty mirage, a ghost town, lucid and splendorous, but empty. Patton had outlined it on the screens for them: an exact replica of the old god Neptune's personal castle; and not empty, but populated with several battalions of Sajorian invaders.

The women proceeded under the barrier with light, swift strokes, setting off no alarms. Then suddenly, "Torches out," Woolf hissed.

As Sterling doused and holstered her flashlight, the darkness was oppressive. She found herself groping along the shelf, wondering where it bottomed out, and felt a myriad of forms touch her in the blackness; along with tinny swashes and yawps, a humming, and a rapping followed by Woolf's signal:

"Don't drop your shield or we're dead."

Gradually her eyes adjusted to the inky dark. On all sides were rocks glowing an eerie yellow-green, and beyond the jagged rocks she saw a bright, clear section where the streets began. And now—

There! in the fold of a big rock: real mermaids, each surrounded by a steamy halo of saffron. They wore breastplates and plumed helmets. Beyond, the gleamingly opulent city extended as far as the eye could see. There were fortifications, all crenellated, with slitlike tower windows. And globe lamps of amber, rose, lilac in a mass of shadow.

Sterling's heart had begun to beat wrenchingly; but Woolf chose to misinterpret.

"Don't let their beauty fool. When we're close enough, I'll use the jelly gas, and when they go screaming out of there on fire, you take it easy. Understand?"

The vampire burst out, "I've got to be able to live with myself." And Woolf retorted,

"We're in their field, pal. Just hug the rocks and get ready to fire."

Then a few seconds later, with a chuckle: "It'll be a massacre. With luck we'll get Beel sitting on his throne. I'll do him like I did Scaulzo."

A smell of sulfur reached them unpleasantly through the otherwise clean waters. Woolf had paused and was running her hands over a slimy rock, unhurriedly exploring what looked like an opalescent shimmer. Finally she slithered her whole body along the frightening beam, and said,

"C'mon! Buck up. Be a human. Let's go."

On they moved, until the machine Woolf carried began to bleat, then sob. Sterling watched, fingers frozen, using clumps of weed to hold herself in place; and was comfortable for a minute in the rise and fall of gentle waves. But she was exhausted by the long swim, and even more by the enigma, so tried to screen out Woolf's information that she would apply pressure and break the seal at this point.

"A precarious balance. Where the four quarters of the universe join." And something about— gradually the lake would seep in and nullify all effects of the tube channeling this energy-picture created by Sajorian mental voltage... Woolf demanded full attention here; no screenouts. She was getting angry about it.

"What do you mean, you don't understand? It's a psychic fact, this is how you humans create your world; what have we been teaching you? But this is a temporary camp in a foreign system so don't get all squishy about it. Watch your shield; you've tipped them off. Too late. It's done. Now, as they spot you, freeze them one by one with your H-2 and finish the job with the magnum. Go ahead. You're on your own."

On her own? The vampire couldn't get her thoughts in line. Her heart contracted sharply, as one of the mermaids stared in curiosity. Then all noises died. The alert had been sounded. The mermaid broke cover. It was approaching in a furious, foamy, tail-lashing path like a watersnake.

"Shoot!" Woolf yelled. "Don't just stand there like a clown!"

At the alarm from this new enemy, the kelpie scuttled for cover and was about to glide into the V of the scummy boulders, when suddenly —

A foaming nugget plunked out of Sterling's H-2 unit. The beam pierced the creature. It screamed silently but horribly, and it shuddered. Then the vampire fired her magnum.

The impact tore the shaky effigy apart. Its organs were floating free; or — no, it was disintegrating! in an obscene tumble, as the face, belly, shapely breasts, and the pubic hair that merged into scales, all went flying to bits. There was a revolting unfoldment of gills, flesh, pink innards, and flashing scales during the course of which Sterling had an incongruous thought. What would some tanker crew think, when they sighted the mutilated body of a mermaid, bobbing to the surface?...

But a larger kelpie came wriggling furiously toward them.

Woolf yelled "Geronimo!" and flung herself onto the beast, wrestling it backward. She yanked off its metal armor and yanked the head back, and sliced its throat, but it managed to break free, and swam off trailing gore.

"Grab 'er, cut off her lips," Woolf screamed excitedly. Clouds of bloody smoke made vision difficult, but another mermaid had rushed in; Woolf and the thing struggled hand-to-hand until the Rysemian got her knife between its ribs. As it was dying, she sang out a boisterous

"Let's hear it for wholesale slaughter."

"I don't like this," Sterling kept repeating from a mesh of horror.

"Think how proud Patton will be of you."

"I don't care" — fighting an urge to vomit as the mermaid she'd slaughtered floated by. Or what was left of it; unseeing eyes wide open and hair streaming. But it was only a messy, twitching clump of flesh. Woolf encouraged her with bold words:

"The eggs of eternity — hunting the waters for prey — "

As the vampire stared blankly and tried to marshal her thoughts, some luminous material rolled aside, revealing a throng of kelpies scuttling back through the gap. They were exposed and were seeking refuge in murky waters, and now, motion for motion, Sterling found herself doing exactly as Woolf wanted.

The two women sidled into the gap, which appeared empty. Creeping forward, melting into sand, thoughts skillfully diffused as protective coloration, Sterling was being taught how to pull off a maneuver like this- when all she longed for was the glow of soft lamps and anything human! but Woolf suddenly glanced sideways; and quickly picked off a mermaid about to attack. Its carcass hit the rock with a silent thud, and bounced off streaming bloody smoke and the others scattered in panic.

"Now!" Woolf yelled. "Finish 'em! Pull the plug, baby, and let's go home."

They burst in, firing. Sterling dodged the first kelpie that tried to escape, as it came at her wearing a death's head, on a curve of hard white light. Luckily Woolf was right behind with the H-2 blazing gloriously, taking careful aim; so remorseless and so busy she failed to notice when Sterling was hit by ricochet. The whole nest had to be cleaned out! But O'Blivion pictured worse plans in the making. She saw a school of remora, roc, and firedrake raddling this world of Beel's. The flood of ephemera threatened the vampire's long-held identity... and so she kept very still, guns in hands; blown into a dreamy ring of degravitized plinth.

"Ya hit?"

Of course it was hard to be certain of another person's motives and feelings. Even another human's. Even your own. Let alone—

Woolf swam close and they touched masks. "How bad?"

Repulsive corpses bobbed and circled. It seemed silly to care. "Nothing much. Curious feeling; slight burning sensation in one arm."

Smiling to herself and apparently satisfied, Woolf took out after the last detachment of mermaids who lurked in dark patches; she hurled her body toward the sheltering rocks, commanding, "Move. Move. Let's bail out."

But Sterling could gather no more strength for fighting. This was a delayed stress syndrome of course, and she was not only making a mistake, but was hemorrhaging badly and would soon die. When Woolf yelled, "Flush 'em out!" the vampire had to say it:

"You're no anthropologist! You're a goddamn evangelist."

"Grab something solid. It's culture shock. We don't wanna lose you."

But Sterling shook her head, gasping, "No. Enough is enough."

"Listen, clown: every night on the tube, your species goes through this. Is it real? Is *this* real? See it all the way through for once! and cleanse your mind."

"Get away, you *thing* in human clothes!"

The vampire was on the edge of hysteria. Woolf hadn't figured she'd get this disoriented. Her guns were waving—

"You *missionary*!" O'Blivion sobbed. "Save your miracles."

The Rysemian knew she should act serious, but couldn't help being amused. "They bought you cheap. It's worse than I thought."

"Who the hell are *you* to test *me*?"

O'Blivion's temper, always hair-trigger, had by now flown out of control. "You're a snake-oil salesman. Ugly. Ugly."

Woolf made a big mistake. She burst into laughter. O'Blivion, gaping and crazed, pointed the H-2 at the Rysemian, who finally realized what was going to happen and shouted, "Don't do it!"

O'Blivion was yelling, "I'm no lab animal!"

"Oh, no? What makes *you* special?"

At that, the vampire pumped her whole chamber of shells out in one spasm. She knew she was about to die; as a matter of fact, was already among the drowned, and had been led into a malignancy she could never overcome. And was surprised when everything began to focus sharply.

Alive and well, Sterling found herself in the body of a laboratory mouse.

Held by the nape. Over a jar of freshly killed white mice exactly like herself.

An enormous, pale hand reached out. Her whiskers trembled, and then she was in searing, agonizing pain, functions all messed up— and Woolf's voice:

"Forget your 'humanism' if this is what it means! If you can do this to animals, you can do it to people."

The H-2 shot had gone wide of its mark. Close but no cigar... wait; Woolf *was* hit! and despite herself, the vampire felt a crazy surge of glee as Woolf doubled over— frozen into her body. Now she could never ditch that carcass full of pipes and wires; she'd be Virginia Woolf forever!, the ultimate security.

"She may hate me for this, but we'll be in the same boat" was the vampire's last complete, terrible thought.

She continued for a few minutes in nervous reflex, as a series of animals in their death throes. A butchered pig. A frog pinned out and dissected by humans while it was still alive.

"Get over thinking you are sacred and the frog is not. Life is life! and if your Bible says no, dump it by the wayside."

Sterling held one idea: "This can't be happening to me—"

She was a lobster, dropped into boiling water.

"As you see, humans can dish it out but not take it," Woolf explained. "You're no holier than any of us, Earthie. Evolve!"

O'Blivion managed to escape these lessons. They were back at the scene of battle surrounded by dead mermaids; Woolf was frozen, and that was good; and now Sterling lifted her Magnum to finish the Rysemian off, according to orders. "Peace—" Arms heavy, vision fading...

Woolf smiled. She raised her Magnum, steadied it with both hands, and fired.

But Sterling (whose heart had already been broken) didn't die right away. She spat out the mouthpiece, which tasted like sulfur, and began swimming shoreward, wobbling like a drunk.

"You've got to see it clearly and whole," Woolf said in a reasonable voice as the cold, blinding water rushed under the vampire's mask. But O'Blivion didn't want to see. Her deeply buried fears had been prodded once too often. She was strangling on her own blood, and death seemed the only way out. Scarlet billows trailed her body.

The last thing she heard was "We're sorry, Mr. File. We did everything we could."

Johnny was standing by the bed and crying. That was very touching; but he was hardly recognizable. He'd blended into another man who existed at the top of time. While Sterling puzzled over that, a voice from still another plane cut in and said,

"She finally went to hell for the crime of vampirism," followed by hollow laughter that spilled over into both the lives or, more probably, shut up one life and opened another.

As the roar of confusion faded, O'Blivion's body drifted to the bottom of the enormous fishtank and after a convulsive shudder or two, she "died."

TWENTY-SIX

It didn't hurt. That was the big surprise.

On the other hand, Sterling File didn't care to touch the crusty, ugly stitches.

A nurse came in and simpered: "Do you know where you are?" Dumb question. Dumb nurse- Patsy Cox, the one Johnny always came on to. Sure, Sterling knew everything that went on in this room. She'd crawled out of anesthesia some time ago. She lay on her back in a narrow hospital bed. The rock music from her dream, with its intrusive, sensual boom, was filtering from a radio down the hall.

There were two other patients in the room; both much worse off than Sterling was. The young woman near the window, paralyzed in a car accident, fresh out of Intensive Care, had ash-yellow hair and lots of noisy visitors, and wore a foggy smile of perpetual delight (from the lovely, lovely drugs they kept you on). The lady by the door was corpulent, white-skinned, and lightly freckled, asleep now. Had been given a needle for a crying jag. Her leg had been amputated a day or two ago (there *were* blank spaces here and there in Sterling's mind) and she'd phoned her husband to bring in "…my beige shoes; you know the ones, the ones with the medium heel I wear around the house" — but the husband brought in the wrong shoes, together with a piece of cake, in a brown paper bag. Lots of human interest here. The woman cried heart-brokenly over bag, cake, shoes, and everything until her husband buried his semibald head in his parka and crept away. Then "the daily fix" (as Sterling's husband Johnny called it) had been passed around, in the paper cups, and now they all felt terrific again.

Imagine not feeling pain. It was a miracle of modern medicine. And Sterling was not being wickedly sarcastic; not any more. She meant it. She meant every word of it.

"What a dream I had," she'd told husband Johnny, who was a bit guilt-stricken and so more attentive than usual after Sterling had almost croaked twice during the night: once hemorrhaging in the ambulance, and ditto in the O.R. "Both of us worked at this dance studio in Chicago. We taught disco. Isn't that a riot? Patsy Cox was in the dream; she was in love with you, and I was a vampire named O'Blivion. A real vampire who sucked blood. I could taste it. Then a beautiful woman came from deep space—"

She told the whole anesthesia-fantasy in a bemused mumble, leaving out the parts Johnny wouldn't approve of, like, when she killed Patsy, and when he himself died; no use harping on the negative; of course Johnny was dead; he'd been born dead. And leaving out her romance with a powerful amazon, "the lost love of her life"- and all that; and embellishing the parts that flattered him. (Even on post-op uppers, Sterling was no dope!, but a discreet wife.)

He was never interested in her dreams, though, and said, "Don't talk now. Get some rest. Don't get upset," and so forth. But Sterling knew a deep change had definitely come over her; and she liked it. Because it was a matter of self-protection. Or as she tried to explain to the red-eyed, jittery hubby as he smoked the last cigarette and crumpled the pack, "That nightmare was as good as a lobotomy. I feel— different. Grown up at last, know what I mean? Like everyone always wanted me to be. And I feel much better."

Johnny was dozing right now, slouched in a chair across the room. He was a bore (what dead person isn't!) but she was glad of his presence. His science fiction paperback had slipped, inch by inch, out of his hairy paw, and was sliding down his immaculate jeans toward his fifty-dollar running tennies. Hubby'd had a bad night too and looked pasty-faced in a gaudy shirt that said "Divers Do It Deeper," and although Sterling loved her 1980s tight-pants hero and closet case (but pitied him even more) it was a sad fact that hubby was no diver at all. He was a hack poet who'd never dived into anything, much less his wife's inner life, and had already been dead for a long time, which is why this society accepted him with all its slavish adoration; and now she'd be "dead" too— in the acceptable way. And Sterling felt positively euphoric about what had happened to her; a profound calm had fallen over her as soon as Johnny walked in and uttered the magic words:

"You're going to be all right, honey! You licked it."

Which could have been the familiar scam they told every victim after "exploratory surgery"; but because she was so used to reading Johnny's frozen little brainwashed mind, Sterling knew it was true... But from now on she'd hide all traces of that telepathy crap, because "you weren't supposed to do that." And for good reason. People deserved their privacy.

The I.V. bottle hung there like teacher's suppressive face, and the TV had been turned on but the sound was off. Silly perhaps, but it was comforting to see two ridiculous twits, one actor, and one actress, in beautiful clothes and makeup, making love in the socially approved fashion.

Beyond the TV, windows looked out onto gloomy, corpse-like, megaconglomerate America: so far beyond "dignity" you couldn't dream it. The drab, sterile buildings over there, with the brown snow on them, seemed enormously satisfying to Sterling; she felt wrenchingly grateful, because she'd been allowed to live. The bed was uncomfortable as hell but she didn't care. It was a warm sanctuary... much better than a cold grave.

The nightmare was over.

She recalled coming to the hospital in the ambulance.

Lots of drama and sirens, and blood, quarts of it; the emergency room chaos, no waiting for once; they were all so certain she'd never walk out of this joint. Layers of Pentothal, the degradation of being shoved, shaved, prodded, and trundled like a strapped-in meat animal— but it was all over now. She'd creep back into normal society, beg everyone's pardon, and stay there, in Johnny's protective presence, and never dream or think again— no, never!, as long as she lived.

Alas! that the mystery had not been revealed to me.

Good, patient hubby, passed out under the TV. He was a despot in his way, but he represented Security. Maybe it was not much of a life, but it was all they had and from now on she'd adjust to it all the way. She'd hold herself back; be a passive clone, keeping up with the mob and its detestable wobbling. If she had to kiss people's feet and flatter them — what the hell, it was a small price to pay for security.

Sterling felt as if she'd been seared, whirled through alien environments and was delighted to be an average, not-responsible human victim once more. By God, any degradation was better than "The Truth"! So from now on she'd be an amputated leg like everybody else— yes— she'd distort her identity to match the average twerp; she'd roll on the conveyor belt with the rest of the cannibals. No more arguing against what she'd called "gross human stupidity." Because it was really *wisdom*. Because it was safe. And painless. Anesthetized but pampered. And that's what counted.

The paralyzed woman's two doctors came twinkling from distant places, all bluff and hearty in their $800 suits. Sterling gave them what she used to call "the sucky smile worn by the people in the TV commercials," and both doctors beamed at her in approval. Then they yanked the curtains together around the paralyzed woman's space, with them inside (along with a tray full of wicked-looking needles. They were always doing strange tests in there. And coming out with jaunty, self-satisfied smiles. Not that they were a pair of gloating creeps; she didn't mean that at all; they were helping, and it was good— their good humor alternating nicely with their ponderous seriousness). But... the point was...

When she was asleep on the table in the operating room, that chamber of illusion, her soul had wandered loose from her body. In the corridor she located a blood-spattered doctor coming from surgery. Like a whipped dog, her soul followed this doctor. Hearing him speak of primary cancer and rap out, "Everyone here is terminally ill! It's the human condition! Carcinoma has seeded the shadow on the film," Sterling's soul knelt and kissed the hem of that doctor's gown, and promised that if he'd let her live, she'd be an obedient robot from that moment on, like all good people everywhere; she'd be semi-sick all the time but she would never, ever, leave her body again—

What did this mean? Well, it meant: when someone is talking to you, you must be interested, no matter how idiotic their speech. You must be respectful, even worshipful. Nod to keep them talking. Flatter them with attention.

Especially if they are "professionals" licensed by the State, like doctors, or politicians. Or some tenth-rate poet with grants and tenure— like Johnny— or like the concerned people who write the TV commercials, and so forth.

That's what it meant.

The knowledge of her own mortality had frightened Sterling so badly she'd give up anything to stay alive. Integrity? It meant nothing. All those high-flown ideals she once had meant nothing. "Spiritual being"— forget it; enjoy the swill, with everybody else. The mass mind was what counted. Encased in fragile meat. Mortal. Never to be exported to fairyland.

Another thing. All those "great writers" she'd always admired: they were wrong. Why raise people's expectations? It was cruelty. The majority had always known that. The majority was smarter than the individual. The hackwork they adored— well, it was *safe*, and that's all that mattered.

The light was falling in a bright patch on the sterile floor. She'd dozed off. Dr. Houghtaling was standing there talking to Patsy Cox, the nervous nurse that Johnny made the most passes at. Houghtaling was angry about something Patsy had done. He was often angry; often well into hysteria. He loomed over the redheaded nurse, his wavy gray hair lit by sun, a juvenile tallboy isolated by his flimsy doctorhood, Sterling noting that the poor jerk was going to die of cancer of the rectum in exactly thirty-eight months but hiding the news from herself *instantly* because people hate it when you probe their secret lives. It's none of your beeswax! as some vague figure out of her past would have said. Sterling strained to hear what they were saying. The sound-deadening ceiling muffled their voices but she thought she heard the nurse gush, "Oh, the miraculous wizardry of modern medicine!" with an irritable, bright-eyed glare.

To which the doctor responded, "Buy and sell. Buy and sell. Bondage-bondage-bondage."

"Bargain-bargain," the nurse sulked back.

At which the doctor snapped, "You have to be ruthless to get the position. Everyone knows the competition is terrible," or gaggle to that effect.

Dr. Houghtaling was invariably condescending to the women in this ward, but Sterling had decided that was perfectly all right. It was enough that he allowed her to survive and lie here watching doctor and nurse stump out together in their usual very quiet frenzy; and as for Sterling File, never would she dream a dangerous dream again. No, it was enough just to *fit in* and be like the others, lying in a warm grave of her own digging. Because it was safe here. And she would forget all that "heroism of the mind" crap she'd been weaned of, somehow during the frightening night, by — something or other.

Oddly, her cheeks were wet... but why bawl about nothing? Only a vision: found and then lost again. The important thing is to feel powerless like the others, and be grateful for the crumbs the world grants you.

"This is no drill! Pull out of it," Woolf had begun yelling.

But Sterling refused to listen. That alien was evil, saying our materialism is just a game. This is no game! This is *real;* a world of ego, petty politicking, diseased and dying bodies, all very serious and important, and you can't pull out of it, because — nothing else exists.

TWENTY-SEVEN

"The truth is greater than arrangements," Woolf brayed. "You can't just throw yourself under a train or into a river and call it 'the end'! What did we teach?"

"I don't remember," I sobbed.

"You either examine your own prophecies, or wallow in the boring conventions of suicide. Take your choice, nitwit."

I'd never seen her so angry.

"I can't help it," I wept bitterly.

"So the bomb drops," Woolf sneered. "Condition is near panic; your 'now' gets pushed out into the wilderness, distorted and frozen into the beautiful static known as The End of Time."

All that worried me was that an alternate Sterling O'Blivion was being wheeled to a morgue at this very moment. She'd wasted her power insisting "this can't be changed" until too late... My tears flowed.

"Quit with the self-pity," growled Woolf. "Develop some guts and you can reverse any process."

"That's not fair. I'm only human, impelled by forces none of us can control—"

Woolf ground her teeth. "You keep pleading 'Help me, what should I do? What should my first step be?' Well, your first step should be to get off psychic welfare. Disconnect from the obsessions of your culture."

"But *how*, in any real sense?"

"Well: we'll get jobs as simple, happy laborers, because hard work is the sweetest thing life offers, right?"

I wiped my eyes. "Fine. I know irony when I see it, but honest work doesn't bother me in the least. Just don't forget the main point: I have a real problem. A serious, *important*, pathological condition, not to be brushed aside."

Woolf snorted. "'Poor me, I'm special. I have a problem.' You know what your problem is? You are genetically advanced but you've been trained to fail. And this vampire thing; what is a vampire? Who projected that image onto you? My guess is, the people of Transylvania *created* you out of boredom and frustration. Don't go getting insulted."

But I was long past insults, merely saying, "Very well. I'll go along with whatever training you care to offer; do I have a choice?"

"Certainly. You can pick up your old life right where you left off."

I didn't think I could stand that any more, and said so. "God forbid. After the last few weeks how could I become what I was, and be trapped in those same conditions? I'd rather die."

Woolf chewed her finger, thinking. "Okay. Apparently I've got to make good on my promise to teach you sorcery. Advanced magicianship, beyond anything you've ever done. First step is to get tough with yourself; quit smacking your lips over the fictions of suicide. That stuff can kill a whole population faster than cyanide in the drinking water. Look what it did to Tolstoy, for corn sake. Killed him deader than a mackerel."

Naturally I was excited. "You mean like in the fairy tale, I'll be able to say 'Little table appear. Spread yourself with good things' and it will actually happen?"

She nodded. "You're talking advanced physics. It'll be common knowledge 500 years from now that you *grow* your reality the way an oyster grows its shell. The idea is to project whatever reality you want. Create it, as a sculptor builds a statue, in all its details— and you'll soon be living in it."

"Then why aren't we doing that already?"

"Lost the knack, I guess. Probably you destroyed some people and property by mistake, out of exuberance (I'm always doing that, dang me) and you went into some kind of a guilt trip and lost your talent. That happens to the best of us. But as in any sport, the point is not to panic if you blow a few shots. You can always get your touch back."

Woolf was feeling happy because she'd negotiated a brilliant exchange with the Sajorians: Scaulzo, freeze-released, in exchange for what was left of our FMTC staff.

"Letting Scaulzo go may be a dangerous move but the way I figure it, good always triumphs over evil in the end, given half a chance."

Our staff had been en route to Sajor as lab animals. Their sufferings were as ghastly as those of Earth's own "research" victims; but the survivors were patched up and offered cushy jobs in ancient Egypt as a form of compensation.

"Sterling and I will follow in April," Woolf promised.

The two of us together, at last, in the springtime; not in Paris of course, but in a mud but with "Home Sweet Home" chiseled over the door in hieroglyphics. We will become simple laborers near Giza, owning nothing but a few jars and boxes, and an unlocked garden full of lettuce, beans, onions, cabbages and cucumbers; sleeping in a reed bed on the roof under the stars, with our two dogs and three cats and nine ducks.

Blake Reardon has wangled a job designing intricate passages and chambers for the project we'll be working on. His wife Susie tells us that Blake's designs will be picked up by the Romans and passed down through the ages as The Draftsman's Bible, which he himself will be forced to use religiously in the twentieth century. Susie writes:

"Egypt, a thousand years before King Tut!, we can hardly believe our good luck. I love our house; palmetto trees, river view, great climate and the kids' school is the best ever. I can't thank you enough, Sterling O'Blivion and Virginia Woolf, for this grand opportunity. Every day is a joy and a delight; easy to see why this civilization endured for 3,000 years, whereas our poor American one seems willing to give up after a mere 200 years— but must rush, going punting on the Nile (water's high at this season which adds to the fun) and again thanks! that my husband is no longer a prisoner on some hideous planet light-years from home. Yours ever, Susie Reardon."

Despite all the letters, documents, visits to the *Vonderra* and other evidence I still fear trickery, I don't know of what kind.

Woolf tries to jolly me out of it. She arranged a touching ceremony in which Vicki Bauer was presented with a duplicate

Marilyn Monroe body.

"Wear it in good health," Benaroya intoned as she made the award.

Vicki is now a novice priestess at the temple of Ra and is delighted with her job, and with the adoring attention she gets.

As for us, I am highly dubious about the future. Can I really trust this Rysemian? "Love" is a concept I cannot fully comprehend, after the terrible life I've led; but Woolf insists we're going to have "barrels of fun" and "peace of mind because you *decide* to have peace of mind and that's all there is to it" (these are direct quotes).

She paints an inviting picture: up before dawn, riding our camel to work, on an enchanting day with fleecy white clouds in a blue sky, the air so clear you can see miles beyond Giza. Our foreman eats bread and onions for breakfast; he has big flappy ears, and a fat little belly bulging over a pleated skirt, and Woolf promises that he will be jolly, and have irregular teeth. Imagine it. I've been *dying* for a glimpse of some good old-fashioned irregular teeth, which I haven't seen in years. But the best part will be our project, the pyramid.

"Slaves didn't build it. Crews of levitators built it." Woolf laid a hand on my neck, telling how our life was going to be.

"Our crew is the Blue Rabbits. The other guys are the Red Hens. Who can lay the most stones by suppertime? Free beer and melons for the winning crew!

"The foreman sticks two fingers in his mouth, we watch as he inhales; the wind is howling... We're way up there gazing at a purple and golden land, a sparkling river, tilled fields beyond it, then dunes rolling away to a misty horizon, and we're dancing with suspense— then the whistle blasts! The Blue Rabbits are off!, hitching ourselves to a slab of shiny limestone. Are we gonna win the free beer and melons? Absolutely.

"We spit on our hands. A lot of little girls with shaved heads are watching in admiration. We grab the ropes and pull as hard as we can. Of course it will be sleight-of-mind that makes the massive block move, but we throw ourselves on the ropes, yank, slip on pebbles, and begin singing the famous Blue Rabbit Song at the top of our lungs... But the limestone slab will not budge.

"After all, it weighs two-and-a-half tons! and to move it by hand is impossible. Any bureaucrat will tell you how unsafe, foolish, and impossible this is. Why, there'll be over two million blocks in all. The pyramid could cover 8 football fields and will be

481 feet high, with a pointed capstone (stolen in a later, dimmer age)...

"We roar out the Blue Rabbit Song even louder, shutting our eyes, straining and hauling at the tremendous weight on its log rollers, until finally— it budges!— the merest fraction of an inch. Then half an inch, a full inch, two inches. And a little more... and a little more.

"Some workers pick up the last log and trot it to the front, where it becomes the first log, and they keep doing that, and soon the huge rock is floating up the incline, easy as a bar of wet soap. And at the top, where our minds merge in a blissful non-effort, nonthought... it almost floats itself into place. Hands, rope, our minds, the wind, the sun; everything seems to work in harmony as the slab glides into its appointed place with a soft click...

"Millennia from now, tourists will stand on this very spot and marvel, 'How did they ever do it? Why can't our modern engineering methods handle jobs like that?'"

Woolf continued, "That's an easy question. There was no self-cheating in it, that's all— because this is the Great Pyramid and we are building it together.

"Not some overpraised man in a space suit, but *us!*"

And then at last it was time for "the action" which is Woolf's name for my grounding in sorcery and magicianship, or "religion" if that is a better word; with the goal of attaining complete mastery over space and time.

"Sorcery is nothing but concentration. You've got to learn to think clearly and steadily, and practice it, like riding a bike.

"Every human once had these powers. You can get them back, but it won't happen overnight; it took years of bad habits to get yourself into such horrible shape. But look at it this way. If a mossback like you can enter a state of grace, anyone can do it."

I had the usual flood of suspicious questions. She handled them patiently.

"Reality is ambiguous. You yourself are fully aware that the people in the physics department agree on something mentally over the years, and then *afterward* find the physical evidence of their creation. Or: what role are you acting? Pick a good one. It will come true."

Certainly I could quit whenever I wanted, but was told, "You'll stagnate and wind up sleeping in a tomb like the others."

Then many exercises: fast gearshifting of emotions so I could get out of grief in a hurry, inventing and creating ideas, building and destroying. I work sedulously and sometimes this is exhilarating, other times a hellish and tortuous grind. My blood-craving has disappeared, yet, instead of turning into a rotting old hulk as expected, I'm becoming more vital and handsome every day. My capabilities are increasing dramatically but still I get these bodily fears and times of overwhelming mistrust when I weep, grow nostalgic over the olden days, and ask, "How long will it take? I can't stand much more of this."

"Who said there's a guarantee?"

With all her patience, Woolf is a terrifying teacher, forever reminding me that a person, like a society, gets back what she projects. "Shun moods of gloom. Live like a champion, act boldly, and throw out doubts every time they arise. Faith is the sword and buckler and momentum will keep you on course."

"But I've been badly used. Denied things—"

"Knock off that 'poor martyr me' crap and get to work. You are the master of your fate. Let's see some concentration, imagination, willpower! Make a firm decision to be serene no matter what. Ignore the world and its problems. Keep being happy in the teeth of all obstacles and soon the world will no longer exist. When you're in shape to help, you'll help, if you still want to. Now back to your corner!"

She said there was no shortage except in people's minds, and that I'd learn to invent, with terrific power and eye-defying speed, such items as a system for feeding an overpopulated planet, or of building thriving new cities in a once-empty desert. Or an endless supply of cures, transportation systems, body shapes, relationships between them, and ways to stop crimes years before they happen, and ways to make war not only obsolete, but uproariously absurd and impossible—

"By the Bulbous-Bodied Pax!" I roared, collapsing with laughter; at which my mentor threw some zany questions.

"How does a black hole emerge into another universe? Can you go out before you come in? Why do you remember the past but not the future? Does it hurt people to tell them the truth? What is matter and what is antimatter, and can the definitions of the two be reversed?"... And, bouncing in her chair,

"Can you *really* become a sorcerer and get your own way a lot, and be happy, successful, and ethical? Yes. This is a solemn promise that I'm making to you now. What do you think psychic evolution is all about?" Woolf yodeled happily.

Musing, I recalled something Dostoevsky once said: "If only we all wanted it, everything could be arranged immediately."

So I calm myself, knowing "the action" is governed by laws rooted deeply in nature and not on the temporary rules (or trendy sciences) of a shaky human society.

But again fear plucks me (oh, the wild dichotomy of the human spirit!) and I find myself asking, "How do I know you won't run out on me? How do I even know this is real?"

Then that slow, green-eyed smile, of the Virginia Woolf I knew long ago.

"Trust me," she says.

ABOUT JODY SCOTT

b. 1923 — d. 2007

B orn in 1923, Jody Scott, or Joann Margaret Huguelet as it says on her birth certificate — Mr. Scott came later closely followed by Mr. Wood, two characters out of P.G. Wodehouse (if Wodehouse had happened to marry Jean Genet) — was born in Chicago of an old-settler family of Fort Dearborn (as the toddlin' town was once called) with loose ties to the underworld.

Ms. Scott attended Daniel Boone grammar school, Senn High, North Park College, Northwestern U. and U.C. Berkeley before crying out in clear, ringing tones: "Enough of this crap. If you wanna be a writer never, NEVER go to college or you'll come out a brainwashed zombie who offends nobody but writes like everyone else or as Monty Python used to say: 'Dull, dull, dull!' — the L's sounding like W's."

Our subject then worked as a sardine packer, orthopedist's office assistant, *Circle Magazine* editor (knew Henry Miller and Anaïs Nin), artist's model at Art Institute Chicago, factory hand, cabbage puller ("in Texas where I was arrested with my buddy Don Scott for hitchhiking and slapped around then thrown in jail for eight days; how stupid can 'The Law' be? Its reasoning was: my gay friend {close pal of Leonard Bernstein and Tennessee Williams} had long hair, therefore we must be criminals"), blue movie maker, headline writer for the *Monterey Herald* ("that's where I got my spare, lean style"), bookstore/art gallery owner, vacation land salesman and at many other fascinating trades, spent six months in Guatemala (in Antigua enjoyed a night alone with Gore Vidal at his house both madly talking) and lived in Seattle in a falling-apart house choked with ivy and blackberry brambles a stone's throw from Puget Sound and was the winner of the 'America's Ugliest Couch' contest upon which she wrote every day from 9 AM to 2 PM Pacific time.

Jody died in 2007.

Visit the official Jody Scott blog at www.jodyscott.info
Visit Jody's Amazon author page at www.amazon.com/author/jodyscott